# Eternal Passage

# *Eternal Passage*

## ELAINE SCHULTE

LIFEJOURNEY
BOOKS

DAVID C. COOK PUBLISHING CO.

LifeJourney Books is an imprint of David C. Cook Publishing Co.
David C. Cook Publishing Co., Elgin, Illinois 60120
David C. Cook Publishing Co., Weston, Ontario

ETERNAL PASSAGE
© 1989 by Elaine Shulte

Edited by LoraBeth Norton
Cover design by Dawn Lauck
Illustration by Kathy Kulin

First Printing, 1989
Printed in the United States of America
93 92 91     5 4 3

Schulte, Elaine L.
        Eternal Passage
        (California pioneer series; bk. 3)
        I. Title.  II. Series: Schulte, Elaine L.  California pioneer series;  bk. 3
PS3569.C5395E84            1989            813'.54            89-23953
ISBN 1-55513-988-4

*In memory of our
sisters and brothers
who brought His love
through the jungle of Panama*

# *Prologue*

**B**enjamin Talbot glanced out the parlor window at the golden hillsides that undulated across the California Territory. Life was vastly different here, yet it presented the usual problems . . . some of which were rendered even more complicated by the great distance to the rest of the country.

"Whatever are you scowling so for, Father?" Betsy asked as she stepped into the whitewashed parlor. "It's not like you to look so fierce."

"I look fierce?" he asked his fourteen-year-old daughter.

She nodded, her green eyes serious and her thick auburn braids brushing the narrow shoulders of her russet frock.

"I am heartened to hear it's not my usual demeanor," he replied with a smile.

She persevered. "What is the trouble?"

"Your cousin Louisa came to mind for no special reason," he replied. "She's an only child—a young woman now, perhaps nineteen years old. If she's still unwed, she can't have a pleasant life with that father of hers. I have such an uneasy feeling about her."

"Louisa . . . the one in Virginia?"

"Yes, in Alexandria."

"I can't help but think how unhappy I would be without

1

a large family," Betsy said. "Why don't we invite her to stay here with us? We have extra rooms."

Benjamin shook his head at his generous-hearted daughter. Indeed, their old Spanish house, Casa Contenta, had extra rooms now that his married children had moved into adjacent quarters in the Californio-style family compound.

"Yes," he said. "I suppose there is room here."

"Shall I bring your writing paper and quill so you can write to her now, Father?" Betsy inquired.

"You're not eager for younger companions in the house, are you?" he asked with amusement.

"I expect I am."

He grew serious again. "To sail here in the midst of this gold rush would be a fearful ordeal for a young woman," he said. "Yet why else would I suddenly think of her?"

"Perhaps we are meant to pray for her, Father."

"Yes, that is precisely what we must do. But I think perhaps I shall write to her, as well."

"Then let me get your writing paper. And if I may, I would like to write to her, too. . . ."

# 1

Louisa Abigail Setter surveyed the drowsy Alexandria waterfront with caution as she approached the red-brick shipping office. Nary a stevedore was in sight, and the few idlers near a decrepit sailing ship took little notice of her. Only the hourly steamship to Washington City moved along the river, its smoke black against the blue sky. *Please, Lord, she prayed, don't let anyone see me here.*

Her fingers closed on the sun-warmed brass knob of the Wainwright and Talbot Shipping door as she heard a horse clip-clop around the corner. Lifting the skirt of her fawn-colored frock with quick decorum, she hurried into the office and closed the door behind her.

"Good afternoon, ma'am." A man rose from a desk behind a counter, his tall, lean body unfolding gracefully.

Louisa's voice held steady. "Good afternoon."

"May I be of assistance?" he inquired as he approached the counter. He was attired like a gentleman in a brown frock coat and high white collar, and his broad smile reassured her.

She swallowed. "Are you the new agent?"

"The temporary agent. I'm working in this office for only a short time."

His face held an aura of kindness. She would have to

3

trust him. The last agent knew Conduff, her husband, and one small slip of the tongue would ruin any hope of escape.

"Allow me to introduce myself," the agent said. "I'm Jonathan Chambers."

"I—I prefer not to give my name," Louisa replied.

His eyes widened slightly. "As you wish."

"I—I need the address of the Talbot family . . . the Talbots of this shipping line. I understand they now live in the California Territory—"

His expression turned doubtful, then his eyes went to her russet-colored hair. "Are you kin?"

He had guessed from her hair, she thought nervously. Aunt Sarah had told her that most of the Talbots were redheads.

"I should not have inquired," he said. "In any case, they now live near San Francisco. I shall write down the address for you."

She darted a glance out the front windows and, reassured, turned to watch him write the Talbot address on a card. "The gold ships to California . . . how much is the fare?"

He blinked with surprise. "It varies, depending upon whether you wish to depart from Baltimore, Boston, or New York. With all of the tales about gold discoveries in California, it has become difficult to book passage." He hesitated. "I should warn you that women rarely go."

She ignored his warning. "Baltimore," she decided. It would be easiest to be traced from there, but the fare would be less. She had only the money hidden in the potato bin in the cellar, the money Aunt Sarah had pressed upon her to hide before she died.

His curious gaze lingered on her a moment longer, then he took up the 1849 rate booklet from the counter and thumbed through the pages. "Will there be one of you . . . or more?"

"One." Please don't make me lie, she thought. She had never been adept at it, and every time Conduff caught her—

"The fare depends upon the ship as well as the journey," Jonathan Chambers explained, looking up from the booklet. "Some sail around Cape Horn, the southernmost tip of the continent. Others stop at the Isthmus of Panama, where passengers travel sixty miles on land, then sail north to California. It is considered a much faster route."

"Which is less costly?"

"Panama. But there are expenses for overland transportation . . . native canoes and burros. And I must warn you of fever and pestilence there."

Louisa thought of the child she was carrying within her. It might not be wise to expose such a fragile life to the dangers of the tropics. Yet if she didn't have sufficient money— "The Panama Route seems best."

"How soon do you wish to sail?"

She kept her eyes on the rate booklet. "I don't know." It depended upon her response from the Talbots, but she could not tell him that.

"Well, then, permit me to write down a list of ships leaving Baltimore and the various fares. You seem to be in a great hurry. I would be happy to deliver the list to you."

"No! It's, you see—it is still too uncertain. May I stop for it tomorrow afternoon?"

"Of course," he replied, then added pointedly, "you can be certain that I am discreet."

"Thank you . . . thank you, Mr. Chambers."

He handed her the card, then nodded politely.

"Good day then, Mr. Chambers," she said as she slipped his card into the pocket of her frock.

"Good day," he replied.

She opened the door and glanced in both directions along the cobblestone street. She could not see Conduff nor any other familiar faces along the waterfront. The Potomac River flowed swiftly past the wooden pilings, and only a few ships sailed by in the distance. Relieved, she closed the door behind her and started for Market Square.

As she hurried along, she caught a glimpse of her reflection in the windows of a chandlery office. She still looked slim-waisted in this frock . . . no sign yet of thickening. Her mind edged back to Conduff and how furious he would be to hear of the child. He'd always said, "If there's one thing I cain't abide, it's squallin' brats!"

At Market Square she manuevered quickly through the crowd gathering at the slave auction block. A dozen or so blacks in chains shuffled toward it, Conduff behind them with a rifle in one hand, his riding crop in the other, and a pistol stuffed under his belt. "A fine lot I got today!" he called out to the auctioneer. "Strong bucks and prime female breedin' stock!"

The crowd buzzed with interest and, nearby, several men broke out in vulgar laughter. Buyers edged forward to assess the slaves, whose eyes were wide open with fear.

Conduff's glance, roving over the crowd, stopped on Louisa. He raised his chin and broke into the engaging grin that women found so charming. If she didn't smile, he would be angry tonight; she could imagine it already. "Cain't you smile at yer man when he's out there up front? If you cain't, honey-woman, there be plenty a woman who cain."

She made herself smile at him across the crowd. She had only to keep him pacified a bit longer, a few more months perhaps. He considered himself the best slave pen man around, and no matter how loathsome she found it, she must pretend to admire the flair with which he paraded out the poor blacks.

A few minutes remained before the auction would begin, and her mind turned back to three years ago when she had first met Conduff Setter. Why hadn't she realized how violent he was? Why hadn't she recognized his overblown image of himself when he worked with her father at the brick quarry?

It had been a Monday evening that spring when her father had brought Conduff home from the grog shops. The two of them had been drinking whiskey in the parlor when Da issued the summons. "Louisa, girl, come in here!"

She had flipped back her thick braids, glad she wore the blue cotton frock that accented the blue of her eyes. As she stepped into the parlor, she stumbled over the fringed rug. "Oh!" she cried out, barely regaining her balance.

The two men chuckled.

"She's a mite clumsy when she's nervous," Da explained, "but—well, jest have a look at 'er."

Blood poured into her cheeks, and the strange tone in which he spoke rooted her to the floor. He had already imbibed heavily, for his face was even redder than usual.

"Da!" she protested. To be examined like this! She stood stiff with resentment as the men appraised her. Finally she said, "You have not remembered to introduce us, Da."

His hooded gray eyes darkened. "Hush up, girl!"

"Da!"

"You hush up or you'll be feelin' the strap!"

She had avoided his strap since her twelfth year, but her father did not make idle threats, especially when drunk. Finally she could endure the men's stares no longer. "If Mother or Aunt Sarah were still alive, they would not allow you to do this!"

"They ain't alive, girl. And jest because you had so much

7

schoolin', it don' make you no judge of what's right. You might be bookish, but you don' know nothin' yet."

He turned to Conduff. "High time I find her a husband, not that it'd be too much trouble with her looks. And she'll be gettin' the house, o' course. No need for you to live on Shabby Street all your life."

*Surely Da is not serious!* Louisa thought.

Conduff's green eyes sparkled. "It bears some thinkin'."

Louisa surmised that he lived on the east side of town, to the north of Queen Street. There, a row of shabby frame houses sheltered ruffians whose drunken brawls kept the neighborhood in a state of turmoil.

Conduff winked at her as he said, "She does look on the spindly side, but I got an idea she'll turn out jest fine."

"Like her ma."

Louisa clenched her fists. How could her mother—a Boston Talbot—have endured his talk? Of course, she had been married to Da for only three years before she died. They had eloped when she was young and rebellious, back before Da's hair turned a muddy gray and his flesh ran to a paunch and double chins.

He said, "I expect, like her ma, she might be partial to Blue Ridge men, especially if they're Scotch-Irish."

Conduff gave her an amused look. "That so?"

Louisa shrugged. Like Da, the darkness of the Irish predominated in Conduff. He was a big-boned man, powerfully shouldered, and more interesting than any of the town boys.

He set down his whiskey glass and moved toward her like a sleek black mountain panther. "Let's jest see if you like Blue Ridge men."

He towered over her, and his green eyes held hers so intently she was unable to tear her gaze away until she

8

smelled his whiskey breath. She flinched only a trifle as he slid his hand up her back and turned her slowly toward him.

He added, "With them big blue eyes 'n that red hair, you might jest amount to somethin', honey-girl."

Her voice quavered as she attempted to sound indignant. "Honey-girl!"

"Yeah . . . honey-girl."

His tone was fluid and warm like honey itself and, without quite understanding why, her resentment toward him began to fade. Conduff's hand was warm, splayed across her back, and after a moment she ventured a shy smile up at him.

"Got a dimple, too," he remarked playfully.

Da said, "Let out yer braids for Conduff, girl."

"Da!"

"I said, let out yer braids!"

"I'd rather not—"

"You heard me, girl!"

Surprised at his vehemence, she turned toward Conduff, who nodded slightly, his green eyes dancing. His voice gentled her. "Won't hurt nothin' to let down yer hair, honey-girl."

She stared into his eyes, then as though in a trance, she slowly began to unbraid her thick hair. As she unbraided, it occurred to her that life might be better if she were married, no longer under Da's strictures. She would have a husband to protect her. She could have supper ready for him when he came home from the brick quarry so they could take a walk in the evening, just the two of them, like other young married couples in town. It might be wonderful to be married, especially to a man like Conduff.

She unbraided her hair more quickly and smiled at him. He was far above the town boys who befriended her. If she must marry someone, she could not imagine anyone more ... exciting or ... manly.

Conduff's lips curved upward as her russet-colored hair tumbled about her shoulders and down to her waist, a shining curtain of thick curls.

"Just like her ma," Da said, taking another swallow of whiskey. "Ain't that a sight!"

Conduff nodded and licked his lips as though they had turned dry. "Yeh." He grinned at Da, and a peculiar unspoken message passed between them.

Louisa backed away a step, but Conduff reached for her hand, engulfing it in his. "Here, ain't no need for you to be scared. Look how you got yer hand all clenched up." Slowly he opened her fist and straightened her fingers before he raised her hand and planted a kiss on her palm.

Her father said, "Well, now, I'll be takin' myself out back. I don't expect you need any help."

Conduff's green eyes never left hers. "I never needed help yet. Expect I won't need it now either."

She heard the words without quite comprehending, though she felt a sense of relief at Da's departure. How weak her knees had become. . . . Her best friend Tess and the other girls in town would never believe this had happened to her. She could scarcely believe it herself . . . a grown man kissing her hand like that, and now he still held it in his.

She dimly recalled Aunt Sarah saying that Blue Ridge men had irresistible ways about them, that her own mother had been trapped by her feelings, and feelings were not enough for a love that lasted.

Yet all concern faded when Conduff said, "I'll jest bet you never been kissed."

When Louisa looked into her bedroom mirror an hour later, she seemed a stranger. Her sapphire blue eyes, remarkable for the charcoal circles around the irises and thick, dark lashes, sparkled with excitement. Her hair, deep rich russet, the color of autumn leaves, curled luxuriantly around her shoulders, and her wide mouth was more red-lipped than ever from his ardent kisses. Conduff liked her very much indeed, she thought, and the dimple in her left cheek deepened.

The next evening when Conduff came to call, her father pointed out the finer aspects of their house. "Better brick on this house than we're gettin' now at the quarry," and, "Most of the furniture come all the way from London . . . her ma and her aunt got it from their Talbot kin. A man's got to watch about property and such when he thinks o' marryin'."

On Wednesday morning, Louisa walked with her best friend, Tess, to Market Square. Tess came from a family of ten children, and her older sisters confided freely about their courtships. Moreover, her mother still pretended to be a southern belle. Most likely that was why Tess had always displayed such a lively interest in boys.

She could ask Tess about courting, Louisa decided. She looked at her overly plump friend, dressed as always in a full pink dress. Nervously Louisa transferred her market basket from one hand to the other. How could she broach the subject? They had already discussed the fine spring weather and passersby.

They were halfway to the market when Tess said, "Let's go out walkin' this evenin'."

"I don't believe I can," Louisa replied.

Tess pouted, her southern accent coming to the fore. "We haven't gone walkin' yet one evenin' this week!"

Here it was, her opportunity to tell. Louisa tried to keep

11

her tone even. "Conduff Setter has called on me every night this week, and he's coming again tonight."

"Conduff Setter!" Tess repeated. Her soft green eyes opened wide, and her pretty heart-shaped face was full of amazement. "However did that come about?"

"Da brought him home."

Tess shook her head. "Why . . . Conduff Setter must be twenty-five years old, if he's a day. He's ten years older than we are!"

Louisa shrugged lightly, looking away. She scarcely saw the neat red-brick Federalist houses that lined the street. "I'll be sixteen in two weeks. Anyhow, that doesn't bother him."

"Not at all?"

"He has not mentioned it."

"Is Conduff serious about courtin'?" Tess asked. "Has he declared himself?"

Louisa faltered. "I—I guess not."

"You guess not? Oh, Louisa, smart as you are, you're such a goose about men. Why . . . I expect you don't know the first thing about courtin'."

"I suppose I don't."

"My sisters say a girl's got to make a man jealous."

"Make him jealous?" Louisa asked.

"O' course!"

Louisa said firmly, "It doesn't seem quite honest."

"Oh, Louisa, you are a goose! Worst of all, I just know you'll be the first in our class to be married . . . and to the most handsome man in town, even if he does work at the quarry."

Louisa's thoughts whirled. It was true that none of the others were yet married. To think that they might envy her!

Tess picked a piece of lint from her pink frock. "What's it like when y'all kiss?"

"Why, why—" Something prevented Louisa from sharing such an intimacy too fully, even with her best friend.

Tess demanded, "You don't mean to say he hasn't kissed you yet?"

"Of course he has!"

"And?"

Louisa felt herself blush. "It's . . . well, it's just fine."

Tess's shoulders drooped with disappointment. "That all you're tellin'?"

"Now, Tess, don't be mad. It's just not the kind of thing to tell. I would just as soon not talk about it anymore."

As the week passed, Louisa's ardor over Conduff deepened, and she had to remind herself time and again that she must not get caught up by feelings.

On Friday night Da said to Conduff, "Expect we ought to invite you to Sunday dinner since you been comin' all week."

Conduff smiled meaningfully at Louisa. "Guess I oughta try yer cookin'."

Her heart pounded wildly. "Aunt Sarah taught me how."

"Good," he said, "glad to hear it."

On Saturday afternoon she baked an apple pie and made all of her other cooking plans.

On Sunday she cooked oyster stew, roast beef, and kidney pies, not to mention peas and potatoes and biscuits and gravy.

When it was almost time for Conduff to arrive, she made a final pass through the dining room. It was a fine room with paneled mahogany walls, a high ceiling and tall windows, and a simple Federal fireplace she had filled with lilac blossoms since it was too warm for a fire. Her eyes noted the polished brass chandelier, the beautiful china and cut glass, and the bouquet of lilacs on the damask-covered table. Despite her nervousness, she felt aglow with pride.

Conduff arrived wearing a handsome black broadcloth suit with a high white stock around the neck. He didn't look in the least like a quarry worker except for his calloused hands. Dressed up, even Aunt Sarah might approve of him.

He and Da sat in the parlor and drank their whiskey until she announced, "Dinner is ready." She desperately hoped that Conduff would like her cooking.

As dinner proceeded, he and her father sat at the table and silently forked the food into their mouths. Occasionally Conduff eyed her with approval.

"Not a bad cook, is she?" her father remarked as they finished off with thick slabs of the apple pie.

Conduff grinned at her. "Not by half."

She attempted to hide her smile.

After they finished, she cleared the table while the men downed glasses of brandy wine.

Conduff said to her father, "Reckon I'd like to take yer daughter walkin' along the river."

Da grinned. "You do that. I don't expect you need my company."

Before long, she and Conduff were walking through town in the bright afternoon sunshine. She noticed that other young women, even some accompanied by beaus or husbands, eyed Conduff in admiration. The women said in impressed tones, "Good afternoon, Louisa!"

"Good afternoon," she replied as though a stroll with Conduff were not in the least extraordinary.

A spring breeze fluttered the bright new greenery and the rush of the river filled the warm air, soothing her nervousness so much that a walk alongside the majestic Potomac River with Conduff seemed the most natural thing on earth. Her senses reveled in the beauty of the scenery: the graceful outline of the green Virginia hills on one side and those of Maryland on the other. By the time he caught her hand in his, she felt so buoyant in spirit that she said, "Isn't this the most beautiful day?"

Conduff laughed. "If you say so, I expect it is."

She laughed herself, then chattered on as they continued along the grassy riverbank. She imagined the two of them in a handsome oil painting: she in her blue bell-skirted frock and Conduff in his black suit, butterflies hovering over the grassy riverbank and the blue Potomac flowing out to sea behind them.

He teased, "You like this, don't you, honey-girl?"

"Do I like what?"

"Courtin'," he replied with such an amused expression that she was sure he already knew her answer.

"I guess I do. Do you?"

He chuckled. "Cain't think of anythin' in the world I like better."

"You've done a lot of it, haven't you?" she ventured.

"Enough." He added with an artful glance, "But never with a little lady like you."

A lady, she marveled. He considered her a lady!

They rounded a grassy hill, and birds twittered from a copse of shrubbery near the riverbank, rising in flight as she and Conduff approached. "Let's jest set by the bank there awhile," he suggested.

The way he gazed into her eyes, she could only say, "If you like, Conduff."

He smiled and laid his handkerchief on the grass for her to sit on, and she settled on it with much self-conscious smoothing of her blue skirt.

He sat down beside her. "Come here," he urged, his voice husky. Seconds later his arm was around her shoulders, turning her to him in the warm grass. "Kiss me, honey-girl."

She could no more resist him than the river could cease its flow down from the mountains and out to the sea.

When they drew apart he said breathlessly, "Reckon you're gonna marry me, ain't you, honey-girl?"

Marry! She stared at him. He had not said he loved her, but he must if he wanted to marry her. "Oh, Conduff . . . yes, I will—"

He laughed. "I expect we ought to get married jest as soon as we cain."

Her heart leapt with happiness. "Yes, I guess we could." She had seen a beautiful wedding at church years ago, and a wish leapt to mind. "I'd like it to be in the church where . . . I used to go with Aunt Sarah."

He had been watching her intently, and at length he nodded. "Let's seal it with a real kiss, honey-girl."

She moved into his arms. "I—I'd rather you called me Louisa."

"Come 'ere," he said roughly. "Come 'ere, honey-girl."


Three weeks later they were married in the pastor's office with only Da and Tess in attendance, since Conduff did not want "a showy wedding." Nonetheless, she was marrying Conduff Setter! Louisa exulted as she stood in the white gauze bridal gown she had sewn herself. Conduff looked wonderfully handsome, though somewhat uneasy, in his black frock coat and trousers. Da wore his black suit, too, and Tess was dressed in a full-skirted pink dress as usual, though this one was new.

When Dr. Norton, the pastor, said, "The ring, please," Conduff placed a small garnet ring on her finger. He kept his attention on her hand, not looking into her eyes as she expected. It was a lovely ring, but for an instant she vaguely recalled having seen one like it on Vinnie Timmons, the black-haired milliner, who had none too fine a reputation.

Louisa set the thought aside. She was marrying Conduff Setter, and he was smiling at her, not at anyone else.

Dr. Norton said, "You may now kiss the bride," and she was overcome with a rush of happiness.

They took their bridal supper at Gadsby's Tavern, where everyone admired them. For her part, Louisa could not take her eyes from Conduff. They dined upon ham and turkey and, though she was unable to eat much herself, she was pleased to see Da, Tess, and Conduff tuck in so heartily. She only wished the men would not drink so much. Da had been imbibing since breakfast, and Conduff's breath had smelled of spirits during the wedding.

By the time they finished the fine dinner, Da was besotted. His words slurred as he said, "Well, girl, I married you off, and at just a mite over sixteen. Got you a strappin' husband, too."

"Da!" Louisa protested. She shot a glance at Tess, who was eyeing Conduff with appreciation and respect.

Her father ignored her. "Now I got an announcement myself."

Conduff asked, "What's that?"

"Quit my job at the quarry," Da said with a smirk:

"You quit?" Conduff asked, incredulous.

Da laughed. "No need havin' two men in the family killin' themselves. Ain't so young as I was."

Louisa felt her mouth drop open. That was why Da had encouraged the marriage—to have Conduff as a means of support! She glanced at Conduff and saw his eyes darken with anger. His voice was ominously level. "We best be goin' home."

They drove off from Gadsby's Tavern in a rented carriage and stopped to leave Tess at her house. "Y'all had a beautiful wedding," she said. "I do believe you are the most beautiful bride and groom I ever did see!"

"Thank you," Louisa replied, giving her friend a wave as Tess started for her front door.

Louisa turned to Conduff. His forehead was furrowed in a dark frown.

They rode home in silence.

When they arrived in the parlor, Conduff brought out a bottle of Kentucky whiskey for Da. "Got somethin' for you."

"Well, now—" Da said, pleased.

Conduff said to Louisa, "You go on upstairs. I'll be along soon."

She nodded and hurried up to her chamber. Their chamber it would be now. Hers and Conduff's! She quickly changed into the white cotton gown she had sewn for her wedding night.

When Conduff finally arrived at the door, he was staggering. "Set me up, yer Da did!" he growled. "All so he could quit work!"

"Conduff—"

His face darkened with fury. "Come 'ere!"

She froze in fear as he approached. His face boiled with fury, and his huge hand reared back, then slapped her across the room so hard that her head cracked against a bedpost. When her vision stopped whirling, her hand went to her hair, and she discovered it was wet with blood.

"Set me up!" he yelled. He grabbed her by the shoulders and threw her onto the bed. "Don't you never try to set me up fer nothin' again, you hear?"

"I won't, Conduff . . . I won't!" she promised.

The next morning when she read her marriage announcement to Mr. Conduff Setter in the *Alexandria Gazette*, Louisa's heart and body already ached with regret.

Feelings were not enough for a true or lasting love, Louisa thought for perhaps the hundredth time in the past three years. Her mind returned to the present, to the slave auction in Market Square.

She watched Conduff shove a huge African man in chains toward the auction block. Tonight Conduff would puff out his chest and ask, "Ain't I more of a man than that big black buck was? Now you tell me, honey-woman. . . ."

Honey-woman! She felt like screaming at the name, which she'd quickly learned had nothing to do with affection or love. Nor had it taken long for the owners of the quarry to see how Conduff mistreated their valued black workers. He had beaten one to uselessness the day he was fired.

Her attention turned to the surrounding auction crowd, and she was surprised to see the temporary shipping agent—Jonathan Chambers—hurry across Market Square. She slipped her hand into her dress pocket, grateful to feel the card with the Talbots' address still there. As he passed near her, their eyes met. He smiled and nodded, then, to her relief, moved on. Terrified that Conduff might take notice, she turned back to the slave auction block.

The auctioneer's staccato voice grated over the crowd as the bidders signaled. She watched Conduff's eyes rove to her again. She understood now why he insisted she be there: he wanted to flaunt his power over her, too. He wanted others to know he was her master, the man who had married into her family's fine Alexandria house. The townspeople's eyes followed Conduff's gloating stare to her. Seeing their pity, she felt newly ashamed and befouled.

Benjamin Talbot stared at his blank sheet of writing paper. Finally he dipped his quill in the India ink and wrote,

Rancho Verde
San Francisco
California Territory
May 8, 1849
Dear Louisa,

Most likely you do not remember me, for we met such a long time ago and you were quite young. You and I are second cousins related on your mother's side of the family. Although she was much younger, your mother and I were very fond of each other when we grew up together in Boston.

I am writing because you came to mind this evening, and I feel a great concern for you. My youngest daughter, Betsy, and I upheld you in prayer, and we want to offer you a place to stay if you are in need. We came from Independence, Missouri, to the California Territory by covered wagon nearly three years ago, and we live in a large Spanish-style house on the outskirts of San Francisco, as Yerba Buena is now called.

Our family includes my sister Jessica, who joined us after I was widowed fourteen years ago. She helped raise my children—Adam, Joshua, Martha, Rena, Jeremy, and Betsy—and has been a godsend. With the exception of Betsy, the children who live in California with us are married and have young families. They live in nearby houses on what is best described as a family compound. We live in the countryside, and the mild climate allows us to be outdoors a great deal, so we are not in the least crowded.

It must seem strange to receive such an invitation, but we have no ulterior motives and require no funds. Our family is established in shipping and trade as well as ranching. We are all Christians and have begun a neighborhood worship service in our house on the Sabbath as there are no churches yet. You would be treated well.

My main concern if you do wish to join us is the precariousness of the journey and the shipmates with whom you would have to contend. Last year, news of the gold discovery spread to our northwest coast, Mexico, Chile, and Peru, and across the Pacific to the Sandwich Islands, Australia, and China, but now word has spread to our own Atlantic community and beyond to Europe. It would not be an easy voyage for you with so many gold seekers under way. I feel obligated to warn you of this. In any case, you are most welcome.

Sincerely,
Benjamin Talbot


Betsy sat down at the small oak desk in her room, took out her writing paper, and wrote with her quill,


May 8, 1849
Dear Cousin Louisa,

Father said that I might enclose a letter to you with his own. Truly you are welcome here. I am most eager to have someone closer to my age in the house. I am only fourteen and I know you are nineteen, but you would be closer in age than Father and Aunt Jessica.

We have outdoor cats and dogs as well as riding horses. We also have what Father jestingly calls "the cattle on a thousand hills," for when we bought the rancho from a Spanish family, all of the cattle and horses were included, as well as the furnishings. At first, it was strange to move into someone else's furnished house, but we were glad not to have to order everything from Boston and wait to have it shipped around the Horn. We have come to like our house, Casa Contenta, very well.

Our house in Independence, Missouri, was made of logs, but this one is made of adobe that has been whitened with a crushed seashell wash both inside and out. The rooms, including "yours" next to mine, are bright white and sunny, and have dark Spanish furniture. Father says it is not an elegant house such as one might find in Alexandria or Boston, but it is most comfortable.

Aunt Jessica was once a schoolteacher, and she has been preparing me to teach, too, since there is talk of establishing more schools soon. There is a private school in town, but I have not yet attended it. I have small nieces and nephews upon whom I practice teaching for now. Our life is very simple, and we do not have grand balls or entertainments such as you might have in Virginia. We look forward to a camp meeting with divine services on our stream one weekend next month. We had one last year, too.

My mother died when I was born, and I know that your mother died many years ago, too. I can only think how sad I would be without a large family. With all of my heart, Louisa, I welcome you.

Sincerely,
Betsy Talbot

# 2

Louisa slipped out of the slave auction crowd once she thought her absence would not stir Conduff's wrath. Nervous, she chose the long way home and hurried along Duke Street, where he was employed at the red-brick prison. The sign over the building spelled out in unabashedly large black letters, "Price, Birch & Co., Dealers in Slaves."

She shuddered at its barred windows and doors, and tried not to inhale the foul smell of the place. Incredible that so many townsfolk took dealing in human flesh for granted, though she had never stated her opinion publicly. Conduff, for one, would be furious, and Tess would probably say, "You're bein' silly, you goose! That's just how life is now."

Be that as it may, Louisa always cringed to see the place. Worst of all was seeing the poor slaves who went unsold at auction being turned out in public view before their trek to Richmond. After having been confined and likely mauled in the loathsome prison, the children and the older women were crowded into wagons, and the others followed afoot, handcuffed or chained together. A week never passed without their being driven through the streets by Conduff, who rode alongside them astride a gray gelding, rifle and whip close at hand.

Why must she object so strenuously to slavery? Louisa wondered. Why couldn't she accept it without question like most of the townsfolk?

Aunt Sarah had often remarked, "It's a sorry sight in a free country to see chain gangs clank through the streets." She had said, too, "You have a strong bent toward righteousness, Louisa. It's a fine trait, but you are going to be disappointed in people. Still, there's the proverb, 'He that followeth after righteousness and mercy findeth life, righteousness, and honor.'"

Aunt Sarah had been right about being disappointed in some people, and the proverb had held true, too, Louisa thought. After committing her life to the Lord, she had rediscovered a measure of dignity and honor in her life. She had also learned to count her blessings, one of which was Conduff's absence for a week every month when he took the slaves south.

As she hurried along, she felt increasingly uneasy. She glanced back and saw no one paying inordinate attention to her. Reassured, she slowly turned her mind to the scenes of Alexandria she would soon leave behind: slave pens, cotton and flour mills, neat red-brick houses, churches with their tall white steeples.

Tonight she would write to the California Talbots, she decided, the thought bittersweet. If it were not for the child inside her, she would probably be too frightened to leave. In any case, no one would know except the temporary shipping agent, and since he was temporary, he would soon depart, too. She still felt unnerved as she approached her red-brick house, and looked behind her again before she hurried in.

"There you are, girl," Da complained from his chair in the parlor, where he sat with his foot up on a stool to relieve his gout. "Thought you'd ne'er get home."

For an instant she felt as though she were a child again, as though he could read her every thought. "I—I started supper before I left."

"Ain't worried about supper. It's lonely when yer out. If I got out to the grog shops—"

"I can't give you another penny, Da. You know I have little enough to run the household. And you know how furious Conduff is when I give you money."

She took off her bonnet and examined her father. In the three years since her marriage, Da's hair had gone gray and his face had wrinkled up like an old man's. His only occupation was to putter begrudgingly at house repairs. "No longer my house," he would grumble, though he was the one who had deeded it to Conduff to stave off foreclosure.

She hung her bonnet on a hall peg. "I'll bring you a cup of coffee."

"You're good, girl."

"I am not so good at all," she responded, guilt-ridden at the thought of leaving him if she went to California.

"O' course, you are. Sometimes . . . sometimes I'm sorry about gettin' you and Conduff together. I expect it hasn't come out like you hoped. I saw it all different myself."

"Yes, I imagined it very differently, too, Da."

"You forgivin' me?"

"I forgave you when I returned to church," she replied. She looked him straight in the eyes. "You weren't alone in my decision to marry Conduff. I could have argued against it. I had to forgive myself and him, too, and I couldn't have done it on my own. It is only through Christ that we can really forgive others."

"Gettin' more like yer mother was toward the end."

"Like my mother?" she asked, for he never mentioned her.

"All blue eyes 'n red hair, 'n standin' straight as a princess, she was, like you. Bookish, too." His throat sounded husky and he harrumphed. "What I meant, I expect, is that you changed, too, after you started back to church."

She had to smile. "I am pleased to hear it was evident."

He gave her a wan smile in return. "Ne'er held with religion myself. Maybe I'll start goin' to church when I'm old."

*You're already old, Da,* Louisa fretted. *You're already old!*

"I'm glad to hear you take some blame yerself fer marryin' Conduff. He's still a mighty good-lookin' man."

"Yes, that he is, though I doubt it will last long the way he lives." She turned wearily toward the kitchen before he could say more. "I'll get your coffee now."

That evening, when Conduff sat down for supper, he blustered at Da. "What did you do here all day, old man? Sit on yer haunches or fix them back steps?"

Da huffed, "I ain't no carpenter!"

"You ain't good at nothin' but sittin' in yer chair," Conduff replied, glowering at him. "I've half a mind to throw you out, then jest see where you'd be."

Da's mouth tightened. "Throw me out of my own house? I don't believe you'd do sech a thing!"

"Don't tempt me," Conduff warned, "or first thing you know you'll be on the street!"

Louisa's breath caught at the anger in Conduff's green eyes. As for Da, it was not the first time he had looked vaguely frightened of Conduff. She pleaded, "Please, let's have peace at the table tonight," and they lapsed into a silence fraught with resentment.

Later, when Conduff departed for the grog shops, a temporary calm descended upon the house. At last Da went to bed, and Louisa went nervously upstairs to Aunt Sarah's old bedroom.

Taking out her writing paper, Louisa sat down at the dressing table. She must write quickly before Conduff returned, though he usually was out till after midnight. Quill in hand, she pondered what she might say to the Talbots. How could she impose on almost unknown relations? Far worse, how could she leave Alexandria and the home she had lived in all of her life? As for Da and Conduff—

*Lord, help me write this if I am to go to California,* she prayed.

While she waited in the quiet, the words began to come.

May 8, 1849
Dear Mr. Talbot,

I am uncertain of how to write to you, since you probably do not remember me. Perhaps you will recall that your cousin Ruth bore a daughter in 1830 here in Alexandria, Virginia. I am that daughter and am now nineteen years old. As you know, Mother died of cholera in the great epidemic of 1832.

Aunt Sarah told me you visited here when I was small, but I regret I do not remember it. She also told me to contact you if ever I needed assistance.

As you might know, Alexandria is in a state of decline. Our city fathers invested heavily in a canal, while Baltimore brought in a railroad and has taken the lead in commerce. At any rate, I find that I must seek employment, and I would like to come to the California Territory. I sew well and can cook a bit, too, but I cannot find work here, not only because of our city's decline, but because there are so many free blacks and slaves to do such work. I read in the

*Alexandria Gazette* that there are few women in the California Territory. Can you please advise me whether I might find work there?

Regretfully my finances are precarious, but I have funds for the trip. I would like to come as soon as possible. Please do not think that I cannot make my own way, for I am strong and unafraid of hard work. I have graduated from our public school with honors, which is insufficient for teaching here, but perhaps I could teach children on the frontier.

I would appreciate any advice that you can give me with regards to the voyage. . . .

She ripped up the letter and began again, rewriting by candlelight until the letter was as good—and as honest—as possible without telling about Conduff or the child. If they knew, it seemed unlikely they would welcome her. Her middle name, Abigail, honored the memory of Benjamin Talbot's mother, and she included it in her signature.

As she folded the stiff sheet of paper, Louisa felt as though she had taken an irrevocable step in the only hopeful direction. Now she must post the letter before Conduff arrived, but how? She glanced out her window into the moonlight and knew it would be impossible to take to town now, not with so many ruffians about. Quite suddenly, an answer struck her. Tess!

Ten minutes later, she stood outside her friend's darkened house and tossed a pebble against her upstairs window, just as they had done in their childhood. She quickly retreated into the shadow of the huge elm tree and waited. Tess's window shone darkly in the moonlight.

Louisa tossed another pebble and hurried to the shadows again. An owl hooted from an upper branch, and she jerked back in alarm, scraping her arm against the tree.

Finally Tess opened the window.

As Louisa stepped out into the moonlight, she whispered, "It's me—Louisa. Can you come down?"

"Just a minute."

Louisa waited in the darkness, uneasy amidst the croakings of night frogs and the chirrings of insects and birds.

Finally, Tess hurried toward her from the house, a shawl wrapped around her ample nightgown. "You gave me a scare!"

"I'm sorry. You know I wouldn't be here unless it was highly important," Louisa replied, feeling strangely formal with her old friend.

"Of course I do. What is it?"

"Will you post a letter for me tomorrow morning? I don't dare have it in the house."

"Well . . . surely I will," Tess replied as she accepted the letter. "Whatever is amiss?"

"Oh, Tess, I would rather not even think about it."

"It's Conduff, isn't it?" Tess asked.

"Oh, Tess, I don't wish to complain. "

"I know, but I'm your friend, and it hurts me to see how he mistreats you. I've seen the bruises on your face and arms ever since the weddin'."

Louisa looked down. "I am grateful to you for helping me."

"Mailin' a letter is nothin'. I'd do anythin' to help. I—I fear I encouraged you in the marriage."

Louisa shook her head. "It was my responsibility entirely. I didn't even ask the Lord about it. I only gave Him directions like, 'Lord, please make Conduff love me' and 'Please make him want to marry me!'"

Tess shrugged. "I reckon I don't see anythin' wrong with that, but I don't believe like you do." She peered at the letter in the dim moonlight. "California Territory!"

"Shh! Yes—I don't know the cost to send it. I will have to repay you later."

"I didn't think of the cost. It's—You're not plannin' to go there?"

Louisa caught a deep breath. "Not only for my sake." Tears welled in her eyes. "I didn't want to tell you or anyone else, but I am . . . with child."

"Oh, my dear!" Tess opened her plump arms, and Louisa caught back a sob as she threw herself into her friend's warm embrace. It was the first time she had told anyone, and a sob escaped from her throat, then another and another.

"It'll be fine," Tess promised and patted her back. "It'll be fine."

At long last, Louisa drew away and blew her nose. "I do forgive Conduff, for his father beat him and his mother. But, oh, Tess, I can't break down again. I must keep a level head so I'm not caught."

"And I mustn't make it harder for you, but I don't want you to leave Alexandria! You're the best friend I have ever had. Nobody else would love someone like me—"

"Of course they would! You mustn't be so hard on yourself." To her surprise, Louisa now found herself the one to give a reassuring hug.

She returned home in the darkness, calmed after her cry until she saw candlelight flickering in the parlor windows. Who lit the parlor candles? she wondered with alarm. She was certain she had snuffed them out before going upstairs to write the letter. Could Conduff be home already?

She ran quietly to the back of the house and let herself

in. The rooms looked undisturbed. Nothing seemed amiss. Perhaps Da had come downstairs again or she had simply forgotten the candles, she decided as she snuffed them out. But starting up the stairs, she grew more and more uneasy.

Light filtered out from under their bedchamber door, and she opened it with trepidation. "Conduff!" she whispered as she saw him awaiting her in his undershirt and trousers.

He grabbed her by the shoulders, his face contorted with rage. "Where you sneakin' off to at night, woman?" he demanded.

"I—I was at Tess's house for a few minutes."

"Liar!" he yelled, giving her a hard shake.

"But I was!" He reeked of whiskey, and the smell made her draw away in fear.

He jerked her back to him. "And what's yer excuse fer goin' to the Talbot office today? I know you were there!"

"I—" He was in another drunken rage, and she could see he would beat her no matter what she told him. She crossed her arms over her stomach to protect the child, but he slapped her so hard she careened across the room, then again, flinging her to the floor.

"I got people watchin' you!" he yelled.

A drunken wastrel at the waterfront? she wondered numbly as she pulled herself up, determined to escape him.

Conduff spewed obscenities as though he were beset by demons, hitting her again and again until his words and the room spun around her. Then she heard Da shout at him in the whirling room, "Stop that hittin'! Git yer hands off 'er!"

At long last she lapsed into a swirl of blackness.

Light and shadow moved through the darkness . . . light and shadow again. Light overcomes the darkness, she vaguely remembered. Light overcomes the darkness.

"Louisa?" Tess's voice sounded far away in the light that flickered in her head.

Groggy, she blinked and thought she saw Tess's heart-shaped face.

"Louisa?"

"What is it?" she asked, then saw that she was in bed.

"Louisa, it's me, Tess."

Louisa focused on the familiar face. Yes, it was her friend right down to the pink dress, but a most solemn Tess.

"I thought you'd never wake up . . . and I didn't know what to do—"

Louisa shook her head slightly. "Oh . . . my head aches!"

"I am afraid your headache isn't the worst of what's happened. Oh, my dear friend—"

"What is it? What's happened?"

Tess shook her head. "I wish I didn't have to tell you—" She drew a breath. "Your Da was found by the back steps."

"Found by the back steps?"

"I don't know what to say, Louisa, but I must tell you."

"Tell me what?"

Tess's lips trembled. "That . . . your Da is dead."

"Dead?"

"He—" Tess hesitated, her face white and her mouth tightly compressed. "The police inspector says your Da was repairing the steps and fell through . . . and broke his neck. And one of Conduff's ne'er-do-well friends claims he came by just then and saw it happen."

Da dead? It was impossible. Yet here she was in bed after such a long time in the darkness, and here was Tess hovering over her.

"Oh, Louisa, he is dead," Tess said. "I saw him myself."

Da is dead! The realization hit her like one of Conduff's hard blows. She recalled that Da had come to her defense and tried to stop Conduff. Suspicion seeped through her shock. "Where is Conduff?"

"He left that mornin' to take slaves to Richmond. They said at the slave pen he'd be back in a week."

"He left before Da died?"

Tess nodded. "That's what Conduff's friend says."

She did not look convinced, either, Louisa thought. Da's death seemed no coincidence after Conduff had threatened him so severely. Yet if Conduff's friend told the authorities he had witnessed Da's death and it was an accident, it would be impossible to prove otherwise.

Surely this was a nightmare, she thought, but—no—everything was real. "What is today? How long have I been in bed?"

"Thursday. It's been three days."

"Three days!"

Tess's lips quivered again. "They had to bury your Da this morning. They said they couldn't wait any longer."

"This morning!" A wave of despair surged through her. Just days ago, when she had spoken to Da about the Lord, he'd said, "Ne'er cared much for religion myself." Every time she'd spoken to him of her faith, he had resisted.

Slowly she sat up in bed. Almost immediately, she knew what the soreness in her abdomen meant. "The baby!"

Tears welled in Tess's eyes. "It's gone. Oh, Louisa, the baby's gone, too!"

"No!" The word of denial echoed and re-echoed in her mind. If only she could escape into the darkness again. Da dead . . . and her baby. "No, God, please no!"

"Sleep, try to sleep," Tess urged, looking devastated.

Louisa's thoughts tumbled endlessly. Da dead and the baby, too. How could she possibly sleep? Yet finally she drifted into the darkness.

She awakened alone. Tess was probably cooking dinner for her family. She always had so much work at home, work her mother should do herself. She reached for the note on the chair by the bed. *Will return in an hour. Tess.*

For long minutes, Louisa lay awash in anguish. If only Conduff hadn't learned of her visit to the shipping office. If only she'd loved Da more. She thought of the child, the sweet babe she had begun to imagine in her arms. How she'd gazed at every newborn in Alexandria these past weeks.

Hot tears stung her eyes, and she brushed them away. Rouse yourself, girl. Think what to do. Da was dead and buried, the house heavily mortgaged—certainly to be lost from Conduff's wild spending.

She sat up weakly. Conduff would be home on Sunday, and then what? Perhaps she should leave for California now. Nothing held her here anymore.

*Lord, help me,* she prayed. She stood up and took hold of a bedpost. Slowly she made her way to the armoire. Staring in it at her clothing, she realized she did not even own a black dress for mourning. She took out her fawn-colored frock and dressed, then daubed the bruises on her face with brown lotion and rice powder. If she wore her matching fawn bonnet, perhaps the temporary shipping agent would not suspect she had been beaten.

As she tied on her bonnet, she scrutinized herself in the oval mirror. Despite her ordeal, she looked passable, though the brown lotion did not entirely mask the darkness under her eyes, and the top of her left hand was a mottled yellow.

Her attention went to her small garnet wedding band. Slowly, very slowly, she removed it from her finger. Conduff could return the ring to Vinnie Timmons, for he saw her openly now, even walked out along the river with her in daylight.

She eased herself down the stairs to the main floor, then continued down to the cellar and to the musty potato bin. She opened it and let out her breath with relief. The bin appeared undisturbed. She rolled the potatoes away from the wall and saw the soiled piece of white canvas she had hidden years ago. Unfolding the canvas, she found the gold coins Aunt Sarah had pressed upon her for an emergency. Louisa placed the coins in her purse, then forced herself back up the cellar steps. Onward, always onward.

Outside, the sun still shone and the sky was still blue. Give me the strength to go on, she prayed.

She must avoid Market Square where she would be recognized, she thought as she started out. Slowly she walked the long way around town to the shipping office.

At the waterfront, she looked about warily. Men loaded a shipment of bread from Alexandria ovens into a nearby sailing ship—the only wharfside activity. If Conduff's "spy" was one of the stevedores or idlers watching her now there was nothing she could do about it. Ahead was the Wainwright and Talbot office.

"Let it be open," she whispered. She turned the brass knob and sent up a prayer of thanksgiving to find the door unlocked.

Jonathan Chambers rose from his desk, obviously pleased to see her. "Good day. I had expected you several days ago to pick up the fare information." Gazing at her face, his smile faded. "I . . . thought perhaps you had changed your mind."

His words took a long time to penetrate her mind, and her own words even longer to speak. "I was detained."

"I see." He appeared disconcerted as he sorted through the files and papers on his desk. "Ah, here it is," he said and handed her a sheet of paper.

At first she could not quite take in the information, then she understood the fare figures—and that she had sufficient funds. "I would like to buy a ticket to the California Territory, but please . . . in confidence."

He nodded. "You have my word. They have found another agent to take my place, so rest assured that no one will question me."

She vaguely comprehended that her departure would remain a secret. "I shall take the train from Washington City to Baltimore tomorrow."

"I also leave for Baltimore tomorrow," he said. "I would be pleased to escort you . . . to see to your safety."

"You are leaving, too?" she repeated with suspicion.

"Yes, my family lives in Baltimore," he explained, then added, "I was raised there."

He had an aura of honesty about him, but she was only slightly reassured. Perhaps he had rescheduled his departure for her sake.

He added, "It is far better to make arrangements for your ship when we arrive in Baltimore."

"I must leave here before daybreak."

"I can arrange for the carriage without arousing curiosity," he replied.

"I appreciate your kindness, but it—it wouldn't do to go only because of me."

"I understand." After an instant's pause, he handed a slip of paper to her. "If you will write your street and number, the carriage will arrive just before dawn."

She penned her address before she could change her mind.

He said, "I do not know your name."

She faltered, unwilling to give either her maiden or married name. "Louisa Talbot—"

His eyes widened. "I wondered whether you were a Talbot when you asked for their address."

"Actually it was my mother who was the Talbot—"

"I see," he said and did not question her further.

"Before dawn then?" she asked.

"Yes, before dawn." A message of trust passed from his eyes to her.

"Thank you. Good day," she finally said. As she closed the door behind her, she gathered strength from her success. Onward, she reminded herself. Onward.

Rays of late afternoon sunshine slanted through the spring greenery as she arrived at the unconsecrated burial grounds between the church and the edge of the forest. It took only a few moments to spot the fresh mound of earth over Da's grave, and she wended her way through the other graves to it.

Tears filled her eyes and she dropped to her knees on the grass beside it. "Oh, Da, I'm sorry, so sorry you had to die this way," she whispered. "If only matters had been different between us . . . and if only you had never met Conduff—"

Her mind returned to her last memory of Da. "Stop that hittin'!" he had shouted at Conduff. "Get yer hands off 'er!"

Perhaps Da led her into marriage, but at least he had repented of it. She hoped he had called out in repentance to God as well, but it was said that few people did in their last moments. Thoughts and memories intermingled, reconciling what might have been with reality, and, after a long time, she rose to her feet. Da was gone, and now she must leave, too.

Inside the nearby churchyard, she stopped at the graves of her mother and Aunt Sarah. "I am leaving," she said softly, her heart aching. She only remembered what Aunt Sarah had told her of Mother, but she missed her aunt most sorely.

At long last she turned away, and her eyes went to the

sky with its puffy white clouds. God had made the earth and the heavens, and she was His child; surely He would take care of her now that her parents and Aunt Sarah were gone.

A sense of peace filled her as she walked in the dappled sunshine among the trees and turned to the white-trimmed brick church. No one was about, and she made her way up the steps, through the narthex, and into the white sanctuary.

Sunlight streamed through the palladian window over the white wooden pew boxes, and she slowly walked across the dark floor to the pew where she had made her decision to accept Christ as her Savior. This would be her last time here. She sat down and allowed serenity to sink deeply into her soul. At last she bowed her head and prayed.

When she left the sanctuary, she felt drawn to Dr. Norton's study. She found him at the door, hat in hand, ready to depart. His ruddy face brightened. "Louisa, come in. What a pleasure to have you round off my day."

"I don't want to keep you. I was just passing by."

"Nonsense. You could never inconvenience me." He ushered her into his study, a room with the same white walls and dark floors of the sanctuary. "I had no idea you were on your feet again. Please sit down."

"Only a moment." How tired she was, she realized as she sank into a parlor chair.

"Not always easy, this life, is it?" he asked. He settled into a parlor chair near her.

"No, it is not."

"But the Christian life is always victorious in the end. Even here on earth we are blessed to be a blessing."

"I am afraid that I do not feel very blessed right now." Suddenly the words burst out in sobs. "The baby is gone—and Da! I didn't like how he lived . . . but I loved him!"

He patted her arm, then waited until she grew more calm. "I pray for you often, Louisa," Dr. Norton said, "I sense great potential for the Lord to use you." He paused. "I have told you before that Christ died for man's sins and that you are not required to die for Conduff's sins, too. He is a dangerous man."

Odd that he should mention it now, she thought. She recalled that Dr. Norton had once suggested leaving Conduff as a way of defense.

"Has Conduff ever asked for your forgiveness?"

"Never," she answered with a sad shake of her head. "The next day he . . . pretends as if nothing has gone amiss."

"Only God can change him, but Conduff is the one who must be willing."

Louisa nodded. She had prayed and prayed for Conduff, but he had no interest in God or in changing.

Dr. Norton smiled kindly at her. "You may not feel blessed now, Louisa, but feelings have little to do with it. You will be better next week, better yet in a month or two, and one day you will see how blessed you truly are."

It seemed impossible, she thought as she blew her nose. Finally she caught hold of her emotions and rose to her feet. She would never see this dear man again and she said, "I am grateful to have you for a friend."

"And I, you, Louisa."

As she bid him farewell, she hoped he'd recall their last words when he learned of her departure.

In the churchyard, she tried to imprint its image on her memory: the white steepled brick church and its graveyard set against the sunlit forest.

She walked slowly to the street and, glancing back against the late afternoon sun, was startled to see a man step furtively from behind an oak tree near the burial ground.

Seeing her, he retreated behind the tree again.

Her heart pounded against her breast. The same man from the waterfront who had reported on her to Conduff?!

Revived by the shock, she set forth toward Tess's house. How could she not have noticed him before! She had felt uneasy since the first time she'd visited the shipping office.

She cast another backward glance down the tree-lined street, but could see only children playing. Was the man only a figment of sunlight and her exhaustion? she asked herself. In any case, it was a good thing she was leaving Alexandria tomorrow morning, although even "before dawn" did not seem a moment too soon.

# 3

When Louisa arrived at Tess's house, her friend's disheveled mother lounged on the front stoop, gossiping with a neighbor. She looked up peevishly. "Guess you're lookin' for Tess. You'll find her back in the kitchen, as usual, probably eatin' more 'n she cooks."

Louisa thanked her politely and let herself into the house. Conduff had once called Tess's mother "a loose-lipped slattern," and, unfortunately, Louisa had to agree with him.

The delectable aromas of beef stew and hot corn bread wafted through the warm house, and she found Tess in the kitchen stirring a huge pot of stew, surrounded by her rambunctious younger brothers and sisters.

Tess stopped stirring in surprise. "Louisa—what are you doin' out of bed already?"

"I have something to confide." The children quieted at once to listen, and Louisa knew they would tell their mother, who in turn would spread the news through Alexandria as fast as a telegraph could. "Can you come see me after supper?"

Tess's soft green eyes danced with curiosity. "I will . . . and I'll bring a bowl of stew. But, please, go on home and to bed!"

"I don't have time to rest."

"Oh, Louisa, take time!" The stew began to bubble wildly, and Tess was reminded to stir it again.

"I shall see you later then, Tess."

As Louisa made her departure, she thought she would always remember her dear friend in the kitchen with small brothers and sisters rampaging about her. It was amazing that she rarely complained about doing her mother's work.

Outside on the stoop, her mother asked with an ingratiating smile, "What y'all stop by to tell Tess?"

"Nothing of consequence." The instant she spoke the words, she realized she had told another falsehood. "Good evening," she quickly added and made a hasty escape.

She peered down the street. No one in sight.

Lacking the strength to hurry, Louisa went on slowly and tried to fix pleasant memories of Alexandria in her mind: the neat red-brick houses, the horses clip-clopping along the fine cobblestone streets, the heady fragrance of lilacs abloom near her front door.

An hour later, she sat on her bed and folded her clothing, then packed it into Aunt Sarah's old trunk. She had sewn two new summer dresses during her lonely evenings, and she would not look like a shabby urchin on the journey, nor upon her arrival in California. When her possessions were packed, she added Aunt Sarah's Bible as a keepsake of the dear woman who had reared her and loved her so much.

"Anyone here?" Tess called out from downstairs.

"I'm upstairs."

Tess came puffing up the steps, carrying a bowl of stew covered with a white linen napkin. "I locked the door. You should be more careful when you're alone."

"I guess I should. It is just that I am so tired."

Tess must have sensed something amiss, for she asked,

"Has Conduff returned?" She could not see the trunk, which was slightly hidden behind the bed.

"No. He never comes home from Richmond until Sunday."

Tess set the bowl on the bed table. "Never?"

"Never yet. I hope this will not be the first time."

"I hoped to find you in bed," Tess said, then spied the trunk. "Why . . . whatever is that for?"

"I am leaving now for California, Tess. Before dawn tomorrow morning."

Tess's hands flew to her cheeks. "Oh, Louisa! Not already! You're not strong enough."

"My strength has little to do with it. I must go now."

"I daresay I don't blame you," Tess replied with a catch in her voice, "but it's so soon. I was only beginnin' to accept your leavin' in a few months. Yet it's better to leave now before—" She hesitated.

"Before things grow worse," Louisa finished for her.

"You are going to need money."

"Aunt Sarah left me a bit."

"I see. Well, I've been thinkin' that you would need a place to keep money, so I guess I'll give this to you now." From her handbag Tess extracted a worn leather money belt.

"Oh, Tess, you must be the most thoughtful friend in the world. What am I ever going to do without you?"

Tess shrugged carelessly and occupied herself with uncovering the steaming stew. "How you goin'?"

"By ship from Baltimore, then through Panama."

Tess straighted up in shock. "Through the jungle? Oh, Louisa—"

"I'll manage, Tess. I promise, I will manage."

"And I'll never rest 'til I hear you've arrived in California."

"I'll write the moment I am there."

Tess nodded uneasily, then finally said, "Sit down and eat. You will need all of the strength you can muster for such an arduous journey."

"I guess I will." Louisa sat on the edge of the bed, took up her spoon, and tried the stew. Delicious as it was, she was almost too tired to swallow.

Tess viewed the trunk. "Is that all you are takin'?"

"It's all I have packed."

"The *Gazette* says California's a raw place with no linens and such to buy there. What's more, Conduff will sell whatever you leave behind! Don't you have another trunk?"

"In the attic, but I didn't have the strength—"

"I'll fetch it."

Soon Tess had packed another trunk with linens, lengths of fabric, and Aunt Sarah's rose-and-white double wedding ring quilt. Watching her dear friend work with such determination, Louisa's eyes filled with tears.

"It's your family's house," Tess said. "It's not fair you're the one leavin' when it's Conduff causin' the trouble!"

"If I hadn't been so drawn to him—"

"You were too young to see what he really was."

"Too young and too foolish . . . and not listening to the Lord. If only I . . . if only—" To her amazement, a sob burst from her throat, then another and another. "I don't even have a black dress for mourning!"

"Oh, phoo! Mournin' clothes just can't be considered now!" Tess's own eyes brimmed with tears. "Please, Louisa, promise you'll write often."

"I do promise," Louisa said unsteadily.

"I know you'll say we should count our blessin's. Well, there are only two blessin's I can think of about your leavin'. First, there's supposed to be a great deal of gold in the

California Territory—and from my viewpoint—" She managed a tremulous smile, "—a great multitude of men."

Louisa made a valiant attempt to return the smile. "Oh, Tess . . . if only you could come, too!"

It was still dark when the downstairs clock rang out four o'clock. Time to rise.

Louisa sat up in bed and fumbled to light a candle. Perhaps this was a dream, she thought as the wick flamed and illuminated her room. But there on the floor were her trunks and the hand baggage all packed for the journey. Sudden panic constricted her throat, and she checked Conduff's side of the bed. Empty. Blessedly empty.

She washed and remembered to put on the money belt with the gold coins in it before she pulled her new blue muslin frock over her head. Finally she donned her matching blue cape and cabriolet bonnet.

The soft knock at the front door, though expected, startled her. She hurried to the entry, flickering candle in hand.

"Ready, Miss Talbot?" Jonathan Chambers asked from the doorstep, his hazel eyes meeting hers in the candlelight.

Miss Talbot? She nearly corrected him, then recovered her wits. "Yes, I am ready. The trunks are upstairs."

"Let me send the driver for them."

Fortunately the driver was a stranger and, before long, he shouldered her trunks and carried them out into the night.

She caught up a bag of buttered biscuits and, numbed by her leave-taking, locked the front door. As she hurried down the walk, she smelled the lilac blossoms on the nearby bush. Would she ever smell lilacs again? Surely she would find nothing so civilized in California.

Jonathan helped her into the hired carriage and sat down

beside her, allowing a proper space between them on the seat.

"Thank you for making the arrangements, Mr. Chambers," she said to him in the darkness.

"My pleasure. And it's Jonathan, if you please, Miss . . . Talbot."

"Then please call me Louisa."

From up on the box, the driver called quietly to the horses, and the carriage lurched forward. She peered back toward her house, but saw only its outline in the moonlight. Her heart twisted. Farewell . . . she thought, farewell!

She closed her eyes. From this time forward her new life would begin. Soon she could write Tess about the train ride from Washington City to Baltimore, about sailing to Panama and the land crossing to the Pacific, then the voyage north to San Francisco. It seemed an endless journey into the future, and she was already so exhausted.

Finally she slept.

"Louisa?" The man's voice sounded vaguely familiar. "We're in Washington City. Time to wake up."

She sat up with a start and immediately remembered why she was in the carriage. "I'm sorry—"

"Apparently you needed a rest," he said.

"Yes." Looking out her window, she saw the first rosy rays of daylight curve over Washington City. As the carriage bumped along the rutted streets of the capital, dawn illuminated the stately new buildings: the domed Capital, the President's White Mansion, the Treasury Building, the Patent Office.

"It's an impressive sight in the morning," Jonathan commented, "even if Charles Dickens did characterize our capital as 'spacious avenues that begin in nothing and lead nowhere.' "

She had to smile. If nothing else, it heartened her to be with a man who at least read. "I hadn't heard that, though I know Jefferson called it 'an Indian swamp in the wilderness.' "

"It might have been true in his day," Jonathan replied, "but not anymore."

Rays of golden sunshine began to brighten the city and, in the morning stillness, the city did achieve an aspect of grandeur. She smiled. "My Aunt Sarah always said that things looked best in the morning, though I don't suppose she was referring to Washington City."

"Perhaps she was," he returned with a chuckle, then he glanced out the window again.

For the first time, she took a good look at him. He was perhaps thirty, and his dark hair was thick and straight, neatly parted, angling over his high forehead. When he turned to her again, she noted the deep cleft in his chin and his hazel-colored eyes, which held an aura of kindness, as did his entire countenance. He was a fine-looking man, even if he wasn't quite handsome.

"Do you have friends here?" he asked.

"No, nearly all of my friends are . . . elsewhere." Back in Alexandria and most now married, but it wouldn't do to tell him that. As for Washington City, Conduff considered its residents and the many free blacks "too uppity." She preferred not to consider his likely pursuit of her, but if he did, going through Washington City would add to his anger.

The carriage slowed to a halt, and Jonathan said, "Here we are. The train is waiting, but we still have time."

She looked apprehensively toward the corner of Second Street and Pennsylvania Avenue. A shiny black locomotive with brilliant red trimmings spewed dark smoke through its smokestack; behind the engine were coal, baggage, passenger, and freight cars, and finally the caboose. The train huffed restlessly on the tracks before the narrow, three-story brick building that housed the Baltimore and Ohio train station.

Uneasy, she dug through her handbag for some of her remaining household money and pressed the bills upon him. "For the cost of my train ticket and the carriage."

He looked as if he might refuse her money, then his eyes met hers with understanding. "If you insist."

"Thank you. I do."

When she stepped out of the carriage, a dozen or more passengers milled about the platform—but no one she knew. Porters carried suitcases and trunks to the baggage car, and horses whinnied as yet more freight wagons pulled up to unload alongside smaller wagons and buggies. Ten or twelve brawny laborers hauled barrels and crates from the wagons, then trundled them to the freight cars. Strangers, every one of them, Louisa thought with relief.

"I shall return as soon as possible," Jonathan said and hurried off to purchase their tickets. Louisa stood uneasily on the platform and watched the porters wheel the trunks to the baggage car. Fortunately, there were few passengers for Baltimore—and the fewer people who might identify her, the better.

The train huffed more loudly, and thicker smoke billowed from the locomotive's smokestack. The warning bell rang in the belfry, and she looked nervously toward the station door.

Finally Jonathan hurried out. "Time to board!" He handed their tickets to the conductor, then helped her onto the train.

She hesitated as they stepped into the aisle of the half-full railroad car, and he suggested, "Shall we take the seat by the window?"

Several male passengers lowered their newspapers and watched as she and Jonathan headed for an empty bench.

"Newlyweds, I'll warrant," someone said.

Heat rushed to her face, and she was grateful that Jonathan seemed not to have heard.

As she sat down beside him, she realized they would be together all morning. It wasn't what she had intended, but there'd been no time to give such matters much thought.

After they'd settled themselves on the hard wooden bench, he took a copy of the *Alexandria Gazette* from his tan leather valise, and she looked out the window.

The locomotive blasted a throaty warning, and the conductor bellowed, "All abooaarrd! All aboard for Baltimore!" The train blasted another warning before the doors slammed shut and the cars jerked into motion.

Louisa gripped her armrest and peered out the window at Washington City for what would most likely be the last time. Smoke billowed all around them as they chugged away from the station and slowly gathered speed.

Jonathan smiled at her. "Is this your first train ride?"

"Yes . . . and my first trip to Baltimore." His tone implied that she was rather young and naive—a refreshing notion, for lately she felt far older than nineteen.

"What do you think of it thus far?"

Louisa looked outside. "I rather enjoy riding along like this and seeing the city go by so quickly. But it smells as if we are sitting by a wet chimney fire."

"So it does," he responded with a chuckle. "To compensate for the smell, however, we will arrive in Baltimore in just over two hours. A far cry from the eleven hours it takes by stagecoach!"

She tried not to think of Conduff and concentrated instead on the green hilly countryside that flew by. She gripped the armrest tighter as they gathered even more speed. "Look," she said. "Even the horses and cows have stopped their grazing to see us pass."

Jonathan laughed. "There was such excitement when the 'iron horse,' as they called it, first came to Washington City, that an operetta was written to celebrate the great feat."

"An operetta? You are jesting," she said, turning to him.

His hazel eyes still flickered with amusement. "An operetta which boasted the unpoetic name of 'The Railroad,' and if I can remember one of the songs . . . ah, yes," and he recited in a comically ironic tone,

"Of each wonderful plan
E'er invented by man,
That which nearest perfection approaches
Is a road made of iron,
Which horses ne'er tire on,
And traveled by steam in steel coaches."

She laughed, then realized it was the first light moment she had experienced in a long time. "Thank you for arranging for the carriage and the train," she said with a surge of gratitude. "The day I first stopped at the shipping office, I had no idea you would have to become so involved."

"I am sure you did not. But it is truly a pleasure to assist such a lovely young lady."

She drew back slightly.

"Forgive me. I meant it as a sincere compliment."

She smiled. "I am overly sensitive lately." After a moment she added, "You have been such a fine gentleman, and now—I wonder what you must think of me."

"Only that you need my assistance to make your journey . . . nothing else."

He regarded her with such a serious expression that she knew she had misjudged him and had to make amends. She smiled. "I thought perhaps you would think I was seized with gold fever and on my way to the goldfields."

A smile began in his warm hazel eyes and moved down to his lips. "No, I hadn't considered that possibility."

"Or that I am an—an indecent woman." She blushed at her words. Nevertheless it was important he understood she was not. If it were a man like Conduff who sat beside her, he would simply assume the worst.

"Rest assured, such a thought never crossed my mind."

"One hears all sorts of wild tales about gold seekers . . . and about others going West."

"Yes, one does hear wild tales, especially in the shipping trade," he agreed.

She spoke on distractedly. "I heard of one woman so anxious to seek gold that she allowed herself to be raffled off as a bride to raise funds for the voyage. She hoped that the man she cared for would win the raffle, but when he didn't, she signed on as the gold ship's cook."

A pleasant laugh rumbled up from his chest. "You are not thinking of raffling yourself off as a bride, are you?"

She had to smile. "No. But my friend Tess, who told me the story, might consider it!"

"She must be eager to marry."

"Unfortunately, she is. She—" Louisa stopped, having nearly divulged the fact that Tess was the only girl from their class who was now unmarried. Louisa quickly suggested, "Tell me about yourself."

Two hours later, when the train ground to a stop at the Baltimore station, she knew a great deal about Jonathan Chambers—and, although modestly presented, all of it was rather favorable. To begin, he was not a shipping agent, but a solicitor with a degree from Harvard. He often worked in maritime law for shipping firms such as Wainwright and

Talbot, whose founder, Elisha Wainwright, had helped to finance Jonathan's education. In return, Jonathan performed various favors, such as closing the firm's Alexandria office. It was strange that he had left his own law office in Baltimore, but neither that nor his departure from Baltimore were her affair—just as her departure from Alexandria was not his.

He asked, "What are your expectations here in Baltimore?"

"Why . . . to go to the Wainwright and Talbot office and book passage immediately. I hope to leave today."

"It would be a miracle if you could sail in a day or two," he replied with all seriousness. "There is a great demand for accommodations on ships to California. As it is, we will have to make certain you don't ship out on a leaky old tub. Disreputable firms patch together any ship they can find, even abandoned wrecks."

"Then I shall have to find a hotel." She dared not stay long in the event Conduff followed her; moreover, room and board expenses would quickly exhaust her funds.

"Baltimore hotels are not always safe places for young women alone, not with the swarms of gold seekers here seeking transportation to California," Jonathan explained. "I thought you might like to stay at my brother and sister-in-law's house near Fell's Point. Their house is well located for making inquiries."

"I hadn't considered—Are you sure about the hotels?"

"Yes, positive. I should have warned you, but you looked so troubled."

"I wish you had." At his pained expression she added, "Perhaps I can stay with them just for tonight until I can get on a ship or find a proper hotel. I do hope your family won't be upset."

His hazel eyes brightened. "Most likely, they will be

pleased. They have such a large household that another person in their midst is scarcely noticeable."

She wished she were not becoming so reliant on him—and now on his family. Yet, if Conduff did try to find her, she might be safer in a private house. She would simply have to continue on, accepting help whether or not it appealed to her.

When they detrained at the railroad station, Jonathan hired a carriage and they rode through the bustling metropolis. The red-brick houses and shops reminded her of Alexandria, only Baltimore had prospered on a far larger scale, and the streets were clogged by buggies, tradesmen's wagons, and carriages, all of which made her feel pleasantly anonymous.

"Baltimore is called the 'City of Monuments,' " Jonathan said, and Louisa soon understood why. Monuments pierced the sky everywhere. Baltimore even boasted the first monument in the country to honor George Washington. Even more surprising was that nearly every storefront displayed banners that advertised "Miner's Supplies!" "Bargains for Gold Seekers!" or "Argonauts' Provisions Here!"

Later, when the carriage rumbled through Fell's Point, she was astounded by the multitude of sailing and steamships moored at the wharfs and anchored in the great harbor. It was no wonder that Baltimore was a prosperous place.

At length they reached the residential area, and the carriage drew to a halt in front of a handsome three-story brick dwelling. "Oakley's house," Jonathan announced. "As is suitable to his name, you will notice it is fronted by oak trees."

Louisa was grateful to see such a large house. If she were welcome, at least she would not crowd the others from their rooms.

"My brother is in the shipbuilding trade," Jonathan explained as he started out of the carriage. "He and Ellie have seven children who range from a baby to six years of age."

"Seven children under seven years of age!" Louisa marveled as he helped her out.

"Somehow Ellie keeps it all under control. Her parents live here, too, and household help."

When they arrived at the door, Ellie greeted them with delight. Her blonde coronet of hair crowned her sweet face like a halo, and her blue eyes beamed with joy. "Oh, Jonathan, how good to have you back!" she cried, giving him a sisterly hug. "And who is this lovely young lady you have brought to us?"

"Louisa Talbot, a friend from Alexandria. I hoped you might keep her here for a while."

Louisa began, "I'm afraid it's a terrible imposition—"

Ellie took Louisa's hands in hers. "You could never be an imposition," she said with a bright smile. "It would be a joy to have you with our family. And, Jonathan, you must stay here, too, now that your house is sold."

"Do you have room?" he asked.

Ellie laughed. "We shall make room, even if you have to stay in the attic. You'll see, we have fixed it quite nicely."

"Perhaps for a few days," Jonathan agreed, then laughed. "You see how much coaxing I require!"

Ellie dimpled. "We are honored. Here, let me take your things."

Jonathan helped Louisa remove her blue muslin cape and waited while she removed her bonnet, his gaze touching hers tentatively.

"Come in and see the children," Ellie urged.

Seconds later, the children descended upon them, from shy six-year-old Adam on through the alphabet: Benjamin,

Christine, Daniel, Elizabeth, and one-year-old Faith, who toddled toward them. Baby Gabriel was apparently sleeping.

"Children, here are your Uncle Jonathan and his friend, Miss Talbot," Ellie said.

The children's faces glowed with delight at Jonathan, and they shook Louisa's hand most politely. She had expected a rampaging lot like Tess's small brothers and sisters, but these children were quite different, their dear faces sweet as pansies. Benjamin, the most garrulous, asked Louisa, "Are you going to marry Uncle Jonathan?"

"Oh, Benji, what a question!" Ellie laughed, as Louisa mustered, "We are only friends."

Jonathan chuckled. "They do get to the essentials rather quickly."

Ellie took his arm and favored him with a mischievous smile. "Yes, they do!"

She turned to Louisa and took her hand. "Come, let's go into the children's parlor. Mrs. Murphy, our housekeeper, will show the driver what to do with your belongings. And here come Mother and Father!" she added as her parents approached. She introduced them to Louisa, who noted the Jurgesons' Swedish accents.

"I can scarcely wait until Oakley comes home," Ellie said. "Won't we have a wonderful dinner now!"

They sat down in the children's parlor, a large sunny room that overlooked the back garden. The children sat on small chairs and on the floor among their playthings. "We were just having a story," Ellie explained. "Would you mind if we continued it? We can visit at dinner and while the children nap. Miss Talbot, what would you prefer?"

Jonathan, obviously charmed by the children, turned to Louisa with a hopeful expression.

"May we have the story?" she asked.

"Good," Ellie said, delighted. "It's an old, old story about a man called Noah and his animals. Now, children, let's continue. Why did Noah build that boat he called an ark?"

Benjamin said, " 'Cause he loved God."

The other children echoed, " 'Cause he loved God."

Ellie turned to Louisa and Jonathan. "Do you know why?"

Jonathan replied, "Because he loved God and because he was obedient to Him."

"Yes," Ellie replied. "Noah loved God, and he did what God told him to do even though other people laughed at him."

Such an aura of love shone about Ellie and the children that the room seemed full of light. If only she might someday be such a mother, Louisa thought with a pang of sadness for her lost child. Tears blurred her view of the children's sweet faces as they listened to their mother.

Louisa blinked at the dampness and turned her attention to Jonathan. He seemed especially happy to be with them. On the train ride from Washington City he had told her he was the youngest of five children and that his parents had died before he was twenty. Like her own mother, his eldest brother and sister had succumbed to cholera in the epidemic of 1832 when they were still children, and another sister died in childbirth ten years ago. This was his only family and home now.

Ellie continued about Noah and, before long, baby Gabriel was carried in by the nursemaid. When the parlor clock struck twelve, Oakley Chambers arrived. He wore a dark, full beard and was as unprepossessing as Ellie was beautiful; his hazel eyes, however, were full of light and his beard often parted to show a white, albeit lopsided smile much like Jonathan's.

"Come meet Oakley," Jonathan urged and accompanied her across the room toward his brother.

Oakley pumped his brother's hand, then eyed her with interest as they were introduced. "Ellie and I are pleased to have you visit us, Miss Talbot," he said with sincerity.

"I am grateful for your hospitality," she replied. She felt like a serpent in their garden, the lie about her name perpetuated.

Oakley turned to his brother and eyed him with an odd expression, too. "Thank you for bringing her here, Jonathan."

Jonathan grinned widely.

In the ensuing silence, Louisa said to Oakley Chambers, "You have a most charming wife and family."

"I am blessed," he replied. "But I have interrupted the story. Please go on."

When Ellie had concluded the story about Noah, Oakley said, "Shall we now praise God?"

Everyone rose to their feet and joined hands in a circle. Louisa found herself held by Jonathan's large warm hand on one side and Adam's little hand on another. Together they sang,

"Praise God from whom all blessings flow,
Praise Him all creatures here below,
Praise Him above, ye heavenly host,
Praise Father, Son, and Holy Ghost."

The children's voices piped out so sweetly and Jonathan's mellow baritone rolled out so fervently that Louisa had to blink away another burst of dampness in her eyes.

Oakley turned to watch his wife lead the children out to their low table and small chairs in the next room, then his blue eyes traveled speculatively from Jonathan to Louisa and back to Jonathan again. "What an unexpected pleasure this is, Jonathan. I hadn't expected you back in Baltimore so soon."

"Matters at the shipping office were simpler to conclude than we had anticipated," Jonathan replied.

"Do Wainwright and Talbot know you have returned?"

Jonathan shook his head and darted a glance at Louisa. "Not yet. I'll go there this afternoon."

That meant, she assumed, he would try to find her a place on a ship to the California Territory, too. Perhaps she could yet leave tomorrow.

In the spacious dining room, the white damask-covered table and mahogany sideboard were graced with bouquets of lilacs, and Louisa felt a pang of homesickness. A French chandelier sparkled over the fine china, silver, and crystal goblets. The table had already been relaid for six people: Oakley and Ellie, her parents, and Jonathan and Louisa.

Jonathan held out her chair and smiled warmly again, as Oakley asked, "Louisa, may I ask what brings you to Baltimore?"

"I am just traveling through your city."

Jonathan asked, "Shall we tell them your destination?"

The information would not go far from here, she thought. "If you like."

The others looked at her expectantly, and Oakley asked, "You won't hold all of us in suspense?"

Jonathan chuckled. "Perhaps we should."

"We'll guess," Ellie said as she took up her napkin. "You are en route to Boston . . . or to New York."

Louisa shook her head.

"Sveden?" the elderly Mrs. Jurgeson asked with a smile.

"No."

"Ach, I know," Mr. Jurgeson put in, his eyes twinkling. "London. You are are under vay to London to visit the

Queen."

Louisa gave a laugh. "No, I am afraid not."

"Paris, then?" Oakley asked.

Jonathan chuckled. "They will never guess."

Louisa smiled herself. "To the California Territory."

"To the California Territory!" they echoed, then began peppering her with questions. Even the housekeeper, who had brought in the roast of beef on a platter, stopped in amazement to listen.

"I hope to be under way tomorrow if Jonathan can find me space on a ship," Louisa said.

A buzz of conversation ensued about how to find the best ships, then turned to fabulous tales they had heard about the gold rush. Oakley said, "Men are so afire with the 'California fever' that they swarm to Baltimore, willing to pay good money for any kind of a ship to the goldfields. And as if ships full of gold seekers are not enough, today's paper tells of mile-long lines of covered wagons heading westward over the prairies, bound for the gold diggings."

Ellie turned to Louisa. "Do you intend to look for gold?"

"Not precisely. I have relations there—"

Oakley asked, "Are you by chance one of the Talbots of Talbot and Wainwright?"

Louisa glanced at Jonathan, then said, "A distant relation." She quickly added, "I hope to open a shop there."

"You will surely have many customers," Oakley replied. "I've read that everything except gold nuggets is in short supply. Merchants can't obtain sufficient merchandise with the arrival of so many miners, some with only the clothes on their backs. Farmers leave their fields untilled and shopkeepers abandon their shops to rush off to the diggings."

Jonathan remarked, "The gold rush is spoken of in some quarters as the greatest mass adventure of all time, the greatest since the Crusades!"

"I am beginning to realize that there may be no space for me on a gold ship," Louisa told him.

"If there is one accommodation available in all of Baltimore, Oakley and I shall find it," Jonathan vowed.

After dinner, the men excused themselves to leave for work. Jonathan reassured her, "I shall investigate ship accommodations immediately. You must promise to rest."

"Well, then . . . perhaps I shall."

His eyes lingered upon her an instant longer before the men took their leave.

Ellie slipped an arm gently around her shoulders. "Let me show you to your room, Louisa. You must have been up since dawn. You look so weary."

"I'm afraid I am." But weariness was only half of it, Louisa thought as the anguish of the past week descended upon her again. As they made their way upstairs she added, "I don't know what I would have done without Jonathan. He has been such a wonderful help."

"The Chambers men always are," Ellie replied with a hint of amusement, "especially to beautiful damsels in distress."

"I assure you," Louisa said, "I scarcely know Jonathan."

"I see," Ellie replied somberly, although the dimples playing around her lips seemed to say, I hope before long you will know him well enough.

# 4

N ow was the time to clarify matters, Louisa decided as she and Ellie stepped into the cheerful yellow guest bedchamber. "I suspect you have the wrong impression since Jonathan brought me to your home," she began. "He claimed the hotels of Baltimore are overly crowded."

"They are indeed full—"

"And that they are not always safe for a young woman alone nowadays."

Ellie blinked as though she finally understood. "I can't imagine what I was thinking. It simply had not occurred to me that he brought you here for that reason."

"I thought not."

"Well, I was hopeful," Ellie said with a sigh. "He has never before brought a young woman to stay here, and we love him so much that. . . . Well, we cannot help being concerned after what he's endured."

"I know nothing of that."

Ellie looked at her thoughtfully. "It is probably best if I tell you, to save him the pain of it. You see, he has had a most difficult time. Everyone thought he should leave Baltimore . . . for a time anyhow. That's why he went to close the shipping office in Alexandria. "

"I have been so preoccupied with my own problems, it never occurred to me that he might be troubled, too."

"The fact is that he was engaged to Olivia Wyatt, a young woman here in Fell's Point," Ellie said with a pained expression. "They had known each other for many years, and everyone expected they would marry. Jonathan had purchased a fine house nearby, and they were to be married next month. He was working as hard as he could at his law practice so he could buy the house and furnishings. Then, to our amazement, she ran off to marry an older wealthy man, one of the social lions of Baltimore."

"Without warning Jonathan?"

Ellie nodded. "With no warning whatsoever. She probably handled her . . . situation as best she could, but there is simply no way to ease such a shock. I often think she truly loved Jonathan best, but loved the assurance of wealth and a high social position far more than she did him."

"So he left."

"Yes. He relinquished everything here and accepted the temporary post in Alexandria. When he brought you in the door today—" Ellie closed her eyes and shook her head. "Well, you might have felled me with a feather duster. I scarcely knew what to think. I suppose I was encouraged to see him with another young woman, but astonished that it was so soon." She stopped and color rose to her cheeks.

"You thought I had caught him when he was most vulnerable?"

Ellie inhaled deeply. "I must admit that it entered my mind. When he left for Alexandria, he said that he wanted to begin life afresh, and then he arrived with you—"

"He was simply playing the Good Samaritan. I am so sorry to have worried you."

"And I am sorry to have allowed my imagination to lead

me astray. Not that I would be in the least disappointed to have him fall in love with you."

"That's very kind of you, but you do not know me well," Louisa said, then remembering Ellie reading to the children, added, "On the other hand, if one could choose a sister-in-law, I should be most happy for you, too."

They smiled at each other, and Louisa felt a quiet joy at this unexpected friendship. It was as though in the midst of her troubles the Lord had sent her a special blessing.

Louisa asked, "What is his ex-fiancée . . . Olivia . . . like?"

Ellie gazed at the sunshine that streamed through the window. "Very beautiful in a dark, exotic way. Not too intelligent, but extremely clever. Her main attribute, as I saw it, was that she looks rather . . . sensuous. Oakley and I never understood what Jonathan saw in her, except for the obvious attraction, of course. To be perfectly honest, I would think a straightforward young woman like you would be more his type."

Straightforward! Louisa's mind echoed. A married woman in flight from her husband? "Please have no concern over that," she said. "I will soon be gone."

"One must never say 'never,'" Ellie warned impishly.

"Then I shall say, 'It is most unlikely.'"

Ellie smiled ruefully and started for the door. "I am sorry to hear it, but you are nevertheless most welcome. Now I must tuck my darlings in for their naps. Call out if there is anything you need."

Before she closed the door, she added, "As Jonathan said, 'Put your mind at rest.' I shouldn't have kept you up so long with talking. You do look weary. Have a good sleep, my dear."

After Ellie left, Louisa unbuttoned her blue frock, so tired she had to resist lying down in her street clothing. How good it would be to sleep now that she felt temporarily safe from Conduff—

Oh, why did she have to think of him! She fought memories of his angry face as she slipped out of her frock and hung it in the armoire. She must try harder to forget.

Catching a glimpse of herself in the walnut-framed oval mirror, she realized how thin she had become from the weeks of morning sickness . . . and even more so since she had lost her child. Sadness began to seep through her again, then she recalled a verse of Scripture: "In every thing give thanks: for this is the will of God in Christ Jesus concerning you."

She forced herself to her knees. *I do not understand why I must do this,* she prayed, *but since it is Thy will, Lord, then I do give thanks in all of this, even the loss of my child.*

Another verse of Scripture leapt to mind. "For thou didst form my inward parts; thou didst weave me in my mother's womb. . . . thine eyes have seen my unformed substance; and in thy book they were all written, the days that were ordained for me."

Her child was with God, and she would see it someday in glory. The thought had passed through her mind before, but it established itself firmly now, and she could imagine her babe in the brilliantly illuminated place she visualized as glory. Instead of wallowing in misery, she must trust God and go on. With that in mind, Louisa lay down under the covers, closed her eyes, and slept.

Hours later, Ellie knocked at the door. "Louisa, are you awake? It's six o'clock."

Louisa opened her eyes and realized where she was. "I have just now awakened."

"You may sleep the entire night through if you like, but Jonathan thought I should see whether you are well."

"Yes, thank you. I feel refreshed."

"No need to hurry. We take supper without the children at seven. If there is nothing you need, we shall see you downstairs."

Louisa's trunks had been delivered during dinner, and she unpacked several frocks. The pale blue dimity she had sewn several months ago was most suitable for supper, she decided, and slipped into it.

When she arrived downstairs, Jonathan sat reading a book in the elegant blue and gold parlor. She had to smile. "This is how I shall remember you when I am in the wilds of California . . . Jonathan Chambers, civilized Eastern gentleman."

Chuckling, he rose to his feet. "You appear quite rested with the exception of impaired vision."

Still smiling, she sat down on the blue parlor chair opposite his. "Yes. I slept the entire afternoon away."

His hazel eyes rested upon her face. "I hope you will be entirely rested before you depart on such a long sea voyage."

"You've secured accommodations for me?"

"Perhaps."

"Perhaps? Jonathan, please do not make me guess!"

He chuckled again. "It seems an outright miracle, for even men of means beg for jobs as cooks and stewards on the gold ships."

"You found a place for me!"

He nodded. "A cancellation for Monday morning on the *Nimrod*, a new Baltimore clipper ship bound for Panama."

"Thank you, I am so grateful—"

"The owner had planned to make part of the voyage, but family problems arose. It is an excellent cabin off the central salon, though rather costly."

When he named the figure, she was astounded. "It is

costly. Yet I have little choice if I wish to go."

He lifted his dark brows. "You do wish to go?"

"Yes." It was no longer merely the need to escape Conduff, but to make a new life for herself . . . to be able to hold her head up again after her shame in Alexandria.

"Louisa—" Jonathan began with uncertainty.

"Yes?"

He cleared his throat as though he had a matter of some consequence to discuss.

"Good evening," Oakley said as he stepped into the parlor. "I hope that I am not interrupting—"

"No, certainly not," Jonathan hastened to assure him.

Whatever had Jonathan begun to say? Louisa wondered.

She had no opportunity to find out in the next few minutes, for the men's conversation drifted from the lovely spring weather to Washington City politics. Before long, Ellie came downstairs from having again tucked in what she ruefully called "my unwilling children," and, shortly thereafter, her parents joined them.

At supper, Jonathan told the others about securing a cabin for her on the *Nimrod*, which Oakley pronounced "a sound ship." As they began to eat, she noticed several times that Jonathan seemed about to divulge something, but checked himself. Whatever it was, Oakley knew, too, for he cast a quizzical glance at Jonathan, who gave an almost imperceptible shake of his head. Apparently Ellie did not know the secret either, for she turned curious looks at both of them.

As supper proceeded, Louisa began to marvel that Olivia Wyatt would relinquish such a charming man as Jonathan. He was most attractive with his smile-creased face and the deep cleft in his chin. If there were any specific detail Louisa could find detrimental to his appearance, it was the darkness of his closely shaven beard—and yet that added to the strong masculine aura about him.

Catching her glance, he asked, "After supper, may I show you around Fell's Point?"

"I—Yes, I should enjoy that," she replied, rather flustered. But she had no sooner than uttered the words than she hoped he would not misunderstand her acceptance.

After dessert, Jonathan said to the others, "If you will excuse us, I am going to show Louisa about the neighborhood while it is still light."

"A fine idea," Oakley agreed.

Ellie said, "I should like some exercise myself."

"Perhaps we shall see you somewhere then," Jonathan replied pointedly as he helped Louisa from her chair, his hand at her elbow.

"Perhaps we can all go together," she suggested, growing more alarmed at his interest. "I am just becoming acquainted with your family, and this will give us more opportunity before I depart."

A slight frown crossed Jonathan's brow, then he nodded amiably. "Of course, I have scarcely visited with them myself."

In the end, all six of them strolled companionably through the tree-lined streets of the neighborhood. Louisa accepted Jonathan's proffered arm since walking on the uneven brick sidewalk was precarious in her shoes. His smile was open and friendly, but she felt uncomfortable.

The next day, she slept until mid-morning and then again in the afternoon. Her body still felt as if it had endured a great shock and could not get its fill of sleep. She didn't see Jonathan at either the noonday or evening meal. Apparently his business matters kept him away.

On Sunday morning, she joined the family in the front

hallway as they assembled for church. She wore her ivory high-collared silk dress and, as she joined the others at the front door, Jonathan remarked, "How beautiful you look, Louisa."

She flushed. "And you, how fine you look in a black suit." He was freshly shaven and his hazel eyes warmed at her compliment.

Outside, the sun beamed through the oak trees as they descended the steps, and a mockingbird sang from among the red roses that climbed a brick wall.

"The sidewalk is still as precarious as it was last night," he said. The lines on either side of his lips deepened as he smiled. He offered his arm again.

"Thank you," she replied," but I can manage now."

He seemed somewhat disappointed as they set off behind the others. It was only natural that she be paired with him, however, for Adam and Benji, who were old enough to attend worship, skipped about and required the attention of their parents and grandparents.

After a while, Louisa glanced at Jonathan and found his dark brows knitted together. "You look so somber," she ventured. "I hope everything is in order about my voyage."

"Yes, it is entirely settled."

"You have paid my fare?"

He nodded.

"Then I must repay you immediately."

"At your convenience."

She waited for him to address whatever was on his mind, but as they walked on, he spoke about nothing more consequential than the glorious spring morning.

As they approached the red-brick church, she felt a pang of sadness. "It's beautiful . . . very much like my church in Alexandria."

"You must miss it."

"Yes, I do."

"Louisa," he began, his voice low and thoughtful as they walked along the church path. "I am unsure of quite how to put this, for I fear you might take it in the wrong light." He turned to her and said determinedly, "I suppose it is best to put it as plainly as possible and, now, without further delay. I intend to accompany you to California."

"You are accompanying me to California!" she repeated.

"Yes. I have booked passage on the *Nimrod,* too."

It was a moment before she could speak. "But why? Why would you leave Baltimore?" Her words were no more than out that she knew. He would never escape the memory of Olivia Wyatt if he remained in Baltimore, the same city where she lived. He had to make a new start, too. "Your family is here—"

He nodded solemnly. "I shall miss them."

"I can't say I am sorry to have your company," she replied in all honesty. "You did say it might be difficult for a woman alone on a ship."

"I considered that, too, when the opportunity for me to go arose, but you must not find my motive altogether altruistic. California offers great adventure. Men all over our country are making the voyage. I had been of two minds about it, even before I met you."

"Then this is not a sudden impulse?"

"No, not sudden. I have prayed for some time about what to do. And now it is as though God has—" He halted, and his color deepened as he looked at her again, "—God has led me in this direction."

*As though God has led us together?* she wondered. Was that what he'd nearly said?

"They are awaiting us at the door," he observed.

She set off with him, still stunned and disconcerted. "Do Ellie and Oakley know you are leaving Baltimore?"

"Yes. When we first arrived, I intimated to Oakley that I wished to go, but I didn't tell them I had secured passage until last night."

"That explains why he looked at you so oddly at supper."

"Very likely."

"What did they say?"

He shrugged unhappily. "They prefer that I remain here . . . and, it is only fair to tell you, they think I am going because of you."

"Because of me! But we scarcely know each other!" She glanced up to find Ellie and Oakley watching them from near the church door. "That is . . . preposterous!"

"Perhaps not."

She glanced at him sharply. "Perhaps not? I fail to understand."

"Only that the notion might not seem preposterous to others."

He meant, she supposed, that he was a man and she was a woman. Ellie had already pointed out on Friday that he had never brought another young woman to their home. What must they think of her now?

As she approached them, Louisa blurted, "Jonathan has just told me about his going to California. I have in no way tried to convince him to go."

Ellie nodded unhappily, and Oakley said with resignation, "So he explained to us."

Louisa cast a sidelong glance at Jonathan and saw the misery etched upon his face. It was as though she—instead of Olivia Wyatt—had caused this new unhappiness for Jonathan and his family, and she shared his wretchedness.

"The organ prelude has already begun," Oakley said. "We

had best go in."

As they entered the narthex, Louisa noticed the pitying looks turned upon Jonathan, and it occurred to her that this was probably his first time in this church since Olivia had jilted him.

Quite suddenly she wanted to help and, mustering all of her charm, she smiled warmly at him. "May I take your arm now?" she asked, reaching for it.

He looked startled. "Yes, of course—"

"I so appreciate your assistance with my problems," she said. She would be gone soon and if she could help him live down his humiliation, what did it matter if his family or the members of the congregation thought she cared for him?

"Good morning," an usher said to her with such an admiring glance that she was glad to have worn her ivory silk dress. He nodded at Jonathan. "What a pleasure to have you back. I was so sorry to hear of . . . your difficulties, but it appears you have weathered the storm quite well."

"Good morning," Jonathan replied and darted an uncertain look at Louisa.

As they were ushered into the sanctuary, she saw pitying expressions transformed to "Who is this young woman with him?" And "My, Jonathan has made a swift recovery!"

She recalled the pity leveled at her in Alexandria over her marriage to Conduff, and it heartened her to see that she brought a modicum of respect, albeit misguided, to Jonathan. She sat down beside him in his family pew, smoothing out the ivory silk of her skirt. Now, she thought, was the perfect time to respond fully to his traveling with her to California. Now was the time to lift his spirits.

Aware that people all around watched, she whispered in his ear, "I am glad you are to accompany me on the voyage, Jonathan."

His hazel eyes brightened as he smiled at her. "I am, too," he murmured, and a warmth passed between them. "Believe me, I am glad, too."

The organ's triumphal strains brought the congregation to their feet. Louisa stood beside him, ready to share his hymnal, and dared not look into his eyes. Grateful as she was for his company on the voyage, she hoped he would not make too much of her comment.

Beside her, Jonathan sang with the others in his deep, resonant voice,

"Joyful, joyful, we adore Thee,
God of glory, Lord of love;
Hearts unfold like flowers before Thee,
Opening to the sun above. . . ."

As she sang out with the congregation, she committed the journey to California and her reception by her Talbot relations to the One to whom they sang.

Benjamin Talbot stood in the California sunshine at the door of Casa Contenta and bid the last of his neighbors and friends farewell. "We shall see you next Sunday!" he called out after them as they went to their horses, buggies, and wagons.

One of the women replied, "Thank ye again for the use of yer house for the services!"

"Our pleasure!" Benjamin returned. "We look forward to worshiping with you again next Sunday!"

Beside him, his sandy-haired young friend, Seth Thompson, waved farewell with him. "Speaking of pleasures," he said, "it was one to preach here today instead of exhorting miners on a San Francisco street corner. Yesterday my pulpit was a plank set on two whiskey barrels at Portsmouth Square."

"You?!" Benjamin asked. He had taken yesterday off from his shipping and chandlery office in town, or he would have surely heard of Seth's preaching in the plaza. It was such a raucous place that it was difficult to imagine a minister there.

"Me," Seth replied with a broad smile. "I felt strongly called to do it, though my congregation thought the wilder miners might mob me."

"And what did Angelica think of you exhorting the miners out on a street corner?"

"She steadied the plank and sang "The Royal Proclamation" with all of her might."

"Angelica?!" He couldn't quite imagine Seth's sedate little wife in such a rough setting.

"Her bursts of holy boldness ofttimes amaze me, too," Seth said, "and the miners are so astounded to find a decent woman here that they soon come around to see what's taking place."

"What transpired?" Benjamin asked, still amazed.

"The first stanza of 'The Royal Proclamation' brought the crowd out and, by the seventh stanza, we had five hundred or so men and as fine as singing as one could ask for in our old Missouri congregation or in any eastern seaboard church."

"You don't say!"

Seth grinned. "I do!"

Benjamin shook his head. "And then?"

"By then I had crossed the Rubicon and the tug-of-war was on. I said, 'Gentlemen, if our friends back East, with the views and feelings they entertain about California society, had heard there was to be a sermon this afternoon on Portsmouth Square in San Francisco, they would have predicted disorder, confusion, and riot. But we who are here believe differently.' I then pointed to our flag waving in the air over the custom house and said, 'There is no true American but will observe order under the preaching of God's word anywhere and maintain it if need be. We shall have order, gentlemen.'"

"An inspired idea."

"Indeed! We had such order that I felt free to speak on deliverance from drink and the lust for gold. I used 'What profit it a man to gain the whole world—and all of California's gold—and lose his soul?'"

Benjamin tried to imagine Seth, his usually mild-mannered pastor, preaching in such a situation.

"To my surprise, Angelica was not the only one filled with holy boldness," Seth continued. "Our faith welled up so that by the time my exhortation ended, several miners made decisions for Christ and said they will come to our church meetings."

"Remarkable!" Benjamin said.

Seth nodded. "We held another service there last night, and two rededicated themselves to Christ . . . one a seminary student who repented of the lusts and the lure of the goldfields and truly sees the light now."

"I never in my wildest imaginings saw you as a street corner preacher," Benjamin said.

"Nor I," Seth admitted with a grin. "If I had known in divinity school what I was in for, I wonder what I might have done! Yet, the truth is, I would not exchange being in California for a nice, quiet church anywhere in Missouri—or on the eastern seaboard."

Benjamin laughed. "If we had all known what was ahead when we set out that first morning with our covered wagons, we might have turned right back to Independence. And if I had thought I would have camp meetings on the stream of my land—" He shook his head. "Yet if we'd known there might be gold, we might have pressed all the harder and killed ourselves on the first mountain pass."

Seth laughed with him. "It is a blessing that we don't know what lies ahead. And it is a strange setting here for our lives, but I am certain that I belong here. Even before these street exhortations, I have seen God work when I tell the gold seekers about Him."

Benjamin's adopted son, Daniel, stepped outside the whitewashed adobe house and joined them. His blue eyes sparkled and his smile split his well-kept dark beard. "I couldn't help overhear you. I have just read Lowell on that very subject."

"And, pray tell, what does Lowell say?" Benjamin asked, half-smiling at Daniel, whom everyone swore remembered every quotation he had ever heard.

Daniel smiled himself, then quoted in his fine deep voice,

" 'New occasions teach new duties;
Time makes ancient good uncouth;
He must upward still, and onward,
who would keep abreast of Truth . . .
God's own arm hath need of thine.' "

"Yes," Benjamin said, "no matter how strange it strikes us, 'God's own arm hath need of ours.' I wonder what His will is for us to do next."

"I am convicted that my 'new duty' is to continue the street preaching," Seth said. "When I see gold seekers rush off the ships into San Francisco, I truly wish to tell them that the most thrilling nuggets in California will be found not in the rivers and mountains, but in the spirits of those who turn to God's gold."

"New occasions teach new duties," Benjamin repeated from Daniel's quotation.

"And you?" Seth asked. "Your neighbors say you preach well. They speak highly of your sermons."

Benjamin shook his head. "They are not like yours, though. I feel as if mine lack badly in form and substance. I am willing to continue with it while there is no one here to preach to my family and neighbors, but I believe my real work lies with encouraging others like you. If I had been thoroughly trained for the ministry like my father—"

"Laymen like you and Daniel are as important as ordained ministers," Seth assured him. "Ministers are expected to preach and to be holy, but unbelievers are sometimes swayed more to see what they might call 'ordinary folk' who live lives fully dedicated to God."

"Perhaps," Benjamin said. "Jessica, however, strikes me as a better example of an ordinary person who has become truly godly," he said of his sister.

Daniel said, "Your life has impressed the whole family to turn to God. Your example made a great impact on me."

"I thank you, Daniel, but I know my imperfections all too well," Benjamin replied. "It is true I learned a great deal from being in a Boston minister's family, but I was as rebellious . . . as full of pride and greed as a young man could be. If I had not married Elizabeth. . . . God surely gave me such a dear wife so I would turn to Christ. Even after all of these years since her death, it takes only the thought of her Christlikeness to fill me with love."

They stood quietly for a while in the midday sunshine and watched the last buggy of worshipers drive away. At length Benjamin gazed at the rolling hills high with wild oats and blooming wildflowers. "A beautiful sight. Elizabeth would have loved it, yet so many who come here scarcely see it."

"When I last rode out to Sacramento," Daniel said, "it

was so beautiful you would think any man would want to settle down and turn a deaf ear to the call of gold. The river lands were covered with waving grasses, and beyond was as wonderful a scene as ever met a man's eyes: a sea of grasses and wildflowers—greens, whites and blues, purples and golds. It seemed a Garden of Eden . . . a paradise. How can gold seekers who pass through there not recognize God from His creation, and see only gold?"

"Those who truly look for God here or anywhere else, see Him," Seth said. "Those who look only for gold, do not."

"A fitting summation of this morning's sermon," Benjamin pronounced.

When they went into the house, Jessica's brown eyes shone as they often did after a worship service. Her hair was grayer than ever, pulled back into its usual bun, but she had grown plump again last winter, filling out after their near starvation on the covered wagon trek west three years ago. She asked Seth, "What is happening in the city with churches now?"

He replied, "C. O. Hosford organized the Methodist Episcopal Church . . . and married a couple bound for Oregon. Three more Baptist clergymen arrived in February, and in March they started a Sunday school. April brought a few more ministers, and Woodbridge organized the First Presbyterian Church of Benicia. This month, Asa White pitched a blue tent on Powell Street for services, and now the First Presbyterian Church of San Francisco is being organized."

"A beginning," Benjamin said. "It's a beginning."

"Yes, a good beginning," Jessica agreed. "I hope you will tell us how we can help."

"Prayer," Seth said, "as much prayer as possible."

Later, when they sat down to dinner in the dining room,

Benjamin looked fondly around the long trestle table at his family: Jessica and his youngest daughter, Betsy; the young couples: Abby and Daniel, Jenny and Jeremy, Martha and Luke; and Elizabeth's and his grandchildren all around them. Even though Elizabeth was with the Lord, they were still mightily blessed.

"Let us sing the 'The Royal Proclamation' in honor of the Lord, and in honor of Seth and Angelica's and the other ministers' work," Benjamin said.

They reached for each other's hands and sang out,
"Hear the Royal Proclamation
the glad tidings of salvation
published now to every creature,
to the ruined sons of nature,
Lo! He reigns, He reigns victorious
over Heaven and earth, most glorious,
Jesus reigns!"

Benjamin hoped they sang with as much love for God and gratitude as Seth's new converts might. As his eyes roved over his family, he suddenly felt led to pray, *Lord, help me keep all of them safe in this rough new territory.*

# 5

The next morning Louisa stood in front of the Baltimore house in her blue traveling frock and cabriolet bonnet, and bid Ellie and her children farewell. The children reached up for Louisa's kisses, which she happily bestowed. Then she turned to Ellie and grasped her hands. "I can never thank you enough for providing this haven when I needed a place to stay. If ever I have seen the Scripture about being a 'lover of hospitality' lived out, it has been here."

"You are far too kind. It has been our pleasure," Ellie replied, her lashes still wet from her farewells with Jonathan. "Perhaps I shall never see you or Jonathan here again on earth, but I shall always pray for you, and see you someday in glory."

"Oh, Ellie—" Tears welled in Louisa's eyes and she drew away reluctantly, heartsick to leave behind not only Tess, but this new friend. "I shall pray for all of you," Louisa vowed.

Behind them, the horses snorted and stamped impatiently with the waiting carriage. Jonathan sounded as distressed as she felt as he said, "Time to go."

"Farewell, then," Louisa said and firmed her resolve. Turning away, she gathered up her blue skirt and allowed Jonathan to help her up into the carriage. Oakley, who would accompany them to the wharf, climbed in and sat in front of them in the warm leather seats.

"Bon voyage," Ellie called out with a tearful smile, and the children's sweet voices echoed, "Bon voyage, Auntie Louisa! Bon voyage, Uncle Jonathan!"

Seconds later, the carriage lurched forward and rumbled away on the cobblestone street. While Louisa waved, Ellie and the children grew smaller and smaller in the distance. Beside her, Jonathan surveyed the house and the neighborhood as if to store away memories himself.

"We are under way," he said.

She nodded, half in dismay. As they left the neighborhood behind, she felt a vague sense of comfort at sitting beside him, though she could not help think—and worry—about Conduff, too. If he did try to follow her, hopefully this stay in Baltimore would throw him off track.

The men began to converse about Baltimore shipping, and she sat back in the seat, bouncing along and half listening. It occurred to her that both Jonathan and Oakley wore black suits and hats, as though they were in mourning, and the sadness about their eyes reinforced that impression.

At length, the carriage drew to a halt at the crowded wharf, and Oakley announced rather grimly, "Here we are."

Louisa's fingers sought out the money belt at her waist and, finding it, she was reassured. She was as ready as it was possible for her to be.

Jonathan looked at her with a tenuous smile. "The great adventure begins."

She nodded, though she must have appeared uncertain, for his smile broadened with reassurance, warming the hazel depths of his eyes. His hands were equally warm as he helped her down from the carriage, and she hastily stepped away from him. He had been reared as a gentleman, and she must not imagine more than mere politeness, she reminded herself.

Breathing deeply of the damp salt air, she started forward into the bustle and confusion that reigned on the wharf. All around them, stevedores rolled heavily laden barrows up the gangways from neighboring warehouses; peddlers hawked their wares; small boats tootled and darted about between brigs and barks and huffing steamships. The tangy salt air mingled with the pungent aromas of hot pitch, sun-dried hemp ropes, bales of tobacco, and the pervasive odor of fish. They hurried along through the tumultuous scene, a porter pushing the cart with their baggage behind them.

"There she is, the *Nimrod*," Jonathan said.

Crates, barrels, and cotton bales walled off a space on the wharf where people laughed and bid their loved ones good-bye, but Louisa scarcely heard their excited chatter as she passed through the crowd and gazed at the majestic clipper ship. "What an impressive sight!" she said.

The *Nimrod's* masts were tall; her lines were sleek; her newly painted white bow and black hull gleamed in the early sunshine. Even the stevedores who loaded the cargo seemed puffed with pride to toil for the *Nimrod's* maiden voyage.

"She is said to be the most beautiful clipper ever to set sail from Baltimore," Jonathan remarked.

"Afraid I must agree," Oakley conceded, "despite the fact that our firm didn't build her. Let us hope that she sails as well as she looks."

They made their way up the gangplank, and all of her nervousness about the voyage abated as Louisa felt the envious gazes of onlookers below. She was sailing on a clipper ship for the first time in her life—and the most beautiful clipper asail. As if that weren't excitement enough, she was sailing for California.

A gray-haired gentleman stood at the head of the gangway. "Welcome aboard, Miss Talbot. Captain Martin at your service."

Her spirits faltered upon hearing his Miss Talbot.

He must have interpreted her reaction as concern about the ship, for he added, "You will find the *Nimrod* the finest clipper afloat. We are extremely proud of her. There is not a safer, sturdier ship anywhere."

"I am sure she must be, Captain Martin," Louisa replied.

She forced her attention to the deck and to the seamen who bustled about. They were an eye-catching lot in their duck trousers, checkered shirts, and black neckerchiefs as they went quickly about their duties.

"Shall we see your cabins?" Oakley suggested. "Ellie will ask for a full account."

"I am eager to see them myself," Louisa admitted.

Below, the interior was quite luxurious, with polished mahogany and gleaming brass. The elegant central salon had an overhead skylight, a mahogany dining table with benches bolted to the floor, a black stove, and two marble-topped sideboards. Companionways led up to the deck on either side of the salon. Aunt Sarah's money had taken her to a far finer place than the dear old lady had likely ever imagined, Louisa thought.

Jonathan opened a door off the salon, and she was disappointed to find the cabin miniscule and dark, without a porthole. "This is my cabin," he explained, then stepped inside and opened another door, displaying a larger cabin with a sunlit porthole. "And this is yours, Louisa. Normally these rooms would be used as a suite for passengers who travel with a servant, but it is all that was available. I hope the arrangement is satisfactory."

How could she object to their traveling in such close

quarters at this late hour? she thought. "Yes, it is fine." In any case, a door with a sturdy brass lock separated the rooms. As for spaciousness, the two berths against the porthole wall made her cabin seem large.

At length, they made their way up to the deck again. When they stood near the rail, they were caught up in the excitement of greetings and well-wishing. Cabin passengers had all boarded and, below, a rougher-looking class of men thronged into the hold, apparently as excited as the rest of them.

"Prospective gold miners, it appears," Jonathan said.

"May they have happiness with their gold, if they find any," Oakley responded. "I fear the dangers of sudden riches and the moral hazards of life on such a remote frontier might ruin them. They will be far from the civilizing influence of home or church."

Louisa asked Jonathan, "Will you search for gold in California?"

"Perhaps," he replied.

He had mentioned no reason for going, and she'd merely assumed he was leaving to avoid Olivia and to seek gold. Perhaps she was wrong; perhaps he had other plans. If so, this was not the time to ask, for the cargo hatches were being lashed down and everywhere a last-minute frenzy prevailed.

"Almost time to sail," Oakley observed, his hazel eyes darkening with sadness as he turned to Louisa and Jonathan.

A bittersweet sadness swept through Louisa and she felt altogether unsteady as she shook his hand. "Thank you for your hospitality and kindness, Oakley."

"It was our pleasure. Take good care of my brother."

Warmth rushed to her cheeks. "I fear I can have little influence on him."

"That remains to be seen," Oakley responded with a

small smile. He turned to Jonathan, and the two men caught each other awkwardly in an emotional embrace.

Quite suddenly, Oakley was departing. "Write to us!" he called back. "You can post letters at Chagres."

"We shall!" they promised. "We shall!"

The lopsided grin so like Jonathan's parted Oakley's beard as he added a jovial, "Send us your excess gold!" He gave a final wave, then rushed for the gangway.

At the bereft expression on Jonathan's face, Louisa turned away. "Lord, give him courage," she prayed, "and me strength."

Nearby the boatswain shouted out orders, and in no time every seaman was in motion, the sails loosed, the yards braced, the men singing out a sea chantey. Unintelligible orders were rapidly given and executed and there was a wild hurrying about mingled with sailors' shouts; the boatswain called, "A-a-ll ha-a-a-nds—"

"We have a fair breeze for our voyage," Jonathan observed, his voice rather husky with emotion.

The white canvas flapped noisily as the men hoisted the sails. Immediately they were filled with the breeze. In moments, the *Nimrod* slipped out from the wharf to the sounds of cheers and the seamen's hearty chantey. From her childhood visits to Alexandria's wharf, Louisa knew that the various sea chanteys put a timing and a will to each job the seamen performed. Now, however, she was on the departing ship instead of ashore, and she wondered whether the songs were also used to divert the sailors' minds from their endless farewells.

"There's Oakley!" Jonathan called out, pointing to his brother in the crowd that waved on the wharf.

Louisa waved, too, and Oakley waggled his black hat at them. The *Nimrod* moved faster, gulls dipping in her wake, and Oakley and the wharfside panorama grew smaller as the ship sailed away, its white canvas billowing in the wind. Despite the sadness of departure, it was heartening to be under way, to be farther away from Conduff and from her memories of him.

As she stood on the deck, she watched the great harbor with its forest of masts and smoke-belching steamships recede entirely. She was leaving not only this port and her old life behind, but her country. True, there was talk in Washington City of granting statehood to California, but most politicians thought it far too distant for such status, even now with the discovery of gold.

"Your first time at sea?" Jonathan asked.

"I have only been out on small boats on the Potomac, and once on the steamship to Washington City." She smiled. He'd asked the same question about her train ride. "Is my inexperience so obvious?"

"No. It's only that you take more interest in what is happening than most young women might."

"Oh?"

"I find it an excellent trait," he hastened to add.

She had almost expected him to make a disparaging remark, since Conduff and her father had always complained about her inquiring mind. Instead, Jonathan watched her quite differently and she wondered if he compared her to Olivia, whom Ellie had called "more clever than bright."

"We scarcely know each other," Louisa remarked without thinking.

He raised his dark brows thoughtfully. "I am sure that will be remedied on this voyage. We will have more time than anything else, except perhaps water and sky."

She nodded and looked out at the bright blue Patapsco River. Beyond Baltimore Harbor and the river lay Chesapeake

Bay, then the Atlantic Ocean and Caribbean Sea—and on the other side of Panama, the Pacific Ocean, which was said not to be as peaceful as its name promised.

"I assume that like most women, you do not swim."

"I can paddle around a bit," she admitted, then at his surprised look added, "I float easily, so it is no great feat for me to move about if I exert some effort."

"How ever did you learn?"

She was half amused and half embarrassed as she explained, "My best friend, Tess, and I were . . . well, I suppose we were more boyish than most girls should be. We played with the neighborhood boys . . . and the summer we were nine years old, we swam with them in a creek."

He laughed in amazement. "And what did your family say about that?"

"Fortunately, they never found out!"

"I can imagine! If you had been my little sister, I am not certain what I might have done."

"I had no older brother to watch over me. Only my maiden aunt . . . and my father, then."

"I see."

It was the first time she had divulged anything about her family to him—or anything so intimate as swimming in a creek—and now she realized what one might think. "We wore some clothing," she hastened to inform him.

He laughed again. "And were you the ringleader?"

"No, Tess has always been the braver of the two of us."

After a while, they sat down on a nearby wooden settee, looking out at the increasingly forested shores. Before long, they sailed past the fortified walls of Fort McHenry, where a great victory had been won in the War of 1812.

Jonathan said amiably, "Baltimore still gloats over that victory. I imagine it always will . . . though pride in its history is a fine thing for a city."

"Yes, perhaps so."

After a while he said, "Something about sailing always makes time more relevant to me. Perhaps it is simply because on a ship it seems we can see the future before us to some extent and see the past just behind us in the wake of the ship. In life, the past often colors the present far too much." He shook his head. "Now how did all of that come from Baltimore and the War of 1812?"

"I believe you mean it is time for us to look ahead."

He nodded, and after a moment asked, "You know about Olivia?"

"Yes, Ellie told me. She thought it would spare your having to explain."

"Thoughtful of her, but Ellie always is." He paused. "I assume you, too, have recently suffered adversity."

Louisa gazed out across the water at the wooded shoreline. "Yes, though it is far better that I don't explain. You will have to accept my word for it."

She worried that he might inquire further, but instead he said, "If you need a friend to lean upon, I wish to make myself available. I have learned a great deal about compassion in the past few months."

"That is most kind of you, Jonathan."

Their eyes held for an instant before she looked away.

At midday, they sat down together at the salon table and became acquainted with the other passengers. With the exception of two wives and a girl of ten, their traveling companions were men, well-dressed gentry of some means, for their fine frock coats made plain that they at least aspired to be gentlemen. Several were merchants, two were Harvard students, one a banker, another a Princeton graduate.

After they had begun to discuss California, the portly

merchant produced a San Francisco *Californian* clipping that claimed gold had been found in almost every part of the countryside.

"A man will be rich in no time," his associate vowed.

"Then there are those of us who crave adventure," the Princeton graduate said. He had been introduced by the captain as Hugh Fairfax, and he was a blond Adonis, surely the most handsome man on the ship. He spoke directly to Louisa. "For my part, traveling to California is an exciting venture into the unknown." His blue eyes settled upon her as though she, too, might be an interesting venture for him.

She dropped her gaze to the food on her plate. The last thing she desired was for men to pay her special attention.

Beside her, Jonathan asked, "Do you know him?"

"No, I do not."

One of the Harvard students remarked to no one in particular, "We cannot even anticipate what we may encounter." He was red-haired and freckled, given to broad smiles, but now he looked quite somber. "Perhaps we shall have to engage in bloody conflict with the native Indians, or be mauled to death by a savage grizzly bear. We may be fated to leave our bones to whiten the plains of the golden land."

The banker harrumphed impatiently. "They say over a quarter of a million dollars-worth of gold was taken from the California Territory already last year."

"All a man has to do is pick it up," someone interjected.

"Many men go armed with no more than a jackknife or a horn spoon to dig the nuggets out."

"They say the savages of the land there are quite docile," another one of the men commented. "They are said to follow the Americans about, eager to exchange gold for glass beads or a looking glass . . . or a pull from a whiskey jug."

Their hearsay and speculation continued, and Louisa

noted that Jonathan did not contribute to it. She nibbled at her dry biscuit and picked at the boiled potatoes, having no stomach for fatty roast pork. Beside her, she saw that Jonathan had not eaten his, either.

When dinner was over, he helped her up from the table most solicitously. "Are you feeling well, Louisa?" he asked, for the ship had begun to roll more noticeably.

She moved away. "Yes, thank you."

"Miss Talbot?"

Hugh Fairfax stepped before her, his blue eyes aglow with admiration. "I thought you might be related to the Boston Talbots."

"Yes, but only distantly," she replied, chagrined to lay false claim to the Talbot name again.

"I am acquainted with Joshua Talbot through trade," he explained. "We have spent many an evening in each other's company." In the ensuing silence he added, "I should be pleased to be informed if I can ever be of service to such a lovely relation of his."

"Thank you, but I have never so much as met him."

"You certainly will in California. He sailed around Cape Horn on the *Californian* last year and arrived at the beginning of the gold rush. I understand that he has married a Rose Wilmington of Georgetown, who sailed on the ship, too."

"I would know nothing of that, though I am glad to learn that there are other young people in the Talbot family." The ship pitched slightly, and Louisa felt Jonathan's hand tighten on her elbow. "Well, Mr. Fairfax," she said, "it has been a pleasure to meet you."

His smile beamed like sunshine. "My pleasure entirely."

Jonathan put in with extreme politeness, "If you would excuse us—"

Hugh Fairfax nodded graciously and moved aside to

allow them to pass, and it struck Louisa forcefully that she was thought to be unmarried, the only unmarried young woman aboard the ship.

Once they were out on deck, Jonathan turned as somber as the gray clouds that obscured the sun.

"You do not care for Hugh Fairfax, do you?" she asked.

Jonathan's dark brown hair blew in the breeze as he looked out across the water. "I have nothing to hold against him. Only perhaps that he is one of those men who are far too handsome. Even the married women and the young girl at the table could not keep their eyes from him."

Could Jonathan possibly be—No, certainly not jealous. It was that he had been jilted so recently. It was normal for him to be wary of other men and needed reassurance. "You are a very attractive man yourself," she commented to that end.

They stopped at the ship's railing. "That is very kind, but you are not required to say it."

"I know it is not required, but it is nonetheless true."

He rubbed his jaw. "With this stubble forever darkening my face, no matter how sharp my razor?" he replied. "Olivia used to say—" He stopped, embarrassed.

Louisa filled the growing silence. "Apparently she did not know a good thing when she saw it."

Jonathan gave a laugh, and she noted the deep cleft in his chin and the fullness of his lips. Apparently Olivia had not only been unfaithful, but foolish. How easy it would be to care for a man like Jonathan far more than was sensible.

"If you will excuse me," she said, "I shall unpack."

At supper, Hugh Fairfax sat beside her at the salon table and his engaging smile elicited one from her. "I hope you don't mind my sitting beside you, Miss Talbot."

"No, certainly not." In any case, she had little choice. She wondered whether he had made arrangements to change his seat with the captain, for everyone else sat in their same seats. On her other side, she saw that Jonathan did not appear overly pleased at Hugh's presence.

Hugh said, "I thought you might be interested in learning more about the California Talbots, since you have not yet met them."

"Yes, I am."

"A fine lot, every one of them," Hugh began with so much enthusiasm that it took a moment for him to realize the captain was asking Jonathan to say grace.

Beside her, Jonathan replied, "It is an honor." He turned to the others and asked, "Shall we pray?"

When everyone quieted, he began with a strong voice, "Our heavenly Father, we come before Thee with hearts full of praise and thanksgiving. We praise Thee for Thy great love for each of us and thank Thee for sending Thy Son, the Lord Jesus Christ, to be our Savior. And we thank Thee now, too, for this food, which Thou givest us from Thy bountiful earth. We pray in the name of Our Lord and Savior, Jesus Christ. Amen."

"Amen," Louisa echoed with the rest of them.

She liked his fervent prayer, and their eyes met for an instant before Hugh interrupted with, "Miss Talbot . . . or may I call you Louisa?"

"Louisa is fine," she replied.

Hugh glanced at Jonathan, then took up his discussion about the Talbots again. From what Hugh knew of them, it appeared that they were a well-educated and mannered family, which buoyed Louisa's spirits more than it unnerved her. It would be no escape at all if she found herself surrounded by a family full of Conduffs. On the other hand, if they did not get on well together, she would go out on her own as soon as possible.

When Hugh finished, he began to press into her affairs, and she quickly said, "I believe I would rather travel by clipper ship to California than by covered wagon as they did."

"Covered-wagon journeys are said to be most arduous," he replied. "We can be happy to have accommodations on such a fine ship. They are difficult to secure, but I am certain that your friend Jonathan, here, has excellent connections."

Jonathan made no comment.

Hugh gave her a brilliant smile. "At any rate, it is a great pleasure to find both of you on this voyage."

"And I am happy to learn more about the California Talbots," Louisa replied. She had been so interested that she had forgotten to eat. She took up her fork and tasted the breast of chicken. It was well prepared and she was famished, despite the fact that several passengers were already seasick.

On the other side of the table, the men were in spirited conversation about the destiny of America. The war with Mexico, remote and unpopular as it had been, had been glorious in its fruits, which included the annexation of California and, close on its heels, this discovery of gold. After a while the discussion turned to the other virtues of California.

"The climate there is said to be so salubrious that a sick person is considered a rare sight," the banker said.

Thus far Jonathan had sat by quietly, but now he asked, "Have you heard of the Californian who lived to be two hundred and fifty years old?"

"Two hundred and fifty years old!" Hugh scoffed.

The others chuckled and cast skeptical looks at Jonathan, and Louisa presumed he was hiding a grin. "Do tell us, Jonathan," she urged.

"Well," he began, "it seems there was a man in California

who had reached the age of two hundred and fifty years. The qualities of the climate there are such that he was in perfect health of both mind and body. But having lived so long on earth, he became bored and desired a new state of existence. Despite his prayerful efforts to move on to the next life, he had no success. Finally his heir advised him to travel into a foreign country."

"Missouri, no doubt," one of their fellow passengers suggested, and everyone laughed.

Jonathan smiled, then continued. "Our hero took his heir's advice and traveled to a foreign country and soon sickened and died. His will required that his heir, upon pain of disinheritance, transport his remains back to California to entomb them. The request was faithfully carried out, and his body was interred with great ceremony and prayers. The Californian was happy in heaven, and his heir was pleased to have him there. But then, being brought back and interred in California soil with the healthful zephyrs rustling over his grave, the energies of life were immediately restored to his inanimate corpse. Such herculean strength was imparted to his frame that he burst the prison of death and appeared before his heir reinvested with all the vigor of early manhood! And so he submitted, determined to live out his appointed years."

Most of their fellow travelers laughed heartily at the preposterous tale, and Jonathan grinned.

"What a storyteller you are!" Louisa remarked. She was pleased to see this humorous side of him. The only hint she had had of it thus far had been on the train to Baltimore when he had told of the railroad operetta. Not that she had shown much humor herself lately.

Captain Martin said, "I am glad to hear that most of you take such California tales with a grain of salt. I have heard the most outrageous stories about the place since gold was discovered. They say that in great areas of the California plains nuggets are clustered thickly about the grass roots, waiting to be garnered like berries along the roadsides . . . that streams are so thickly covered with gold flakes the water racing over them glows amber." He shook his head. "I say they are fanciful tales imagined by those who wish to avoid working."

The captain was probably right, Louisa decided. Nonetheless, when she considered the state of her finances, it was agreeable to contemplate finding gold so easily.

After supper she went up the companionway with Jonathan and Hugh, and they stepped out on deck to a glorious sunset.

"May I accompany you about the deck?" Hugh asked, his eyes bespeaking more than mere friendliness.

She glanced at Jonathan.

"Perhaps the three of us—" he began.

"Yes, that would be lovely," she responded rather quickly. Two was said to be company and three a crowd, and she wished to give neither of them false expectations. Moreover, it was better to be with them than to brood in her cabin about Conduff and Da and the baby.

Long after the sun set, the three of them continued to stroll around the deck. Opalescent clouds lit the velvety black heavens, and Louisa thought it was the most magnificent night sky she had ever seen.

"Looks like a storm brewing to the east," Hugh observed.

"Perhaps not," Jonathan countered.

"The pessimist and the optimist?" she asked, and they chuckled. In any event, they seemed in opposition.

As they conversed, she divided her attention as evenly as possible until she realized how tired she was. How long it was taking her body to recover from losing the child. "If you will excuse me, the air is becoming quite damp."

"I should be honored to see you to your cabin," Hugh offered immediately.

"And I," Jonathan said.

"Thank you," she responded, "but I can manage by myself. I bid you good night, gentlemen."

Below deck, the central salon was unoccupied and the mahogany dining table gleamed from its recent cleaning. She passed through the salon and let herself into the suite through Jonathan's cabin. He had already organized his belongings, and his frock coats hung neatly on the wall pegs, his trunk set under his bunk. Uneasy as she felt about the proximity of his cabin to hers, it reassured her to know he would sleep between her cabin and the central salon, rather like a buffer to the world. And certainly she preferred him to having Hugh in this room.

When she realized where her thoughts had drifted, she stopped in shock. Why would such a preposterous notion present itself to her . . . a married woman? She had chosen a husband three years ago, even if she'd been far too young and foolish—and she had no right to think of other men. Thoughts, it was said, were forerunners to deeds—and thoughts, even if not heard on earth, were heard in heaven.

She let herself into her own cabin and locked the door as much against herself as against Jonathan. Trying to constrain her thoughts to her actions, she undressed and unbound her hair, then slipped into her white nightgown.

As she knelt at last beside her bunk, she prayed, *Lord, help me to sleep this night, and not think or dream of anyone or anything.*

She lay down on her bunk and pulled the covers up to her chin. Turning to her side, she slowly surrendered to the rocking of the ship. She kept her mind on the sounds of the sea and imagined the *Nimrod* as it sailed across the magnificent blue water. At long last she fell asleep. It must have been hours later when she heard Jonathan enter his cabin and move about quietly. She rolled over and slept on dreamlessly.

Benjamin Talbot reined in the horses and called out, "Whoa, boys!" As the buggy stopped, he glanced uneasily at the crowd of miners who milled on the San Francisco streets. "Are you certain you want to get out here?" he asked his sister Jessica.

"How else can Betsy and I call on Angelica?" she replied reasonably. "Benjamin, you know we haven't been in town for months. Sometimes it is difficult for women to be stuck out in the country."

He drew a deep breath and climbed from the buggy to help her and Betsy down to the street. It was one thing for them to call on the pastor's wife in Independence, Missouri, but quite another in the tent town of San Francisco. Hundreds of miners arrived daily to head for the diggings, and those who struck it rich often returned to town to spend their nuggets and gold dust on hard drink, gambling, and other dissipations.

"It is against my better judgment for you two to be here," he said as he helped Betsy down from the buggy.

"Don't worry, Father." Her green eyes sparkled with excitement at their visit to town. "What could happen to us so early in the morning?"

Not replying, he turned to help Jessica down.

She eyed the crowd of miners. "Sometimes I wish James Marshall had never seen that gold in the saw-mill tail-race."

"You are not alone in that wish," he said, "but we cannot

turn time back anymore than we can turn back the flow of the miners who come in. We must go on with life as it is."

She gave a laugh. "Now, Benjamin, there is no need to lecture an old schoolteacher. I merely expressed a wish."

"I know." He gazed at the miners again—Americans, Chileans, Chinese, Dutch, English, French, Greeks . . . everyone wanted California's gold. "I expect my trouble is that I would often like to return to our old pastoral existence myself."

She nodded, then straightened her dark blue cotton bonnet and smoothed the full skirt of her matching frock with determination. "In any case, it won't do for us to look so grim."

He half smiled. "Now who is lecturing whom?"

Her brown eyes flashed with amusement, then grew serious as she looked away. Already a crowd of curious miners had stopped to gawk at them, particularly at Betsy, whose auburn braids and lively green eyes always drew attention to her. In her new green calico frock, it was obvious that she was becoming a young woman.

"It will suit me a lot better when you are in their house," he said. "I intend to wait right here until you are."

"It is just that these men rarely see women on the street," Jessica replied quietly. "We'll be fine. You'll see. Come along, Betsy!" she added briskly, and they started down the dusty street.

One of the miners asked, "Betsy, are ye?"

Benjamin watched as his daughter nodded uncertainly.

A bleary-eyed one called out, "Ain't ye a pretty thing?"

"Ye must be the one we been singin' about, sweet Betsy from Pike!" one declared. He sang out tipsily,

"Oh, do you remember sweet Betsy from Pike,
who crossed the big mountains

97

with her husband Ike,

with two yoke of cattle, a large yellow dog—"

Benjamin started forward, but Jessica had already taken Betsy by the elbow and used what she called her old schoolteacher voice. "Gentlemen, if you will excuse us, I am sure you must have business to attend to."

"Business!" a tall, black-haired one laughed. "Here's our business!" With that he took a swig from his bottle.

Jessica replied, "A bad business that is, sir. Your poor mother's heart would likely be broken to see you now."

"Yer right there," the fellow replied with a grin as he wiped his mouth.

"Young man, I hope you know you can ask the Lord to deliver you from drink," Jessica told him. "He can make your life worth living, too."

"You askin' us to take the pledge?" one laughed.

"That's up to you," Jessica replied. "There comes a time for everyone to decide for the good or the evil side."

For a moment Benjamin wondered if she planned to recite Lowell's poem on the subject, but the miners chuckled, then drew back and let Betsy and Jessica pass.

In spite of his concern, Benjamin hid a smile. Jessica was good with children, and miners often required the same kind of management. Just last night she had said, "When men leave their responsibilities behind as some of these miners do, you have to treat them like children, too."

He climbed back on the buggy and watched as Betsy and Jessica made their way along the dirt street. If nothing else, the Thompsons now lived in a wood house instead of a tent. The rental of houses was so expensive that Seth and two friends had gone to Oakland for lumber and shakes, and built a one-room house on the lot to serve as the church meeting place as well. Out back, Seth had a garden, chickens, and a cow, right here in town.

At last Betsy and Jessica were in the Thompson house. Benjamin sat on the buggy seat watching until the miners wandered on.

"Gid'up, boys," he said and flicked the reins lightly over the horses. If only Betsy and Jessica hadn't yearned so to come to town for the day, he thought as the buggy moved along the dusty street. Everywhere he'd ever lived, there had been lowlifes and ruffians, but nowhere else had there been so many of them. Unfortunately, these had gold dust in their pockets and plenty of time to spend it.

He glanced out at the sunshine sparkling on the blue water of the bay, and it reminded him of the One who had created the earth and its beauty. That same One loved him—and every last one of those miners. The thing to do was to remind them of it, or to let them know; the trouble was the lack of sufficient ministers for the booming population. The few here like Seth Thompson worked day and night and ruined their health.

Just last week Seth had said, "The Pacific Coast was once called the Rim of Christendom, but that period passed when the Mexicans won the land and took the missions from the church. The time's ripe to spread the reformed faith. You and I have been called, and maybe plenty of other believers, too. I pray they will come and not be lured by gold dust instead of telling all who'll hear of God's grace."

"Amen," Benjamin had pronounced. "Amen."

Seth had added with vehemence, "If I had a hundred bodies and as many tongues, I would be glad to lay them all on His altar in California. What better expenditure can be made? California is the beacon of the world."

Benjamin recalled a hymn he had heard they now sang on the eastern seaboard,

"Go where the waves are breaking
on California's shore,
Christ's precious gospel taking,
more rich than golden ore."

At Wainwright-Talbot Shipping and Chandlery, he bid the clerks good day and hurried to his office. Two ships had sailed in this morning and his adopted son, Daniel Wainwright, was already out with their supercargoes as they unloaded. Hopefully, among the miners, shovels, and picks, they would unload a few gold-resistant ministers.

At three o'clock, Benjamin set out with the horses and buggy for Seth and Angelica Thompson's house. He seldom worked such a short day at the chandlery, but something in him had risen up and urged him to immediately go for Betsy and Jessica. He'd come for them early whether they liked it or not. He had grown more or less accustomed to the crowds of drunken miners on the streets, but this afternoon they made him feel uneasy. As he neared the Thompson house, he saw that a large crowd of miners had gathered on the street in front of it.

Urging his horses on, he viewed the scene from his buggy seat: Two drunken miners held Betsy in their grip and were trying to kiss her, while others held Jessica and Angelica Thompson back.

Such a fury rose in him that he rode the buggy into the midst of the crowd. "Take your hands off my daughter, you ruffians!" he yelled. "Unhand her right now!"

The crowd parted and the men dropped their hold on Betsy.

"You women get in the house," Benjamin ordered. "As for you men, don't you ever touch my family again. You hear that? Don't you ever touch a one of my family again!"

The men backed off and he added, "Something must be

done to make this place safe for people to live! Something must be done!"

The words had no more than left his lips than he remembered: it was man who was the agent for the temporal advancement of either good or evil; man was the focal point of the conflict between God and Satan. All too often, man forgot that living on earth was to exist between the two spiritual kingdoms in conflict.

He disliked politics and preferred to avoid the law and order issue, but he was suddenly convicted that he must become a part of the solution whether he wished to or not. As Betsy and Jessica stepped into the Thompsons' house and closed the door behind them, Benjamin prayed, *If I am to help fight this lawlessness, Lord, I ask Thou wouldst show me how!*

# 6

As Louisa stepped out on deck the next morning, the *Nimrod* sailed smoothly across the glistening water of Chesapeake Bay. The warm wind caught her fawn-colored bonnet and skirt, and as she turned to retie the bonnet, she saw Jonathan striding toward her. "There you are, Louisa," he said, his expression far more cheerful than when they had departed Baltimore. "I am already on my fourth circuit of the deck. Would you care to walk with me?"

"Yes, with pleasure. I daresay walking will do me good after sleeping so late. I scarcely knew where I was when I awakened."

"I hope I didn't wake you."

She fell in step with him. "Not at all. It was the sun streaming through my porthole." It would not do to tell him that in the mesmeric state of half-sleep she had wondered about him. Before coming to her senses, she had even imagined how vulnerable he would be in sleep with that deep cleft in his chin. She looked at him for an instant now. He wore a brown frock coat and trousers that suited him perfectly.

He shortened his stride to match hers. "Best to walk now. The captain thinks we are in for a storm on the Atlantic."

A bank of dark clouds did indeed lurk on the eastern horizon. She must have looked worried, for he said, "We shall be fine." He took note of her dress. "Are you warm enough?"

"Yes, thank you, though I may need my cloak when we sail into the Atlantic." She wore the same dress she'd had on when she'd come to the shipping office to ask about the voyage to California. How much her life had changed since then, since she left Conduff—No, she must not think of it. Better to thank God for this beautiful morning.

As she and Jonathan circled the deck, they spoke of the beauties of the sea and the sky, of the voyage ahead, and of the sailors' endless chores. Everywhere about them seamen went about their tasks: reefing, furling, and bracing sail; tarring, greasing, oiling, varnishing, painting, scraping, and scrubbing other parts of the *Nimrod*. Jonathan quoted what he called the sailors' "Philadelphia Catechism" with amusement:

"Six days shalt thou labor
and do all thou art able,
And on the seventh,
holystone the decks and scrape the cable."

Louisa laughed, remembering that he had mentioned his interest in maritime law on the train ride to Baltimore. "How did you become interested in maritime law?"

"Through reading Dana's *Two Years Before the Mast* and his *The Seaman's Friend*. Then I met Dana when I was at Harvard, and I've often thought of becoming a seaman to see the world, but here I am, traveling in luxury. I am doubtless too old to be a seaman now—

"Too old?"

"I am thirty years old."

"I had no idea you were a modern Methuselah."

He chuckled, and she was pleased to see he could laugh at himself. "Will you practice maritime law in California?"

"That and much else remains to be seen," he replied.

"A great deal remains to be seen in my life, too."

They fell into a companionable silence, which pleased her as well. She and Tess had called such comfort without discussion "the trying of friendship," and friendship was precisely what she wanted with Jonathan. Surely it must be possible for a man and a woman to be no more than friends.

Breakfast was not well attended because several of the passengers were seasick. Out on deck afterwards, Captain Martin spoke privately with Louisa and Jonathan. "I would like the men in the hold to take fresh air, and some of them speak coarsely. Perhaps you would prefer to be on the quarterdeck."

"Yes, thank you for warning us," Jonathan replied.

He escorted Louisa up the short flight of stairs to the quarterdeck, his hand solicitously at her elbow. If he were Conduff, she thought, he would take pleasure in subjecting her to foul language. Nor would Conduff wipe off the slatted bench for her as Jonathan did with his neatly folded handkerchief.

She sat down beside him and looked below through the rigging as the men from the hold pushed out on deck. They were a rumpled, bedraggled lot. Apparently several had been seasick and hadn't bothered to wash the stains from their clothes. She cringed as they took notice of her, leering and grinning, and she quickly redirected her attention to the sunlit sea.

Before long, several of their fellow passengers in cabin class joined them on the quarterdeck. Last evening, they explained, some of the men had drunk and gambled at cards far into the night and now slept off their folly. Hugh Fairfax, they said, had been the greatest winner.

At midday, when he arrived at the dinner table, they taunted, "Finally here, Fairfax!" and "Thought you'd sleep all day!" and he laughed heartily with them.

He took his seat beside Louisa and smiled his Adonis smile. "Are you going to chide me?"

"Certainly not. I have no reason to."

His blue eyes probed hers and, before she could draw away, he took her hand and bestowed a lingering kiss on her fingertips. "How beautiful you are in that fawn color with your chestnut hair," he murmured. "Though the dress you wore yesterday enhances the sapphire of your eyes. I presume that men often present you with sapphires."

She nearly laughed. "No, never sapphires." For the most part, men had presented her with a life full of difficulties.

"Then I shall bring you sapphires," he vowed. "Sapphires mounted on California gold."

Louisa realized that the others were waiting to say grace. A wave of heat flooded her cheeks and she bowed her head while Jonathan prayed. She was still embarrassed after the final "Amen," and she concentrated on eating the chicken dinner, carefully forking up the peas and buttered spring potatoes.

After a while Jonathan inquired stiffly, "Is Fairfax annoying you?"

"No . . . no, he is not."

Later, when Jonathan discussed a joint gold mining venture with those at the table, Hugh murmured near her ear, "I understand that you share Chambers's suite."

She replied as calmly as she could, "We do share a suite, but we certainly do not share a cabin, if that is what you wish to imply. As matters stand, I was fortunate to find any accommodations at all. I hope you will clarify the situation with whoever was gossiping about me."

Hugh's expression became contrite. "I beg your pardon. I was unsure what to think since you seem a fine young lady. I only wished to be certain—"

"I see." Somewhat mollified, she decided that he had been putting her to a test. Like most men, he wanted to discover what her reaction to such a notion would be. She hoped she had made her opinion quite clear.

Turning to Jonathan, she realized that he had not overheard. His eyes went to Hugh Fairfax before returning to her. "If you will excuse me this afternoon, several of these gentlemen have asked me to draft a mining contract."

"Of course. You must not feel obligated to entertain me."

"Obligation has little to do with it," he returned.

Shortly after dinner they sailed out of Chesapeake Bay near Norfolk and into the vastness of the Atlantic Ocean. It was only minutes before they turned in a southerly direction, though they could not see the North Carolina coastline. The sea was so beautiful, Louisa thought she could stay forever out on deck and admire the glorious sight.

Before long, however, Jonathan had to depart for his meeting, and Hugh began to pay her such ardent court that she retired to her cabin. Complimentary as it was to have the handsome Princetonian's interest, she preferred not to upset the fine balance of friendship between herself and Jonathan, and she suspected that Hugh's presence caused Jonathan to become—at the very least—uneasy.

The wind rose later in the afternoon, and the *Nimrod* rolled with the heavier sea. Feeling queasy in the cabin, Louisa returned to the quarterdeck for fresh air. Jonathan and several of her fellow passengers, she discovered, shared the same idea. Nodding at them, she proceeded to the railing. A stiff wind buffeted her bonnet and tore at her cloak, but being out in the elements did relieve her queasiness.

Beside her, Jonathan suggested, "It would be sensible to forego supper since we are nearing the storm."

"The weather does appear to be worsening. Perhaps the cabin boy could bring us biscuits to eat here."

"A sensible idea."

"Are we nearing Cape Hatteras?" she asked. "One hears so much about shipwrecks along the Carolina coasts."

"Yes. Cape Hatteras, then Cape Lookout. It is one of the most treacherous stretches in the Atlantic because of the shoals. But we will be fine," he assured her before he left to search for the cabin boy.

At sunset, they sat on the bench and ate the biscuits. The wind blew harder by the minute, and the eastern sky darkened. At length, only a narrow shaft of red-gold sunlight pierced the blackness. Thunder echoed and lightning zigzagged through the sky, making Louisa's nerves as taut as the *Nimrod's* white sails.

Darkness fell like a sudden clap, and the winds howled in the rigging. A cry sounded, "All hands aloft!" followed by loud and repeated orders by the mate, the trample of seamen's feet, and the creak of blocks.

Huge waves began to pound at the *Nimrod's* hull, and Louisa braced herself against the wind and the roll of the ship. The great sails whipped and snapped overhead, and she took note of the nearby quarter boats. Could such small boats survive such a fury if a clipper ship did not?

Lightning split the nearby sky, and the sea pounded the *Nimrod's* bow like a sledgehammer before breaking over the deck. Loose ropes flew about as the sailors chased them and yelled hoarsely. The black sea heaved in ever higher waves, the crests breaking into bright white foam around the ship.

A seaman, battling the wind, hurried out to the small

knot of passengers with lighted kerosene lanterns. "Ye best go to yer cabins!" he shouted, and the others departed.

At Louisa's frightened glance, Jonathan called over the storm, "Best to stay out as long as possible!"

She clung to the ship's rail and tried to train her eyes on a point in the darkness where she imagined the sea met the sky. Buffeted endlessly by the wind and loud claps of thunder, she feared she might not be able to hold onto the rail much longer. "I must go down to my cabin!"

Great drops of rain began to splatter on the already sea-drenched deck, and Jonathan grabbed her arm. "Let me lead!"

The ship's kerosene lanterns spread pools of light near the companionway, and the two of them caught onto handholds as they battled their way down into the central salon.

Jonathan appropriated one of the salon's lanterns, and they struggled toward their suite. Although the thunder and the howl of the wind in the rigging was not so dreadful here, the ship rolled and pitched dangerously, and Louisa had to hold the lantern as Jonathan labored to unlock their door.

Light glimmered among the shadows of his cabin as they staggered in, and the ship heaved as he opened the door to her room. She clutched the doorjamb.

Even here, Jonathan had to speak loudly. "Take the lantern, but be sure to extinguish it before you sleep!"

The instant the ship's rolling ceased, she took the lantern from him. Its circle of light surrounded them, and their eyes held as though they had been stunned by lightning.

"Will you be all right alone, Louisa?"

She tore herself from his gaze. "Yes, thank you. Good night, Jonathan."

"You need not lock the door."

Not lock the door between them? At this moment, she trusted the storm more than she did her surfacing passion. What folly to hope they might be no more than friends.

Lantern light danced around her cabin as the *Nimrod* heaved with the storm, and it took a great effort to lock the door. Once again she thought that perhaps she should confess to her marriage—but once her secret was out, who knew how far such information might go?

Her trunk slid across the cabin's slanting floor, returning her to her senses. She pushed the trunk back, but the instant she stepped away, it skidded across the floor and smashed into the opposite wall. It was equally impossible to undress, though she did pull off her shoes and extinguish the lantern's light before getting into her berth.

The storm raged as though intent upon unleashing its full fury upon them and, as she lay there, the conviction came upon her that she was being punished for leaving Conduff. Lord, forgive me! Forgive me!

She remembered, "But the Lord was not in the wind . . . and not in the fire . . . and, after the fire, a still small voice." She clung to her berth, tossed to and fro, until finally she dropped into a fitful sleep.

When at last morning light filtered through her porthole, waves still crashed over the thick glass, though with less frequency. The storm appeared to be abating, but the ship's movement felt strange.

She attempted to sit up, holding onto a berth post. Suddenly the *Nimrod* crashed, shuddered to a stop, then lurched forward to another crash. Her lantern shattered and the reek of kerosene filled the room. Outside, bells clanged.

"Louisa!" Jonathan called, trying the door. He pounded on it. "Louisa, the ship is foundering!"

Struggling toward the door, she tried to keep her bare feet

from the glass sliding across the floor.

"Louisa!" Jonathan shouted.

"Wait! Wait a moment!" The ship pitched violently as she tried to unlock the door.

Finally the lock turned and Jonathan threw the door open, dressed and wide-eyed with concern.

"My shoes—"

"There's no time!" He grabbed her arm, and they began to struggle toward his door.

*We're going to die. We're going to die right here at sea,* she thought.

In the salon's dim light, everyone was white-faced as they hurried from their cabins. Jonathan grabbed her hand, and she followed through the crowd in his wake toward the aft stairs. The ship lurched, and they tumbled against the steps.

"Are you hurt?" he shouted over the din.

"No!" She pulled herself up on the handrail and toiled her way up the stairs with him.

Outside, dawn streaked the sky, and the rain had ceased. The clouds were white now, more benign in appearance.

"Hurry!" Jonathan looked wide-eyed at the water pouring in through the broken hull. "We have to abandon ship!"

*This cannot be happening—* she thought, terrified. *It's a nightmare—*But the *Nimrod* crashed again, shuddering as a horrible ripping and rending filled the morning.

"A shoal . . . we've hit a shoal!" Jonathan yelled, propelling her down the slanting deck toward the rail.

White water boiled around the *Nimrod's* disintegrating bow. Heavy beams and planks splintered as the ship reared and ripped, tattered wood lifting into the air.

"Hold onto the rail!" Jonathan ordered as he pulled her along to where men were lowering the quarter boat from the side of the ship. They were gold seekers from the hold, except

111

Hugh, who was too preoccupied to see her.

Grasping the rail, she turned again to see the *Nimrod* rushing forward yet another time as if intent upon destroying itself and all of them.

"Now!" someone shouted, and the quarter boat was over the side, bouncing on the sea. The men jumped into the churning water and pushed the boat away from the *Nimrod*.

Jonathan forewarned her, "I'll throw you overboard."

Before she could speak, he lifted her and she was up over the rail, then falling into the inky-dark blueness below. "Help me, Lord!" she cried.

She hit the sea with such force that she lost her breath, then plunged deep into the cold water. She fought her way to the surface, her lungs almost bursting. Waves broke over her head, and she finally caught a painful breath. "Help! Help!"

Men swam around from the quarter boat, trying to pull themselves aboard, but apparently no one heard her cries. She struggled to stay afloat in the icy water, the heaviness of her wet frock pulling her head beneath the frequent waves. She stroked the water with her arms and tried desperately to kick her feet, but her efforts seemed useless.

A wave lifted her and, though her eyes stung from the salt water, she glimpsed her surroundings. Some distance away, the *Nimrod* was disintegrating on the shoal, and men were trying to push the quarter boat ever farther away. The other quarter boat was crowded with passengers, who rapidly rowed away. The churning water was full of passengers who clung to debris or tried to swim.

Debris floated everywhere in the icy water. Indeed, a wooden keg bobbed toward her, propelled along by the wind. Even in her terror, she knew such a buoyant keg would keep her afloat. Here it came . . . She grabbed it with all of her might and held on doggedly.

What a relief to float. She succumbed to it as the wind propelled her and the keg through the cold sea. As she rose on another wave, she saw two men in the second quarter boat, rowing it away from the *Nimrod*. Other passengers held onto splintered fragments of the ship, but with the sea surging all around, she was unable to identify anyone. "Jonathan!" she shouted. "Jonathan!"

No one replied, and the *Nimrod* battered against the rocks again. She wondered whether Captain Martin was aboard, for men still leapt off. The ship smashed against the shoal again, and she turned away, unwilling to further witness its destruction.

The quarter boat lifted on the waves, full of passengers rowing in her direction. She called out and waved. As the boat moved nearer, she saw it was badly overcrowded. Yet surely they'd make room. Hugh would save her. "Help!" she cried, gulping a mouthful of salt water.

She choked and tried to call out again. Didn't they see her in the midst of all of the debris? Lord, let them stop! she prayed, but the boat moved onward across the waves, the men's backs turned as they let a body slip out into the sea. Someone had died, and they were preoccupied with that.

She waved and waved until they were nearly out of sight. Lord, I cannot believe I am to be abandoned here in the sea!

She recalled hearing that God regarded death very differently than mortals might. Nevertheless, she was not ready for death, and it was a distinct and immediate possibility.

The sea was a bit calmer, she thought. When she had another glimpse above the waves at the *Nimrod*, she felt heartsick to see that the fine ship was a complete wreckage.

"Louisa!"

At first she couldn't believe she'd heard a voice, then it

came again amidst the sounds of the sea: "Louisa!" She turned and, to her astonishment, found Jonathan paddling to her on some kind of a platform. "Thank God I've found you!"

A sob burst from her.

"Please . . . stay calm, Louisa—Here, let me try to come close."

She nodded, still sobbing and unable to speak.

He manuevered the makeshift raft about with a long oar, and despite the skirt tangled at her feet, she tried desperately to kick her way closer to him. When her keg was as close as possible, he lay down on the raft and slowly pulled her aboard. Finally she lay as bedraggled as flotsam on what she realized was the *Nimrod's* hatch cover.

"Hold on here," he ordered, transferring her grip from his hand to what appeared to be a metal handle.

"Thank you . . . oh, thank you, Jonathan!"

"Let me secure you to the raft." He encircled her waist with rope, then strapped her to the handle.

When he had accomplished it, she threw herself into his arms. "Oh, Jonathan—" She was shaking with shock and then weeping against him.

"You must hold on to the handle," he said, pushing her away. "What we do now, Louisa, will make the difference between living or dying."

She loosened her grasp on him and grabbed the handle.

"Can you hold the oar?" he asked. "I want to bring your keg aboard. If we could find another—" She took the oar, and his words trailed off as he set to work, his face full of determination. Five or six inches of water covered the hatch cover, more when the waves rolled over them.

He wrestled the keg aboard and tied it to the handle. "Hold onto it, too."

She nodded.

He sat down on a coil of rope beside her, blinking and shaking his head vaguely.

"Please rest," she begged. "You have a bloody cut on your forehead." His dark hair was plastered over it, just as his soaked clothing was plastered about him.

She glanced down and discovered that the top of her fawn-colored skirt was ripped and ragged. Her bare feet were white and scratched, and she tucked them under her, though it brought little warmth in the icy water.

Jonathan took the oar from her. "Let's look for other survivors."

He rowed toward the wreckage of the *Nimrod*, and she surveyed the sea with him, but there was no sign of others in the debris that was slowly spreading over the sea.

"The water is too cold," he said as they rowed through the debris.

"I saw people holding onto the wreckage before."

"I tried to help," he replied with anguish. "I tried—"

What had he seen? she agonized as she looked away at the undulating sea. She had been spared the sight of death except for the body released into the water from the quarter boat. It seemed now that they were the last people on earth, abandoned in the vastness of the sea.

By the time the sun's rays burst through the clouds, she and Jonathan had cut away a small section of sail and rigging from the debris and brought aboard another empty keg and a broken oar.

"Best to leave," he decided and began to paddle with the shorter oar. "Nothing else we can use."

"Won't others come here to find us?"

He glanced out at the calming sea with her. "Better to sail for the shipping corridor. If the sea rises again, it is best to get away from the debris."

"Can't we rest . . . just a bit?"

"No," he replied sternly.

She clutched their finds from the *Nimrod's* wreckage as he began to paddle. They manuevered some distance before Jonathan handed over his oar to her to hold. "We need the kegs under us for buoyancy and to keep us above the water," he explained, then showed her what she must do with the rope while he tied the kegs beneath their raft.

He dove into the water, and she prayed, *Lord, don't let him drown! Please, don't let him drown!*

It took what seemed hours for him to tie the kegs beneath them. The raft rode much higher in the water, then finally he was climbing up onto it again. "We can float awhile," he said wearily. He rested only a few moments, however, before setting to work on fashioning a rudder from the broken oar.

Finally he was finished, and their rudder was attached to an eyebolt behind him. He pulled out his pocketknife again to cut away at their scrap of canvas. "Now to make a sail."

By midday, he had rigged a small sail. He attached it to the longer oar, then stood the oar upright and tied it in place with ropes to the handles on all four sides of the hatch cover.

Louisa held onto the rudder as the wind caught their sail. "We're moving! Perhaps someone will find us yet!"

"I'm a man who believes in miracles," he said.

After he had made adjustments to the rudder and sail, he cut a length of rope and tied himself to a handle, too. "In the shipping corridor, the Gulf Stream, it's warmer and we are more apt to be seen."

Warm water was said to flow north from the Gulf of Mexico, she remembered as she watched their progress over the sea. Turning, she realized how the knob on Jonathan's forehead had risen. "Jonathan, I think you must have been hit hard."

He nodded, wincing in pain.

"Does your head ache?"

"Yes," he admitted and rubbed his temples. "Let me rest awhile. But don't let me sleep."

She wanted to sleep in the warm sunshine herself, but she had not worked as hard as he, nor been hit on the head. She tore off a bit of her ragged skirt hem, dipped it into the cold water and folded it into a compress, then placed it on his forehead. His dark lashes parted for an instant, then he smiled and tugged at the rope around his waist before lying down. His clothes were sodden; he wore only a tattered white shirt, trousers torn at the knees, and brown woolen socks.

After a while, his chest rose and fell in the rhythm of sleep. How vulnerable he appeared, she thought. Despite the darkness of beard around his jaw, sleep imparted a boyishness to his expression. How could it hurt if he slept a short while?

She appraised her own appearance. One sleeve of her wet dress had torn off at the shoulder seam and the other sleeve at the elbow, three bodice buttons were missing at the neck, her hem was even more tattered now, and the damp rope around her waist tore at her skin. Her hair had slipped its pins and blew in the breeze.

It was disheartening to have lost all of her belongings, even Aunt Sarah's Bible. On the other hand, she and Jonathan were still alive, while many of their shipmates were not. How excited they had all been yesterday, especially the red-haired Harvard student who thought their bones might whiten the plains of California. Instead, his bones might be enriching the sea. She hoped the two wives and the ten-year-old girl at their table had been rescued in the quarter boats.

At length, she knew she must direct her thoughts to cheerful avenues, and turned them to Ellie and Oakley and their family.

How sleepy she was. Could it matter if she lay down for a minute or two while she held onto the rudder? She lay back and was far more comfortable, though she had to close her eyes against the sun. Before long, she caught herself drifting off.

Opening her eyes determinedly, she held sleep at bay, then slowly, slowly her eyes closed again. She dozed for a few seconds, roused herself to check the rudder, then dozed for another second or two.

Awakening with a start, she saw a red and gold sunset shimmering across the water. "Jonathan!" She sat up. He was still asleep. "Jonathan! I'm sorry! I slept, too!"

He lay on his back, not responding, and she crawled nearer. "Jonathan?" Dared she shake him?

She reached for a muscular shoulder and shook it tentatively, then harder. Fear seized her. What if he were unconscious from the blow on his head? One heard of people who didn't awaken for days and even weeks, some never. "Jonathan!"

She leaned close. To her relief, she felt his breath on her cheek, then saw his lashes flicker. His hazel eyes filled with confusion, then brightened.

Before she could think, his arms gathered her to him. "Let me hold you a moment, just a moment," he murmured.

"No, you must not. Jonathan—"

Her protest faded as his mouth neared and touched hers. His lips tasted of salt, too, but his kiss was warm and tender, like none she had ever known, and she found herself beginning to return it. His arms drew her closer, and she allowed herself to touch his strong shoulders. How warm and comforting he was. How could this be wrong when they might drown any moment? How could it be wrong when he was the finest, most caring man she had ever known?

"My lovely Louisa," he whispered as they caught their breath. The water bobbed below them and the sun warmed them, lulling all reason. His mouth moved to hers again, their kiss slowly deepening.

Finally the rope pressing her money belt into her stomach brought her to reality. She backed away. "No, Jonathan—"

He sat up, his eyes holding hers tenderly. "How I want to hold you in my arms forever."

She closed her eyes in anguish. "I should not have allowed it—"

"I am not trifling, Louisa. I have cared for you from the first . . . in the shipping office. I hope you care for me."

Despite herself, she whispered, "I do, but—" She had no idea of how she might explain herself without revealing the truth about Conduff.

"When I awakened earlier and found you sleeping beside me, being shipwrecked seemed a wonderful dream—"

"You awakened earlier?"

He gave her a small, guilty smile. "How do you think that my socks came to be on your poor feet?"

"On my feet?" She stared down at the wet and overly large brown socks she now wore. "I . . . hadn't noticed."

"You're not angry?"

"I scarcely know. I—I imagine your motive was noble."

"Entirely so," he vowed, though he smiled.

As his hands reached for her hair, the last rays of sunshine glistened across the sky and the sea. "What a picture you are, Louisa. You are like a beautiful sea-maiden with flowing red tresses whom God has cast here on the ocean with me."

At the thought of God, she removed Jonathan's hands from her hair. "We had better see to the raft. Are we on course?"

His eyes appraised her, then looked up at the stars in the darkening sky. "It appears that our raft holds better to the right course than I."

She met his gaze uncertainly. "We must not . . . Oh, Jonathan, we cannot—" She turned away, desperately wishing she were free to love and be loved by him.

As she gathered her resistance, she saw the sun was gone and total darkness was falling. The wind turned cold. They would spend the entire night together, and already she would like nothing more than to bury herself in his arms again. *Lord, help us,* she prayed, for only He could. And only He knew when, if ever, a ship might rescue them.

# 7

**B**enjamin Talbot stood at the railing of the ship as it sailed into the Bay of Monterey. "Sheltered from all winds" Sabastian Viscaino had written about the bay in 1602 and, remembering the words of the Spanish explorer, Benjamin wondered how long this bastion of Spanish and Mexican rule would be sheltered from the winds of the gold rush.

They sailed past the old Mexican fort and its cannons, then to the harbor of the unimposing capital of the California Territory. Despite its past and present honors, Monterey was little more than a dusty village set between hills on the sparkling blue bay. Its whitewashed presidio, the oldest military establishment west of the Rockies, had been founded by the Spanish nearly eighty years before and took up most of the place. Outside its high walls stood the custom house and adobe buildings. Here and there, rustic ox carts for carrying hides from neighboring *ranchos* to the ships stood outside the walls.

Disembarking from the ship, it seemed impossible that the change he sought might come from such a quiet place. He hoped General Riley, the new commander of the presidio and governor of the territory, would see matters his way.

"Benjamin Talbot!"

He was pleased to see Thomas Larkin, former U.S. consul to Mexico, waiting for him on the shore. "How kind of you to welcome me, sir."

"A pleasure," Larkin said. "Our friend Walter Colton is occupied with his alcalde duties and asked me to come."

"The judge, jury, and jailer of Monterey?" Benjamin asked with amusement.

Larkin laughed. "Colton handles his power well, though an alcalde is as powerful as the Czar of Russia these days."

Benjamin chuckled and they shook hands heartily. "I am pleased to hear that our naval chaplain doesn't let his power go to his head."

"As are we all," Larkin replied.

Benjamin took the man's measure again. Though nearly fifty, Larkin's efforts to bring California to the American side had not grayed his dark hair and thick brows. He was sober of eye and said to be a tolerant man who made allowances for the crudities of the gold rush. Within limits, tolerance was a fine trait, Benjamin reflected; the real question was how much he would tolerate. Would he, for example, tolerate a girl like Betsy being manhandled by miners?

Benjamin picked up his valise again, and they started toward the custom house. "It is a pleasure for me to enjoy the quiet of your town after the raucousness of San Francisco."

"Yes, it is especially quiet now," Larkin answered. "Many of our residents are off to the diggings or the excitement of San Francisco. Rachel and I were glad to hear of your coming." He gestured to his house some distance up the dusty calle principal. "We have comfortable quarters and hope you will stay with us."

Benjamin glanced at the well-known house, the

forerunner of what was being called the Monterey style of architecture. Its whitewashed adobe walls rose two stories high and were topped with a hipped roof, and the verandas on three sides served as protection against the California sun. It was a style that appeared well suited to the territory.

"Thank you. If Colton is occupied, I shall accept your invitation. I have heard of your fine hospitality and admired your house. Indeed, Colton and I bought supplies downstairs in your store a year ago, but you were in San Francisco."

"I am sorry to have missed you then," Larkin said. He eyed Benjamin carefully. "I understand you are in favor of writing a constitution for California as soon as possible."

"Indeed I am! It is precisely why I've come. I know you are one of the most highly respected men in the territory, and I hope you will help us with the governor to obtain territorial law."

"Alas, my influence with our new governor is limited," Larkin replied. "I am interested, though, in how you think you might influence him."

"We must point out that the Mexican system of law may be fine in a quiet town like Monterey where there is a conscientious alcalde like Colton, but it is hopeless in a teeming place like San Francisco, and worse yet out in the diggings. Matters are so bad the miners take the law into their own hands and whip or hang those they judge guilty."

"And . . .?" Larkin prompted.

"Unfortunately, they often wait until matters go too far, and then do not always act fairly. Last week at the diggings a man was sentenced to two hundred lashes for a minor matter, and the lashing killed him."

"I'm not surprised," Larkin said unhappily. "What do you propose?"

"At the least, to form a provisional government based on

the American system of elected representatives. Nearly five hundred people met in San Francisco in February to organize a government along American lines, but Smith, the former governor, refused his support."

"So I heard," Larkin replied.

"We feel if California is to be American, we can't have a government that's part military and part civil and, as the miners put it, 'part no government at all.' The law-abiding people want elected officials like they had at home, and they want them as soon as possible."

"The governor will say it is up to Washington," Larkin responded. "He maintains that the Mexican laws must continue in force until changed by a competent authority. In other words, we must wait for Congress to act."

Benjamin shook his head. "Congress is so deadlocked by the slavery question that they will take years to establish a territorial government for us. If only Riley would issue a proclamation for a general election to a state constitutional convention, it would hurry us toward statehood."

"If is the question," Larkin said, "if the governor will."

Benjamin recalled the miners grabbing Betsy, and he moved on with determination.

At ten o'clock the next morning, Benjamin entered the whitewashed presidio office and shook hands with Governor Bennett Riley.

"A pleasure, Mr. Talbot," the governor said. "I have been hoping to meet you. Your shipping firm is well known and respected."

"Thank you, sir." At the governor's gesture, Benjamin sat down on a black leather chair across from the man's desk. After exchanging pleasantries, he said, "I wish to come straight to the point, sir. The lawless element in San Francisco is out of control. It is becoming more and more unsafe for law-abiding citizens to be out on the streets."

"So one hears," the governor replied. "Nonetheless, I am eager to hear your view."

"Thaddeus Leavenworth, our San Francisco alcalde, is inundated with cases, and many miners refuse to recognize his authority."

The governor nodded. "You are not the first man to speak of it. Mr. Leavenworth has appealed to both my predecessor and to me for support, and we have both given it to him."

"But if we could take broader action against the lawlessness, sir," Benjamin said. As calmly as possible, he reiterated the problems of San Francisco and the diggings.

When he'd concluded, the governor raised a curious brow at him. "What is your motivation for coming here on this matter, Mr. Talbot?"

"There is, of course, the consideration any decent citizen has for living in a civilized place," Benjamin equivocated. "The reason—" He drew a deep breath, for Riley looked him straight in the eye. "The specific reason is that drunken miners manhandled my young daughter in broad daylight . . . in front of my sister and numerous other witnesses. If I hadn't been nearby, one can only wonder what might have transpired."

"I am sorry to hear it, Talbot," the governor said. "You have my sincere sympathy, but it does not alter the fact that the Mexican laws must continue in force."

"Why not make a beginning toward broader action? Why not begin a provisional territorial legislature such as they have in Oregon?"

"Oregon is a different matter. It was without laws when our people came," the govenor replied. "In California, the

Mexican law was already in place."

"Perhaps if we form a provisional legislature—"

"The people of California cannot form a popular government without my consent," the governor argued. "Even the town council in San Francisco is an illegal body. They have no right, even if they had my consent, to begin a town or a state government before Congress admits California as a state."

"Legally, you are probably correct, sir," Benjamin agreed, "but being legally correct does nothing to establish law and order. I believe our only hope for a better government soon is for you to call for a general election for delegates to draft a constitutional convention. With a good constitution, Congress might move more quickly to give us statehood."

"And who would write such a constitution?" Riley inquired.

"We can use the Iowa and New York constitutions as models," Benjamin replied hopefully. "We have copies of them."

Riley considered the suggestion, then shook his head. "There are other problems, like the slavery question."

"I believe it can be decided with one vote," Benjamin replied. "Most Californians do not favor slavery."

"Still, there is the controversy of our eastern boundary . . . the 'small state' faction advocating the line of the Sierra Nevada and the Colorado River, and the 'large state' proponents arguing to include the Rocky Mountains, creating a state so large Congress would refuse to admit it into the Union."

"That, too, can be solved, sir," Benjamin replied, "but we must take action now before the lawlessness becomes worse."

"I shall take it under consideration, Mr. Talbot." The governor rose to his feet in dismissal. "Do not be too hopeful.

I am, however, impressed that you would come to Monterey to speak to me of this. I still believe that right now the Mexican laws or military rule, if you wish to call it that, are our only alternative to anarchy."

Benjamin left the office downhearted. Even Riley realized how futile it would be to strictly enforce military rule. Doubtless that was why he allowed the miners free rein in handling their own affairs. Regular law and order would require effort and money, neither of which transient miners were willing to expend. It appeared that miners' law—lynch law—would prevail for some time to come, but at least he had planted seeds in the governor's mind.

As he made his way out of the presidio, he recalled Alex de Tocqueville's recent words: "America is still the place where the Christian religion has kept real power over men's souls. . . . Nothing better demonstrates how useful and natural it is to men, since the country where it now has the widest sway is both the most enlightened and the freest." If de Tocqueville were right about Christianity keeping men's souls under control, what would he say about the godlessness in San Francisco now?

That evening Benjamin dined on roast beef at the house of Rachel and Thomas Larkin, with Walter Colton and other Americans in attendance. After he had told them of his meeting with the governor, the others nodded with resignation.

Colton asked, "Have you heard of a Simpson pamphlet that the new gold seekers now bring with them?"

"Indeed. I have seen it myself," Benjamin replied.

"What is it about?" asked one of the men.

"It's an outrageous tale written by this Simpson, who was in Stevenson's regiment," Benjamin said. "Simpson claimed to have made his fortune shortly after gold was found last year, and he printed the pamphlet in New York after his return. It describes a life of leisurely gold gleaning and assures the reader that all streams are lined with gold. Just as bad, it says that in the course of three weeks, one goes in quite impossible stages from Sutter's Fort to the foot of the 'Shastl' peak, evidently Mount Shasta, and returns. One walks that far, not because gold is scarce, but solely because one wants some notion of the size of the gold region!"

"Outrageous is right!" Larkin said. "And, according to him, what does one do during these leisurely three weeks?"

Benjamin had to smile, exasperating as the pamphlet was. "Ten days are spent by two men, with almost no implements, in picking up $50,000 of gold. The rest of the time, the yield is much more moderate because one is wandering, or discussing theories about the great central gold vein, from whence all gold 'streamed' or was 'thrown out' in the 'volcanic' days."

At their appalled response, he continued, "He says that one's companions are the best of fellows and the life is perfectly happy. The whole idea of the pamphlet is 'Why should one not come and bring all of his friends to this inexhaustible treasure house?' Worse, he uses facts to make it all sound plausible. Descriptions of the landscape, of people, of geographical matters, with names and dates freely given. In short, the pamphlet is persuasive and plausible."

"No wonder men stream in by the thousands!" Colton replied. "With such misinformation abroad, it will never stop."

Benjamin nodded. "And no wonder men are furious when they must actually work hard for the gold now. Few ever did just pick lumps of gold off the ground as this fellow implies."

"Men who are convinced by such pamphlets are in no

mood for sober state building," Colton remarked.

"God help us!" someone said.

At length, their talk turned to hopes for statehood, then to the godly men who had written the U.S. constitution.

"If American law and godly living aren't instituted in California," Benjamin said, "we can only subdue it with a totalitarian government."

One of the other guests objected to a godly approach to California's constitution. "California has one of the best educated citizenry in the country. We need only our intellects and ingenuity."

"I do not believe mankind can solve its problems with only intellect and ingenuity," Benjamin replied kindly. "We must ask for God's wisdom and blessing. George Washington said it best, that it would be impossible to govern this nation without God and the Ten Commandments. It is from those roots that our federal constitution grew, and it is from those roots that we must base our state constitution as well. If we stray from those roots, democracy will soon be brought down."

The next morning as Benjamin stood at the railing of a San Francisco-bound gold ship, he felt thoroughly frustrated. Monterey's serene whitewashed presidio and houses receded into the distance and, all around him on the ship, unwashed and bearded miners packed and repacked their provisions to be ready for the diggings. Their belts were stuck full of guns and bowie knives, and each of them seemed determined to strike it rich at all costs.

*God help us*, Benjamin prayed. *God help us*.

Louisa smelled the sea air and opened her eyes, full of fear. Bright rays of sun attacked her startled eyes, and she was shaking with cold. Carefully, she tried to change her position on the hatch cover. She was stiff, and her face and the back of her neck stung with sunburn.

The raft still sailed along over the waves and Jonathan still slept, his trousers as sodden as her skirt. The ocean stretched all around her as far as she could see. She was so thirsty her tongue felt huge and swollen. In the darkness, with no horizon to look at, both she and Jonathan had retched time and time again. "I am . . . so embarrassed," she had confessed.

"It is nothing to be ashamed of," he had replied, though she sensed he was himself. He tucked leftover canvas pieces from the sail around her. "Try to sleep. I'll keep watch."

It had been a miserable, if fitting, conclusion to last night's ill-considered kisses. Now their ramshackle raft rose and fell more distressingly than ever, and she knew it was unlikely they would survive a storm on this raft.

Jonathan groaned, and she reached out from under her canvas to touch his hand. "We are still afloat," she told him, hoping the sunburn on his face did not pain him as badly as hers did on her face, arms, and neck.

His eyes opened, and he squinted against the light. "Are you all right?"

"I'm fine." Her reply stretched the truth considerably, but if nothing else, they were alive.

"If only we had fresh water and bread," he said.

She smiled a trifle, though it made her lips hurt. "The driest crust would do, but we mustn't think of it." Touching her lower lip, she realized a painful blister was rising on it from the sun—or was it from their kisses? Trying to evade the thought, she looked out across the sea. There was nothing but blue water and bright sky.

Beside her, Jonathan said, "A ship will come for us!"

"How can you be sure?"

"I know in my spirit that it will."

"Pastor Norton sometimes spoke of spiritual assurance," she said. "Perhaps you should have become a pastor, too."

Jonathan gazed out at the sea. "I thought so for a while. When I was growing up, our neighbor was a pastor. I'm his namesake. Before I was born, he led my family to Christ."

Louisa waited to hear more, but Jonathan lapsed back into silence.

The sun beat down upon them without mercy as it made its journey through the sky. She fell asleep time and again, waking once to find Jonathan rearranging a piece of canvas over her face to shield her from the sun. Later, she saw he had moved so that his shadow shielded her from the brilliant sunset. "Your feet are burned, Jonathan. You must take back your socks." She bent down stiffly to remove them from her feet.

"I'm fine," he insisted, catching hold of her hands. "I'm fine, and it is nearly night again. The socks have dried out and you will need them for warmth. It's you who were shivering and crying out in your sleep."

A slice of her nightmare resurfaced.

Conduff was striding toward her, his face contorted with anger. "Thought you'd run off on me, did you!" he'd shouted, his hand raised to slap her. "Ain't no wife of mine runnin' off!"

"No!" she screamed. "No, Conduff!"

"Ain't you the one who said you loved me?"

"I love you! I love you, Conduff!" she cried out.

She asked Jonathan, "What . . . what did I say?"

Jonathan touched her forehead. "You are still feverish."

"What did I say?"

"Nothing of importance. Rest, Louisa. Sleep."

But it was of importance. She had called out in her sleep

to Conduff. What had Jonathan heard?

"Sleep," he said again.

That night when she awakened, she realized he was holding her close. He wanted to shield her body from the cold now, nothing more, she told herself. Even holding her, Jonathan was a gentleman. The sea heaved restlessly and she huddled with him for warmth. "The Lord is my shepherd," he prayed softly. "I shall not want . . . . He maketh me to lie down in green pastures . . . He leadeth me beside the still waters—"

Comforted, she relaxed in his arms.

The next morning she felt him withdraw his arm from around her shoulders, then slowly move away from her. Opening her eyes, she saw the sun's rays flare from the shimmering water on the horizon. Morning. They had lived through the night.

"A ship—" Jonathan said, rising unsteadily to his feet. He grabbed a piece of canvas and waved it wildly toward the tall-masted vessel. "Help!" he shouted, his voice cracking, then more loudly, "Help!"

Louisa rose to her knees and feebly waved a bit of canvas herself. "Lord, let them see us!"

But the ship sailed serenely across the blue sea, its white sails taut in the wind.

"See us, oh, see us!" she wailed, then while she watched, the craft slowly changed course.

Jonathan flagged his bit of canvas victoriously. "It's an American ship . . . an old brig. Here they come!"

The brig was bearing down upon them, and Jonathan said, "They're slowing for us—They're slowing—"

Louisa felt only a twinge of gladness as she slipped into darkness. Later, she only half realized they were carrying her aboard. Rough seamen gaped at her as she regained her feet and tottered backward. Her last glimpse was of Jonathan and a seaman as they helped her into a miniscule cabin and lay her on a bunk. "Thank You, Lord," she murmured. "Thank You, Lord."

For days her mind wandered in and out of darkness. Sometimes she found Jonathan at her side with a bowl of broth. "Try a spoonful," he would urge. "Here . . . just one more spoonful so you can regain your strength."

"You look like Oakley," she said once, for Jonathan wore a beard now, too. During a lucid moment she supposed it was difficult for a man to shave with a sharp razor on a heaving ship. And this ship heaved and creaked steadily.

"We're on the *Berta*, a New York gold ship bound for Panama," Jonathan explained.

"A gold ship?"

He nodded. "The hold is full of Northeasterners . . . men determined to make their fortunes in California."

"How did you secure . . . this cabin?"

"You must not concern yourself with such matters, Louisa. Set your mind on getting well. That's of foremost importance." He ignored her words as he propped her up in her bunk. "Can you sit up and drink this broth?"

She swallowed a bit of the warm chicken broth. "Where do you sleep?" she asked as she lay back.

His color heightened. "In the upper bunk."

"Right here in this cabin?"

He nodded uneasily. "They assumed we were married, and I didn't disabuse them of the notion. It's your best protection with no other women aboard. Now, another swallow of broth."

That evening, between spoonfuls of broth with rice, she nibbled on hardtack. The next day, she felt strong enough to eat bits of salt beef and potatoes, and drink China tea.

The day after, she saw he had shaved off his beard and looked quite the gentleman again.

Slowly she regained her strength, slowly but as steadily as the endless creaking of the ship. One morning she was strong enough to mend her tattered dress with a sewing kit Jonathan borrowed from a seaman—not that the frock would ever be truly presentable again.

When she was well enough to walk out to the deck, sunshine flooded the sky and sea, and she marveled at the magnificence of the day. "The ocean has turned aquamarine!"

"The Caribbean Sea," Jonathan explained.

"A welcome change," she said. "I have seen enough of the Atlantic Ocean to last a lifetime!"

He chuckled and she smiled. It was the first light moment they had shared in a long time.

He helped her to the quarterdeck's wooden bench. "One often hears the sea described as a lady of many moods."

"That is putting it mildly, though I see no reason not to compare it with a changeable man."

The lines around his mouth deepened. "Touché!"

"I was not referring to you," she said. Conduff was the one who had been changeable, though his storminess, his inner rage, had always predominated.

Jonathan tucked the blanket around her feet. "Warm as the weather is here, you must not catch a chill."

She thanked him, unnerved by the intimate gesture, but feeling grateful to be cosseted.

With the sunshine beaming down on them, she saw that his face was no longer sunburned.

"Is something amiss?" he asked.

"Your face is brown as a nut."

He laughed. "As yours will soon be, I hope. I should like

to see you aglow with health, like the girl who went swimming in an Alexandria creek."

"You've remembered that?"

He nodded, his hazel eyes shining. "I have tried to imagine what you might have looked like then."

She smiled, remembering how strong she had been then, how brown from the sunshine, even if it was unfashionable. "I shall be strong again," she vowed.

"Yes, when you look that determined, I know you will."

After a while she realized that the rough gold seekers were watching her from down on the main deck, and she turned her attention to the sea. "How did you acquire a cabin for us?"

"I had no choice but to tell the captain you are a Talbot. He often has work from Wainwright and Talbot, so he became agreeable enough."

There it was, the lie again.

Louisa's hand went to her hair, wondering whether its red color had been confirmation for the captain. In any event, her hair hung loose about her shoulders, knotted and snarled. She had never in all of her life felt so bedraggled. "You have already done so much, and now I have yet another request," she said, "water to wash myself."

"I shall see to it after our midday meal."

Their conversation turned to the gold seekers below, who Jonathan said included farmers, engineers, lawyers, and doctors. The majority were Americans from all over the Union; the rest were English, French, and German. "No matter what their social or financial standing," he said, "they are all roughing it."

In the afternoon the cabin boy brought a pitcher of water, a basin, and soap to the cabin. Louisa bolted the door behind him and undressed as the ship rolled and creaked across the sea. How thin I've become, she thought as she washed herself. As for her hair, it took almost more effort than she had to work out the tangles.

She enjoyed simply being clean again. Unfortunately, there was no choice but to wear her tattered frock, and she pulled it over her head. Jonathan had purchased a brown coat and trousers that fit him within reason, as well as shoes from a gold seeker who had gambled away most of his money. Jonathan had also secured socks and a pair of men's shoes for her, both enormously large for her feet. The seamen traded and sold their belongings with impunity, it appeared, for he had even bought himself a journal from one of them. Dressed, she clumped up to the quarterdeck to join him while she dried her hair in the sun.

He glanced up from writing in the journal and rose to his feet. His eyes took in the sight of her long hair blowing about her shoulders. "You must stay out of the wind. There's a sunny place behind the quarter boat, out of the gold seekers' sight. They look at you too much, Louisa."

"I am sorry to be such trouble—"

"I do not think of you as trouble," he replied. "If only—" He hesitated, then remained still.

Yes, if only she were not married, she thought.

They sat down in the sunshine, and she continued to work the knots and tangles from her drying hair with her fingers while he wrote. Wanton as it was to allow a man to see her with her hair down and all about her shoulders, she had little choice. Jonathan, she noticed, kept his attention on his writing. Something between them had shifted. *He must have heard me cry out about Conduff,* she thought. Whatever had existed on the raft had come to an end.

When Jonathan glanced at her she asked, "Are you writing to Oakley and Ellie?"

"I have already written to them. I'm concerned they will learn of the *Nimrod's* disaster and assume we were drowned, so I must post their letter at our first opportunity."

"And I must write to my friend Tess as well. She had no idea which ship I took, but I should let her know how I'm faring. Most likely, she will envy me, shipwreck and all. She has an adventurous spirit, despite her dull life."

He tore out several pieces of paper from the back of his journal. "Let me pare a quill for you," he offered.

As she watched him sharpen the quill, the breeze fluttered a page in his journal. He had been crossing out and rewriting—

He scrutinized the quill's new point and smiled at her perplexity. "I am attempting a newspaper essay," he explained. "A Baltimore editor suggested I write about 'seeing the elephant' for his paper."

"'Seeing the elephant'?"

He smiled. "It's an expression for the gold rush. Haven't you heard it?"

She shook her head.

"It began with a story about a farmer who longed to see an elephant," Jonathan said. "When a circus, replete with elephant, arrived in a nearby town, the farmer loaded his wagon with eggs and vegetables and made for the town's market. En route he met the circus parade led by the elephant. Well, the farmer was thrilled, but his horses were not. They bolted, scattering bruised vegetables and broken eggs as they ran away. The farmer, however, said, 'I don't give a hang! I have seen the elephant!'"

Louisa gave a laugh. "And that's what the editor wants you to write?"

"Yes, traveling to the goldfields and seeing what happens . . . the adventure of it. I hadn't fully agreed to it, thinking I might not have enough of interest." He added ironically, "Thanks to the shipwreck, I have an interesting experience with which to begin."

"And I have something of interest to tell Tess," she agreed. She smoothed the blank sheets of journal paper he had given her and sat back, rather liking the expression about seeing the elephant. Despite the shipwreck and the fact that she hadn't set out to seek gold, she now looked forward to the adventure.

But how to begin? Best not to mention Jonathan, for the less even Tess knew of him, the better. Yet if she eliminated him, her rescue from the shipwreck would not seem possible.

Finally she wrote the date and began with the day she left Alexandria. Once she had written about him and the shipwreck, she turned to other matters that would surely interest Tess.

You would be delighted to see so many men on the deck below, but they do not look too wonderful. I shall attempt to describe the scene.

To begin, most of the argonauts sailing with us are young, "in the prime of life." Nearly all, however, are rough-looking and unkempt from the journey. Since our arrival in Chagres is imminent, they practice the reloading and firing of their pistols. Apparently a revolver and a bowie knife are considered of foremost importance in a "California outfit."

Sadly enough, thirty of these fierce adventurers on our ship have already died of cholera. Many are also equipped with pots, pans, kettles, drinking cups, knives and forks, spoons, pocket filters for water, india-rubber contrivances (that blow up into a bed, a boat, or even a tent), and astonishing amounts of medicine—all of which they constantly trade or unpack and repack on deck.

Most of them gamble; others read, write, sketch and whittle; several sew bags, shot pouches, etc., to contain their anticipated hoards of gold. All in all, I do not see one worthy of you, my dear friend.

Our "bill of fare" is not good and the men complain heartily. Would that you were cooking! If the others had been adrift on a raft for days, however, they might not mind weevils in the hardtack and endless salt pork so much. Yesterday, they added a delicacy to our bill of fare by killing dolphins. They are good eating, if one does not think about what joyous creatures they once were. They come in small groups of a dozen or so and cavort before the bow of the ship, giving the men an opportunity to harpoon them.

The trade winds here provide delightful weather. It is very hot, but with a strong breeze at night, rendering it sufficiently cool to sleep in comfort. The weather, however, is not the most engrossing topic of conversation on the ship; I overhear the men forever speaking of the heaps of gold to be found in California.

We are to arrive at Chagres, Panama, in a day or so and, though it is said to be one of the worst pest holes in the tropical world, I heartily look forward to standing on solid land again.

Oh, how you would enjoy this adventure, Tess. I shall write again to let you know of the passage through Panama.

Affectionately,
Louisa

P.S. Please destroy this letter. I would not want it to come into Conduff's or anyone else's possession.

The next morning, Louisa had her first sight of palm trees and the lush tropical growth of Chagres. The almost landlocked bay looked like a friendly place from a distance: palms fringed the sandbar and heavy green foliage stretched along the river and up over the surrounding bluffs.

When they went to bid their bewhiskered captain farewell, he became quite anxious. "Hopefully your rescue wasn't for naught, madam. Panama is rotten with cholera. People die one after another on the trail to the Pacific."

Jonathan replied calmly, "We have both lost members of our families by cholera. I believe we can endure this port."

"Even so, the natives' food is abominable and the water is poison. It won't suit you at all—"

Before the captain could continue, Louisa said, "We appreciate your concern, but we shall survive."

"Then tarry only long enough at Chagres until you find a native *bungo* to transport you upriver. And ask our ship's cook for all of the hardtack and apples he can spare."

Shallow water prevented a near approach to the land, and the ship dropped anchor some hundreds of yards from shore not far from two brigs, an aged barque, and a new side-wheel steamer. Small boats were crowded with passengers being rowed ashore, and throngs of men already swarmed over the beach.

Jonathan started down the rope ladder before Louisa could begin the terrifying descent. "Allow me to help you. I'll place your feet on each rung."

"Thank you, I shall manage on my own." She swished her tattered skirt out behind her and started down the swinging rope ladder in her oversized shoes. She must do something on her own! she told herself and tried to ignore the heavy swell that caused the *Berta* and the quarter boat below to roll heavily. She had become far too dependent on Jonathan during the journey; her health was better and, at the very least, she must accomplish this.

The *Berta* rolled with each swell and Louisa's legs trembled as she climbed down the rope ladder rung by rung, slowly making her way to the bobbing boat that awaited them in the turquoise sea. At last Jonathan handed her into the quarter boat, and she sat down, shaken. Arranging her skirts around her, she made a pretense of composure.

Finally, they were rowed toward the village of Chagres, where the natives apparently endured the humidity by living in windowless bamboo huts with thatched, palm-leaf roofs.

In an attempt to sound brave, she said, "It's a picturesque setting, humid though it is."

"Yes," Jonathan replied, "picturesque."

As they neared land, however, Chagres became less and less picturesque, and the stench of rotting fish on the beach mingled with the smells of sewage.

When they disembarked, she was appalled to see that the village was surrounded by heaps of filthy offal and greasy, stagnant pools bordered with blue mud. Worse, the dark natives strolled about all half clad, prompting the seamen and gold seekers to make coarse remarks. Louisa's cheeks burned as she attempted to keep her eyes away from the villagers and on the emerald hills, and her legs wobbled as she walked on land again.

Argonauts from the ships swarmed all around, yelling and cursing in English, German, French, and assorted Indian and Spanish dialects. They motioned impatiently across the white sand toward the great piles of valises, trunks, and other paraphernalia they wished the natives to transport.

Jonathan said, "It may be a blessing that we have no possessions to possess us."

Louisa turned an ironic smile upon him. "I would consider it a blessing to have other clothes and a pair of women's shoes!"

"Perhaps we can find something, though it looks unlikely here. The terrible reputation preceding this place was not disagreeable enough. We shall have to find a safe place for you while I arrange transporation up the river."

The only woman in the vast confusion, she was stared at by both the argonauts and the natives. She tried not to take notice, but kept her attention on the town. It straddled the river and consisted of miserable bamboo and mud huts as well as two equally wretched wooden houses, hotels someone said were kept by Americans. On top of Chagres's southerly bluff, nearly concealed by a luxuriant tangle of trees and tropical creepers, sat the ruins of a picturesque Spanish castle.

Jonathan settled her on a split-log bench near the coffeehouse hut. Here, the stench from the beach was not as overpowering, and it mingled with the smells of coffee, tea, and cinnamon. "I'll order coffee for you," he said.

"You could write an amazing article about this place!"

"Amazing indeed." His hazel eyes reassessed the scene, and it was with obvious worry that he departed for the river.

He had no more than left when she heard a gold seeker say, "A lady like that will never make it 'cross the Isthmus. She'll object to the Indians bein' naked . . . she'll get one o' them savage fevers. She'll never stand it."

Other blustering fellows gawked at her, their belts so stuck full of pistols and bowie knives that she thought they might be more trouble than the unarmed natives. Shaken, she looked at the sea and watched the boats ferrying in more gold seekers. If matters became unbearable, she could reboard the *Berta*, which still lay at anchor. She was just considering that when a young, breechcloth-clad native woman brought steaming coffee.

Louisa dropped her eyes in shock. "Thank you," she finally managed without quite looking at her. *Please, Jonathan, make haste!* she thought frantically.

She felt even more miserable as she sipped the hot corrosive brew. She was already drenched with perspiration, and these few minutes of sitting here already seemed an eternity.

"Louisa? Is that you?"

The familiar voice astonished Louisa so, she thought she had lost all reason. Was that truly Tess approaching through the squalid scene?! Her dear heart-shaped face glowed with happiness, but this was an almost thin Tess. "Tess?"

Tess laughed. "In the flesh, though there is not nearly so much of it!"

"Oh, Tess!" Louisa threw herself into her friend's arms. "What are you doing here? I have never been so amazed . . . and I just posted a letter to you on the ship—"

"And here I am in person for you to tell everything!" Tess said. "I've been watching for you on every ship that comes into port."

"But . . . what if you had missed me?"

"If I'd missed you here, I planned to find you through your Talbot relations in California. I wasn't going to give up!"

Louisa embraced her friend again. "I have never in my life felt so pleased to see anyone!"

When they pulled apart, Tess looked her over. "My land, do you look bedraggled!"

They sat down on the split-log bench together, and Louisa told briefly about the shipwreck. Finally she asked,

"Why did you leave Alexandria?"

Tess lowered her gaze, then her soft green eyes raised to Louisa's again. "It sounds selfish, but I was so tired of takin' care of the young ones, much as I loved them." She hesitated. "Even your awful marriage to Conduff was better than my life. I had to get away, Louisa. I had to begin livin' on my own. With so many men goin' to California, it seemed a perfect chance to find a husband and to have an adventure."

"Oh, Tess—"

"I said it poorly. Can you understand?"

She embraced Tess again. "I surely do, my friend."

Tess sighed. "So far though, a lot of my time's been spent cookin' and bein' seasick."

"Then it's seasickness that has made you become thin—"

Tess smiled ironically. "A blessin' in disguise."

"How did you ever get here?"

"I went down to visit my aunt in Norfolk, then signed on as a cook on the *Estelle,* that old Norfolk brig in the harbor."

"You were a seasick cook?"

Tess laughed. "I never did quit cookin', though I surely couldn't eat. Guess I couldn't abide flour acrawl with weevils and maggots in the meat. But I was the only unmarried female aboard . . . and I got myself a beau."

"Oh, Tess!"

Her friend's eyes sparkled. "He's up seein' about a boat to take us upriver. How about you? Are you alone?"

"Not entirely." She glanced past the bamboo huts to the lush foliage by the river. Throngs of men milled about to secure passage across the isthmus, but she couldn't see Jonathan. "The temporary shipping agent from Wainwright and Talbot in Alexandria accompanied me. I suppose one might call him a friend and protector."

"I see." Tess hesitated, then asked somberly, "You want to hear about Conduff?"

Louisa cringed at the thought. "No, but I should."

Tess drew a deep breath. "Well, after he returned from deliverin' the darkies, he came to my house mad as a hornet, wantin' to know where you'd gone. I flat out said I wouldn't tell if I knew. He'd been drinkin' fierce, and I guess he took it to mean I didn't know, so he didn't come around again."

"Good."

"No, the real good news is that he went up to Baltimore and heard you'd gone to New York."

"To New York?"

Tess nodded. "So few women go to California, I doubt he would dream of your goin' there. Anyhow, talk of your disappearance was dyin' down in Alexandria. Most folks didn't blame you a bit. And I surely didn't speak one word about your plans."

"That is something, I suppose. I would hate to have people think badly of me." She faltered. "I haven't told anyone of my marriage, Tess. I hope you won't speak of it."

"A good idea," Tess said. "Consider it forgotten."

"If only I could!"

Tess glanced at her uneasily. "There is more about Conduff, but I hate to tell you right off."

Louisa steeled herself. "I had better hear all of it."

"Well, besides being mad at your runnin' away, he was upset because the bank was foreclosin' on your house."

Louisa's heart constricted, even though she had guessed financial matters would go to that extreme. "Now I shall have to forgive him—and Da—for that, too."

"I'm truly sorry."

Louisa let out a deep breath. Somehow she knew Tess was holding more back. "What else?"

Tess looked heartsick. "Conduff swears he will find you, no matter what! He says you and your Da caused all his problems!"

"That we caused all of his problems?" It was as though Conduff had struck her another blow.

"He doesn't know where you are, so you mustn't let it worry you too much."

It would be impossible not to worry about him, Louisa fretted. Neither he nor his threats were easy to forget.

"Enough of that," Tess said. "Tell me of your journey before the shipwreck."

It took an effort for Louisa to wrench herself from the onslaught of hurt and anxiety about Conduff. Finally she told about the train trip to Baltimore and their stay with Ellie and Oakley. "It was one of the best visits of my life," she was saying when a blond bearded man headed around the nearby bamboo hut. His blue eyes widened at seeing her. She must be dreaming, she decided, for he looked like Hugh Fairfax.

"Louisa Talbot!" he exclaimed, his handsome face as full of amazement as she felt. "I never thought to see you again!"

"Nor I you. The last I saw, you were rowing away from the shipwreck in a quarter boat, and I was in the Atlantic clinging to a water keg and calling for help."

Hugh looked heartsick. "If I had only seen you—"

"You mustn't blame yourself."

"How could I not?"

"There was such a turmoil with people plunging into the sea and the *Nimrod* thrashing itself to pieces against the shoal. I am sure it was impossible for you to see or hear me."

He gazed at her gratefully. "It pained me to think you had drowned . . . and now here you are! It seems impossible."

"We had all planned to cross at Panama," she pointed out. "In any case, I am happy to see you again, Hugh." It was not only a pleasant surprise, but his appearance had eased her new pain over Conduff. "May I present my friend, Tess—"

Tess looked like a kitten peering up over a platter of cream. "Hugh and I met sailin' on the *Estelle* from Norfolk, though I didn't know y'all knew each other."

Hugh reminded her tenderly, "You were too sick to want to hear about shipwrecks."

"That I was. And you didn't want to talk much about it yourself," she replied with a fetching glance at him.

Hugh was Tess's beau! It made perfect sense since she had been the only unmarried female aboard ship. Likely Hugh didn't let the sun set on a day he didn't take interest in the opposite sex—and Tess was not only thinner, but almost beautiful.

Hugh asked Louisa, "Do you have transportation upriver?"

"Jonathan Chambers is making the arrangements now."

Hugh grinned. "So Chambers survived the shipwreck, too."

"Indeed he did. He saved my life!"

"I am not surprised. And now he is making arrangements for himself and the lovely Louisa Talbot."

Louisa Talbot. Again, the lie about her name. Blanching, she turned to Tess.

The confusion in her friend's soft green eyes turned to understanding, then a promise: She would not divulge the secret about the Talbot name, nor about Conduff.

Despite a stab of guilt, Louisa turned a steady gaze on Hugh, as though nothing were amiss. Now she had caused her best friend to become an accessory to the lie, but the deception would end when they reached San Francisco. Surely that would be soon enough.

# 8

Two hours later, Louisa sat beside Jonathan in a grimy deep-water boat, chugging up the wide Chagres River with Tess, Hugh, and a dozen argonauts. Overhead, the boat's palm-leaf canopy shaded them from the scorching sun and, on either bank, a tangle of greenery grew to the edges of the river. Before boarding, one of the passengers had eyed their two half-clad native boatmen and whispered, "I heerd they're cannibals."

Louisa looked at the dark-skinned natives warily. They kept sharp machetes close at hand, and they looked sulky, like the sort who might kill for mere pleasure. She whispered to Jonathan, "Do you think they are truly cannibals?"

"We would have heard of it earlier if they were. Likely whoever said so is overly nervous."

Her own nervousness lessened somewhat. It was difficult enough to try to forget what Tess had just disclosed about Conduff without thinking about cannibal-minded guides or other trials of the journey ahead. Instead, she would count her blessings. Tess's presence was one. Another was that she was no longer falling over her feet in ungainly men's shoes, as Tess had given her a pair of black shoes from her trunk. A third was that the boat, though heavily laden, moved upstream steadily against the strong current, passing a wide assortment of whaleboats, ships' boats, skiffs, and native bungos, some of which carried fifteen or twenty passengers.

Moreover, as they left the huts of Chagres behind, the tropical scenery became breathtaking. Scarlet and white flowers bloomed in the midst of the luxuriant vegetation growing down to the river, and even the roughest argonauts took an interest in the tropical flowers and foliage.

Jonathan wrote about their fellow passengers as the pop-eyed argonauts stared at the natives and the jungle fearfully. The sun's torrid rays beamed down through the clouds—clouds so thick and gray that they seemed symbolic of her life, now that thoughts of Conduff crept over her.

As she watched, one monstrous black cloud overtook them and, quite suddenly, torrential rain poured down. Neither the boat's palm-leaf canopy nor the flimsy umbrellas they had purchased at Chagres helped much, and they sat there drenched. Minutes later, when the sun shone through, the jungle steamed, and Louisa felt as though she were steaming herself.

The boat chugged along through clouds of mosquitoes. Two figures broke through the luxuriant foliage of the riverbank and stopped to stare at them. "Monkeys!"

From the seat behind Louisa, Tess exclaimed, "Just look at them lookin' at us!"

The passengers laughed at the monkeys, startling two brilliantly hued parrots from vines in nearby trees.

"We'll probably remember this sight all of our lives," Louisa said. "I have only seen such exotic things in pictures—" She saw Jonathan smile at her, and she added in confusion, "I doubt that you have seen them elsewhere yourself."

"You're right, of course. It's just that I am unaccustomed

to seeing you so . . . enthused."

"You have mainly seen me shipwrecked and sick."

"It is not so difficult to imagine you enthusiastic and full of life," he said.

At that, her spirits lifted.

As the hours passed, the novelty of the jungle lessened, and Hugh groaned from the seat behind them, "If only we had water we could safely drink—"

He did not look well, Louisa thought. Those with light coloring were said not to tolerate heat well, but she was a redhead and terribly thirsty herself. Only the stoic natives, their dark skin glistening with sweat, did not complain.

The boat's engine coughed, then coughed again, and Hugh said, "I had doubts about a steam-powered boat in the jungle. Let's hope we make it to tonight's destination."

"And if we don't?" she asked in alarm. "There are said to be snakes and alligators in the rivers."

"Let's not think of it," Jonathan replied. He turned to Hugh behind them. "Thank you, Fairfax, for working matters out in Chagres. I shall look more kindly upon Princeton men from this day forward."

Uncomfortable as he appeared, Hugh grinned. "My pleasure to help, though such practicalities were not taught at Princeton. How fares your Harvard education on this journey?"

"Not too well. I do, however, recall that the first white men who invaded Peru carried their loot down this river on their way back to their ships and to Spain."

Despite the heat and awful humidity, Louisa was gratified again to be with an educated man. When he discovered her looking at him, he explained, "Fairfax did most of the convincing to get us on this craft. The deciding factor turned out to be our lack of baggage. We took the places of two argonauts with piles of belongings that could not possibly fit on the boat."

"I see."

The other men who sat nearby listened to them, she realized and looked away. They were for the most part a silent lot, who apparently had nothing better to do than eavesdrop. Nearby, a native bungo—a hollowed-out log—was being paddled upriver by Jamaican Negroes. Those aboard, jammed in and half hidden by their baggage, scowled as they were passed.

"At least we are making good time," she commented.

"I am sure that even the bungo passengers are better off than the walkers," he replied.

"People are walking across the Isthmus?"

"Desperate people will try anything, and I suspect a great many desperate people are under way to California."

She hoped that Conduff would not be one of them.

After midday, they shared the hardtack and apples with Tess and Hugh, who divided up some of their jerked beef. One of the rougher argonauts sitting near them said, "You ladies want a pull from my jug?"

Appalled, it was a moment before Louisa could say, "Thank you . . . but no—"

"No, thank you!" Tess said a trifle too vehemently.

Jonathan struck a conciliatory tone. "We appreciate your thoughtfulness, sir, but these ladies do not drink spirits."

Hugh offered, "I would be glad to take a drink in their stead. I am thirsty enough to try poison."

The heavily whiskered man laughed and handed over his jug. "Poison it is!"

Louisa watched uneasily as Hugh drank, for the jug looked as dirty as the rough gold seeker. The man, whom the men called "Old Whiskers," was even more unkempt than most of them, his eyes bloodshot and yellowish.

Nearby a huge snake slithered down the thick trunk of a tree and onto the riverbank, and Louisa whirled away with a shudder, making the men laugh gleefully.

"When we comin' in?" the argonauts demanded over and over of the boatmen, only to be answered with a peevish poco tiempo, which someone translated as "by-and-by."

After a while, Louisa rode along in a vague bewilderment, trusting in Jonathan and his calm manner. She allowed the cries of the jungle to drift around her, trying to ignore them except when they were too close, too frightening.

Finally they had covered the eight miles to their overnight stop, and the boat was swerved into the overgrown shore, where numerous bungos and another deep-water boat were tied to the trees.

Jonathan remarked, "Hopefully it won't prove more unpleasant traveling by bungo the next few days."

Unnerved, Louisa scrutinized the native boatmen, all of whom carried long knives; they congregated around their craft at the river's edge, as noisy as the cabmen at the Baltimore and Ohio Railroad Station in Washington City. "I should think you could get a colorful paragraph about them," she told Jonathan.

"Just what I was thinking," he replied and stopped alongside the river to take notes. If the men and their knives worried him, he did not show it.

Louisa and Tess moved on slowly, noticing a group of bedraggled white men ahead on the trail.

One of them leered at them drunkenly. "White women!"

Louisa exchanged an uneasy glance with Tess.

"Ignore them," her friend advised. "We had plenty of that sort on the ship from Norfolk, and even I ignored them!"

"Hugh's presence must have deterred them."

"I guess it did," Tess replied, pleased.

The boisterous miners moved on, and when Louisa looked back she saw that Hugh and Jonathan were catching up with them. They smiled brightly, evidently unaware of the welcome effect of their presence.

As the four of them continued along the trail through the vines and creepers, Louisa's attention was diverted by a reddish-gray animal moving in the nearby tangles of undergrowth. "Something is under the vines!" she said.

"Where?" Jonathan asked.

She pointed. "There—"

The creature's scaly body had limbs, even toes. A monstrously huge lizard! It moved steadily toward them, its beady eyes glistening and its long tongue darting out. As it lumbered out from under the green vines, there seemed no end to the grotesque creature. Horror-stricken, she was unable to move.

Jonathan tugged at her hand. "Louisa, come away!"

She came to her senses, aware that everyone else had backed far off. She ran with him to the others, stumbling through the chopped stubble of the clearing.

"Iguana! Iguana!" the boatmen yelled, waving their long knives and carrying on as more natives gathered to capture it.

"Hugh says they eat the awful things," Tess said.

"Oh—" Louisa replied, her stomach turning over.

Finally the boatmen and the iguana disappeared from sight along the riverbank, but for all she knew the beast's family lurked under the surrounding foliage.

"Lizard sceered ye, din' it?" an argonaut asked. "Think it was one o' them big 'gators?"

Louisa smiled weakly at him and moved on.

Ahead, in the clearing, fifty or sixty disheveled argonauts

lounged about, many with whiskey jugs in hand. Jonathan began to write about them and their surroundings. A dozen bamboo huts stood alongside the river at the far edge of the clearing and a wooden floor had been laid down in the middle of the remaining green stubble and stumps.

"Whatever is that floor for?" Tess asked.

"It's our hotel for the night," Hugh replied.

"We are to sleep on that floor?" Louisa asked, recalling the iguana.

"We are to have the privilege of dining upon it as well," Jonathan said. At her incredulous look, he added, "They told us at Chagres, but we decided not to inform you in advance."

"What else haven't you told us?" Tess asked.

"There are bamboo huts at the other stops," Hugh said. "When they told us about this floor and the bamboo huts, they acted as though they offered the highest class of amenities of the Astor Hotel."

In the ensuing silence Louisa said, "I am certain you and Jonathan did your best under the circumstances."

"Indeed we did," Jonathan replied.

Louisa's attention wandered to the edge of the floor, where native women cooked over an open fire. The smell of the meat was vaguely familiar.

"At least it's pork they're cooking," Tess said. "I like to try new dishes, but I am surely not ready for lizard."

Several argonauts demanded, "When we gettin' supper?" accompanied by eating motions so the natives might understand.

"Poco tiempo," the natives replied irritably.

Finally the native women piled heaps of roast pork and thick beans on wooden platters. There were no forks, knives, or spoons, only rustic wooden plates and wooden cups for a caustic black brew everyone took to be coffee. Louisa and

Tess sat down with the others on the wooden floor, waving off swarms of mosquitoes as they ate even the beans with their fingers.

Night fell like a sudden thunderclap. Stars gave a dim light in the velvety black sky; beyond the clearing, tall jungle trees darkened the firmament. Below, the cook fires flickered, and wild animals screeched and chattered from the dark jungle, their eerie cries chilling Louisa.

"I suppose we had best get to sleep," she said uneasily. Perhaps even worse than sleeping in the middle of the jungle was the thought of sleeping in the midst of the argonauts, some of whom drank and swore horribly.

"Maybe they'll keep the fires burning all night," Tess said.

"If you and Tess lie close together, Hugh and I will sleep on either side of you," Jonathan offered. He handed her one of the blankets he had purchased from a gold seeker on the beach in Chagres. "Wrap yourselves up in your blankets."

Hugh took a gun from his valise and stuck it in his belt. "One of us should look as warlike as the rest of them."

"I'm sorry—I know it's more difficult because of us," Louisa apologized.

"I didn't understand it would be this bad myself," Jonathan said.

Louisa bestowed a wry look on him. "I expect a wooden floor to sleep on is better than nothing in the jungle."

"And probably better than a raft in the Atlantic," he remarked, "though I do have some fond memories."

She swatted at the mosquitoes and said nothing. It was the first reference he had made to their romantic interlude.

Tess began to wrap herself up in a blanket. "Well, Louisa, we'd better try to sleep."

"Yes." Her gray blanket was rough and grimy, but better than nothing. Feeling especially self-conscious after

Jonathan's comment, she lay down next to Tess. Shortly thereafter, she heard him lie down behind her.

"Good night, Louisa," he murmured.

"Good night," she replied firmly.

An animal's cry of sudden death in the jungle filled the night, making her tense, and several men swore again. It was a long time before she began to relax. Difficult as it was to lie in the midst of mortal danger and the argonauts, it was worse yet to lie in such close proximity to Jonathan.

She forced her thoughts to the hard, uneven floor and to the wild animal cries that pierced the darkness. Finally she remembered to pray and, at long last, she surrendered to her body's exhaustion.

Quite suddenly she was running through the darkness . . . running and running in terror. Behind her, he gained rapidly. "Come back here, woman!" he yelled. "You come back here!"

"No!" she cried, for he would certainly beat her. "Leave me alone, Conduff! Leave me be!"

"Louisa!" Tess whispered, "you're having a bad dream."

Louisa opened her eyes. She saw the starlit jungle sky and Tess leaning over her.

"You were having a nightmare," Tess whispered. "You'll be all right now. Go back to sleep."

But Conduff's angry face remained imprinted in her mind's eye, and it was a long time before she slept.

With the rosy glow of dawn, the jungle came alive with exotic cries, chirpings, and hammerings. Stiff, she sat up quietly and glanced at Jonathan.

His eyes met hers and he mouthed a smiling "Good morning." His jaw, dark and unshaven, heightened his aura of masculinity. She hastily lay down again, rolling over and staying as far from him as possible.

The sounds of the jungle rose in a crescendo. Tess still slept, and it seemed an eternity before she and the others began to stir.

They breakfasted on more beans, roast pork, and corrosive coffee, then the boatmen began to load passengers. Jonathan and Hugh secured a hollow-log bungo that barely held four passengers and the two breechcloth-clad boatmen. Like yesterday's deep-water boat it had an overhead canopy of palm leaves, but that was its only amenity.

Tess asked Hugh, "Shall we sit in front?"

"Yes, we'll take the scenic seats."

"Let me help you in, Louisa," Jonathan said. He was solicitous enough, but it did seem he had no other choice than to sit with her in the backseat.

Louisa sat down with him. Their ride yesterday had begun with such an air of anticipation, but now she felt miserable. Her nightmare had reminded her all too clearly of Conduff . . . and now to sit so close to Jonathan, his arm pressed against hers!

Finally the boatmen pushed the bungo out from the riverbank and into the strong current, poling slowly upstream while they chanted in rhythm. Once they had poled beyond the clearing, the jungle pressed in all around them, its savage beauty tempered only by chattering monkeys and bright-plumaged birds. Sometimes the bungo was poled midstream in the hot sun, but more often they stayed close to shore and glided lazily under the arching trees and canopies of flowering vines.

From the jungle around them came the incessant screams and chattering of monkeys and parrots. The boatmen chanted endlessly to ward off evil spirits, and their chants heightened the eerieness of the vine-choked river. When they encountered bungos en route to Chagres, the boatmen exchanged shouts in their strange tongue and waved their long knives at each other, then they would pass and begin to chant again.

After a while Louisa saw the vines that twisted around trees as hideous coiled serpents. The logs at the water's edge turned into lurking alligators, and jungle cries evoked images of wildcats poised to pounce on them.

The boatmen's chants pervaded the jungle hour upon hour until she was sure she could not endure it any longer: not the eerie jungle and its dreadful humidity, not these naked natives and their chanting, and not forever having to resist Jonathan.

"What is it, Louisa?" he asked.

Tears filled her eyes.

"It has been a terrible journey for you."

Before she fully knew what had happened, his arm reached around her and she was sobbing quietly against his chest.

He patted her back awkwardly and his soft reassurances blended with the chanting boatmen and the rush of the river. "It will soon be over," he promised.

"That's what I dread most," she blurted.

"I fail to understand—"

"Oh, Jonathan, I don't want to be away from you!"

His eyes held hers. "I had hoped—" He pulled a handkerchief from his pocket and daubed the tears from her cheeks. "At this moment, I want nothing more in this world than to kiss you," he murmured.

She turned away. "No, Jonathan, I cannot—"

He gathered her closer. If only she never had to leave his embrace. He was a good man, a kind man.

Before she could pull away, he kissed her forehead and cheeks. "My intentions are honorable," he said.

"No!" The word escaped her so loudly that Hugh turned and, at the sight of them in each other's arms, hastily faced forward again.

"No?" Jonathan asked softly.

She shook her head. *God, forgive me for going this far,* she thought.

"If you think I still pine for Olivia, please banish the notion. When you are near—"

"I beg you, I don't want to hear it."

"What is it then? You must tell me."

She shook her head. "Please, Jonathan, no words. Please hold me a bit longer."

"With pleasure, though I don't understand. It's been a terrible journey, and I expect everyone including the roughest argonaut has been unnerved."

Yes, let him think that. It was better than telling him of her marriage.

Finally she forced herself from his arms. "No more," she whispered. "Please, Jonathan, no more!"

The jungle grew more dense and alligators, drowsing along the riverbanks, bared their teeth at them. When the boat could no longer advance against the thick vines, the four of them had to slosh ashore and wait in the dank foliage while the boatmen cut a trail in the river with their long knives. Finally the natives returned for them and half pulled, half pushed the bungo through the chopped vines to the bank.

Louisa took Tess aside. "Please let us sit in front of the bungo now."

Her friend's soft green eyes assessed her. "Oh, Louisa, Jonathan is such a fine man. It breaks my heart to see what's happened. If you hadn't met Conduff—"

"And if I hadn't been in such a rush to marry then. You were right . . . what a silly goose I was about love. Now I can repent the rest of my days."

"Hush! Here they come!"

Tess and Hugh exchanged words, and Louisa quietly advised Jonathan, "I've asked if we might sit in front."

He drew back. "You had only to tell me to desist."

"It is far too difficult for me to do so."

A woebegone smile played around his lips and he helped her into the bungo. "A rather startling admission, which I wish to take as a compliment."

"Wasn't . . .?" She caught back the thought. *Wasn't Olivia attracted to you?* she had almost asked. Some women, it was said, had too little passion—and perhaps just as well. Look where it had led her with Conduff.

The boatmen pushed on, poling and chanting. She must keep her thoughts on the river and the jungle, Louisa told herself. She must not let Jonathan so much as touch her again.

The day became hotter and more humid. The boatmen often jumped into the river to cool off or to cut food from the tropical plants on the banks, while Louisa and the others suffered agonies of heat, thirst, and hunger.

That evening they put in at a village, and there was roast pork and thick beans again, then bamboo huts with hammocks to sleep in. Their steep palm-leaf roof, however, leaked copiously when the sky unleashed a torrential rain. Louisa scarcely slept, terrified of snakes and lizards—and of nightmares.

Tess's romance with Hugh flourished before their eyes, making it even more tempting for Louisa to let her attraction to Jonathan overcome her. Instead, she tried to put more and more distance between them.

"What have I done to deserve such cold treatment, Louisa?" he asked. "I understand discretion and resisting temptation, but the way you are treating me amounts to abandonment."

"It's my fault entirely. It is nothing you have done."

He frowned. "Can't we discuss it reasonably?"

"No, we cannot. We simply cannot."

She hardened her heart at his every overture until finally he began to withdraw from her as well.

On the river the current grew stronger, and the next night darkness overtook them far before the stopping place. The boatmen could not see six feet in front of them and were obliged to chant louder to avoid a collision with other boats. Several times they nearly capsized on snags, and Louisa clung desperately to the bungo rather than to Jonathan. At long last, the boatmen tied onto a tree until the moon rose.

On the morning of the fourth day they made Gorgona, a small village where they would transfer from the shallow vine-choked river to a mountain trail. Louisa no longer marveled at the profusion of oranges, bananas, and coconuts, nor at the myriads of monkeys screaming and chattering.

At midday they sat at a bamboo table in an open hut, and it seemed they had at least reached a more civilized part of the country. As they sat at their table, a native boy brought in lunch on a huge baking dish and popped off the cover with a flourish. Louisa let out a horrified gasp at something on the platter that resembled a roasted baby.

"Ringtail monkey," the boy announced. "Muy bueno."

Louisa swallowed the bile that had risen to her throat.

"Bananas?" Jonathan suggested in a strangled voice. "Do you have bananas . . . or beans . . . frijoles?"

The boy was incredulous, but finally covered the huge baking dish again and carried it to another group of argonauts who were less squeamish.

After Jonathan had obtained beans, bananas, and oranges for them, he remarked with a wry expression, "Now that was a sight to write about—my fellow passengers confronted with a ringtailed monkey repast."

Tess grimaced, and Hugh said with a wry smile, "You may write that all of our faces turned green, including yours!"

They all had to laugh. As it was, Hugh's face was pale, even under his sun-browned skin and blond whiskers. Louisa had observed that his Adonis smile had been absent for some days until now.

They consumed their fruit and beans, then were led out to the precipitous mountain trail, where they mounted mules. Louisa counted thirty mules, four cows, and twenty passengers in the caravan, their luggage packed on mules' and on the natives' backs.

When they were all ready, their native leader gave a wild whoop that was repeated down the line, and her mule began to move forward. The trail followed the rugged contour of the mountains, winding its way to the top and down again into the valley; it was an old trail that must have been traveled for centuries, for in places down the hillsides there were steps worn smooth several feet deep in the solid rock.

Louisa peered down from a treacherous ledge that fell off deep into the jungle. *Lord, if I die here, if I go over the ledge* . . . she began, then was unable to continue.

They rode on slowly: Jonathan, then Louisa, Tess, and Hugh. Mango trees and alders edged the narrow trail, and coconut palms towered over them. Their canopy of trees protected them from the intense glare of the tropical sun, but not entirely from the intermittent cloudbursts.

That night Louisa collapsed in exhaustion on the

ground, not caring about snakes, lizards, or the clouds of insects.

"Hugh, you're burnin' with fever!" Tess said. "How long have you been this hot?"

His voice was so low that Louisa could not hear.

"You look terrible," Tess added.

Louisa raised up on an elbow to look at Hugh in the dim evening light. His teeth chattered and he shook visibly.

Jonathan got up and knelt on the other side of Hugh, touching his hand to Hugh's forehead. "There's no water we can trust. Only whiskey and rum, and he'd be better without them. I'll see what I can find."

Tess whispered to Louisa. "I never felt anyone's head so hot, not even the young ones at home. I dosed him with pills, charcoal, and sulphur, but it's growing worse. Please pray, Louisa. You know God so much better than I do."

"It is not a matter of who knows Him better, but of who knows Christ as their Lord and Savior," she said.

"Please," Tess begged.

"Of course I'll pray," Louisa added.

Jonathan returned with a tin cup of water. Dirty as the water was, Tess used it to wet a cloth for Hugh's burning forehead. Jonathan covered Hugh with yet another blanket, for he shivered unceasingly.

Weary to the bone, Louisa drifted off to sleep, waking in the night when Hugh cried out in delirium. Once he shouted, "A quitter I'm not!" quite loudly, then "No! Begone! I am not ready!" causing a deathly quiet among the awakened argonauts.

"It's all right, Hugh," Tess said soothingly. "We know you're not a quitter. I'm right here beside you. Let me change the cloth for your forehead."

*Lord, let him sleep peacefully,* Louisa prayed, *and let me sleep dreamlessly, too.*

At dawn Hugh was less feverish, and he insisted Jonathan tie him to his mule. "In case I die," Hugh rasped as he handed over a business card to Jonathan, "please notify my kin."

"If it brings you peace of mind, I'll take it," Jonathan said. "Scripture tells us we are to call upon the Lord in good times and times of need. Are you calling upon Him?"

Hugh nodded shakily and allowed Jonathan to finish tying him to the mule.

All morning poor Hugh swayed from side to side on his mule along the perilous mountain trail; by afternoon he was half delirious, scarcely holding on.

The long day debilitated Louisa until she felt weary beyond human endurance. After dark, they halted several hours short of Panama City. They were busily getting Hugh settled when the tent whirled about her and she collapsed on the hard-packed dirt floor.

"You must eat, Louisa," Jonathan urged when she came to herself. "I've brought you beans wrapped in tortilla bread. Tomorrow we'll reach the sea. We will all feel better."

What does it matter? she thought.

The past months unreeled in her mind: Conduff at the slave auctions in Alexandria, the deaths of Da and her child, the shipwreck, the endless Chagres river through the jungle, and now this horrifying mule trek through the mountains. What could matter now?

"Louisa," Jonathan whispered, "please eat."

As her thoughts blurred into the darkness, she knew what would matter: losing Jonathan.

# 9

Louisa awakened refreshed and heartened by a light breeze that wafted its way from the distant Pacific Ocean and stirred the jungle humidity in the native tent. Only half a day to Panama City. Surely the worst was over.

She ate a breakfast of bananas and salt pork with the others, and everyone felt better, even Hugh, though he had fallen asleep again after eating a banana.

While they waited to leave, a line of argonauts swayed by on mules en route to Panama City. One of the men, whom they had met on the boat from Chagres, greeted them in high spirits as he rode past, then sobered as he turned to shout, "Old Whiskers died yesterday morning of cholera."

Louisa's eyes met Jonathan's in shock.

Jonathan drew a deep breath. "If only Hugh could have a good long rest . . . days or even weeks of it. And you, too, Louisa. You don't look well."

"No one looks well," she replied. "No one."

When they mounted their mules, Hugh said, "Tie me on again, Jonathan." He was paler then ever, but he smiled weakly as he said, "Ah, the adventurous life!"

"You'll be fine, Fairfax," Jonathan assured him. "Only hold on a while longer, then you can rest on the steamship to California. When we arrive, you will be your old self again."

"I hope so," Hugh replied, apparently unconvinced.

Tess said from her mule, "You will, Hugh, you will. Tonight we'll find a hotel in Panama City so you can rest."

As their mules moved slowly down the trail, Louisa hoped their short stay in Panama City would be that simple. Three centuries ago Panama City had been a Spanish port of great consequence, and it was still considered a more civilized place than Chagres, but so far nothing in Panama had been very comfortable. *Lord, help Hugh through this day,* she prayed, then, *Give all of us strength!*

After several hours, the trail began to wind out of the mountains and flattened into a roadway that cut through cultivated fields and passed by two-story houses. Produce carts and water carriers joined the mule-back travelers. As their long line of mules plodded along, Louisa looked into the distance. To her amazement, she saw a walled city with brightly painted buildings and an ancient cathedral, its spire shimmering over the horizon like mother-of-pearl. Behind the city, the blue sea sparkled in the tropical sunlight.

"Do you see it?" she asked Jonathan, who rode the mule ahead. "Look ahead!"

"Panama City!" he exclaimed.

The scene before them looked like an illustration for *The Arabian Nights.* The hardships of the journey were forgotten for a long moment as they marveled at the sight.

At last they reached the bay bordering the city, where Indians waited to carry them across the shallow water. Exhausted, Louisa made no protest when Jonathan hired a carrier to take her on his back and other carriers to transport Hugh and Tess.

"This must be the first time I have been carried since

childhood," she said, feeling helpless and foolish as the native carried her through the water.

Jonathan sloshed wearily alongside the natives and smiled. "Would I could carry you myself!"

She drew an anguished breath.

When the Indian carrier finally set her down, they continued on another ancient roadway, Jonathan and Tess supporting Hugh. Finally they passed through the city gate with their fellow argonauts.

The bustling town looked as if it had been built and worn out in earlier centuries; its colorful buildings had faded unevenly and bore the marks of age. Creepers—even bushes and trees—grew from cracks and crevices in the walls, and the houses' sagging balconies leaned so far out that they almost touched over the narrow passageways.

On the streets, donkeys carrying bundles of leaves and water jars trotted through the chaos of men and carts. Dusky Indian women, more modestly dressed than their jungle sisters, went about their affairs in white garments. Most surprising, though, were the hordes of bearded men dressed in the red flannel shirts and the rough trousers of gold seekers. Jostling through the dusty, weed-grown streets and plazas, they made the decrepit old city look as though it straddled different cultures as well as different centuries.

Jonathan asked a group of American men, "What are so many of you doing here in town?"

"The gold ships ain't comin' back from San Francisco."

"Not coming back?" he replied.

A man with a great white beard explained, "Seamen are jumpin' ship and goin' to the goldfields themselves. Our ship was due in three weeks ago, but it never come back."

"Is there space for us in hotels?" Jonathan asked.

The gold seekers guffawed. "Everythin's packed and full

o' vermin at that. Most men are buildin' shacks out yonder."
They pointed to a vast shantytown sprawling over the hill.

"It's a mean settlement and gettin' worse," another
warned. "Cholera and Chagres fever are killin' off men every
day."

Louisa flinched, knowing Hugh had heard him.

"My family has business ties here," Hugh said weakly,
"people who have lived here for generations. We shall have
to turn to them."

None of them wanted to impose, but there was no help
for it. They walked through the crowded streets toward
Cathedral Square, where the Indian carriers were to transport
their baggage. Nearing the cathedral, they saw vines
entwined in its cracked and creviced walls. Its shell-
ornamented tower and pinnacles, however, shone through
mold and mildew in the sunshine, imparting an exotic
elegance.

When they arrived, Hugh rallied sufficiently to send off a
note to his family's acquaintances. While they awaited a
reply, the cathedral bells rang out midday, sounding and
resounding across the blue sky, only to be joined by fife
playing and drumming in front of the church, followed
by the loud booms of cannons, then chanting in the
cathedral.

The messenger returned in no time with a Spanish
woman wearing a black mantilla over her dark hair. "I am
Senora Rodriguez. Your family opens their house to mi
esposo—my husband—in New York. I like to return su
cortesia."

They thanked her profusely, and even Hugh seemed to
revive a little. They followed her through the plaza, past the
bandstand and along a paseo where pigeons fluttered out of
their path.

Her huge pink house was of Spanish architecture, and, inside, it featured towering ceilings and vast windows that looked out on a green courtyard. She escorted Louisa and Tess upstairs, chattering in half English, half-Spanish all the way. She ushered them into a damp bedroom furnished with a lounge covered in red velvet, two hammocks suspended from the ceiling, a huge gilt-framed mirror, and a great wrought iron chandelier with wax lights. Despite the heat, a fire burned in the fireplace "to dry the walls," their hostess explained.

"Come here to see." She led them through French doors to a wide balcony overlooking the town and the cathedral. Beyond sparkled the blue Pacific.

"You like to bathe before dinner?" she offered as though it were a usual suggestion for guests.

Louisa caught sight of herself in the gilt-framed mirror. "How disreputable we look! What must you think of us?"

Senora Rodriguez's dark eyes danced merrily. "I have—how you say it?—seen worse coming into our city in these past months. I send you my maid."

Tess unpacked her trunk and laid a pink cotton frock across a hammock for Louisa. "It will be far too big, but I daresay it is better than your dress."

Louisa gave a laugh. "I hope never to wear it or any other fawn-colored dress again!"

Half an hour later, she and Tess took turns in an outside bathhouse, where great clay jars of water were dumped on them from a high ledge by Senora Rodriguez's maid. Later, when Louisa inspected herself again in the mirror, she felt clean at last. Even her hair, now wound in a simple coil atop her head, was clean and free of tangles. The pink frock hung like a tent around her, as did Tess's.

When they stood together before the mirror, Tess

laughed. "We look like girls wearin' our mothers' dresses!"

Downstairs, the dining room was barnlike in size and the furniture dark and rustic in contrast with the French crystal chandelier suspended over the vast table. Jonathan said grace, a prayer full of praise and thanksgiving, much to the interest of Senora Rodriguez and her numerous relatives. They ate roast chicken, served with mild red peppers and rice—a relief from beans and pork.

Their hostess said, "Now you have siesta. It is muy importante after dinner because of the midday heat."

"I have to secure passage on a ship," Jonathan protested.

"No California ships here today," the Rodriguez relatives countered. "Manana is soon enough."

"Then we had better rest," he replied, and they slept the remainder of the day away.

The following morning after breakfast, Jonathan installed Hugh on a black iron bench in the enclosed courtyard. Louisa sat down in a chair beside him, needle and thread in hand for taking in the seams of the pink dresses from Tess's trunk.

"Tess and I shall return as soon as we've made arrangements for a ship," Jonathan told them. "If I can't make use of my shipping connections, Tess intends to offer her services as a ship's cook to secure places for all of us."

"Oh, Tess, it would be such hard work to cook for a ship full of men again," Louisa said.

"But I truly like cookin'," Tess insisted.

When they left, Hugh fell asleep on the bench. Hummingbirds flitted among the exotic plants and flowers, and Louisa sat back, finding it pleasant to sit and sew while the cathedral bells rang out the hours.

At midday the bells were again accompanied by a fife and drum, followed by the booming cannon, and Hugh roused himself. "I regret I am such poor company," he said groggily.

"I enjoy sitting here away from the noise of the city."

"I'm too much trouble. Jonathan even has to shave me."

"I am sure he is glad to help. He believes in . . . doing unto others as he would have them do to himself."

"Yes, I have noticed that."

Hugh straightened up on the bench, squared his shoulders, and eyed her with a hint of his old Adonis smile. "Tess won't say a word about you and Jonathan. She claims it is none of our affair, but I am not stilled. Are you betrothed?"

Louisa pierced her finger with the needle, drawing a drop of blood. "No, we are not."

"Then he's a fool. With so many men and so few women around, he shouldn't let such a beautiful woman escape. I certainly would not."

*Is that why you have attached yourself to Tess?* Louisa was tempted to ask, but resisted.

"Had I known you were available on the *Nimrod* . . . I assumed you and Chambers—Perhaps I should not speak of it."

"No," Louisa replied quietly. "Please do not."

"Would that I had returned to New York after the shipwreck." He sighed. "The return of the prodigal."

"The prodigal?"

He nodded. "I ran from spending my life at work in my family's bank. I thought I needed freedom and adventure, and now that I have it—The saying must be true. Be careful what you hope for . . . you may get it."

The courtyard door clattered open, and Tess and Jonathan came to join them. They had been unable to book passage on the next ship, but would try again in the afternoon. Although Tess appeared dejected, Jonathan remained in good spirits. "At least we are learning our way around the city," he commented.

"Counting your blessings?" Louisa asked.

He nodded. "When I see how most of the argonauts are surviving, I know it could be far worse for us."

The days passed, a week, then two weeks without a seaworthy ship sailing for San Francisco. New gold seekers arrived daily in search of a ship, no matter how bad its condition.

Every morning Louisa sat with Hugh, plumping his pillows and sewing. Cloth was in good supply in Panama City, and Tess brought back a length of dark blue sprig muslin—a plain woven cotton patterned all over with tiny sprigs of white flowers.

Louisa asked her, "Shouldn't I wear black to mourn Da?"

Tess shook her head. "It's too late now. What would Jonathan think if you suddenly appeared in mourning?"

"I hadn't considered that."

Her new dark blue frock was such a success that she sewed another in pale blue for herself and one in yellow for the delighted Senora Rodriguez, who upon modeling it in the courtyard exclaimed, "You are a true seamstress!"

"I am delighted that you think so, for that's what I intend to be in San Francisco," Louisa responded.

"You work while su esposo—your husband—finds gold?" Senora Rodriquez asked, darting a glance toward Hugh, who was now well enough to read the hours away. Apparently she thought Hugh and she were bethrothed.

"Oh, no—" Stunned, Louisa was glad Hugh was engrossed in his book. Her telling him she wanted nothing more than friendship had, if anything, brought about the wrong effect, for he was beginning to seem more interested in her and less in Tess. "We are only friends," she explained to Senora Rodriquez.

"What of Tess and Senor Chambers?"

"They are also friends. The four of us are . . . merely friends."

Senora Rodriguez's dark eyes remained perplexed.

Louisa was perplexed about Tess, too. When the two of them had gone shopping for fabric, her friend basked in the appreciative stares of the hundreds of men in the streets and plazas. And during dinner on the servants' day off, Tess had captivated Pierre, the small, dark-eyed French argonaut who, awaiting a ship, ran the city's best restaurant. Tess had been so vivacious that the restaurateur had even sent her a bouquet of exotic flowers, addressed "Pour l'enchanteresse, Tess."

Enchantress indeed! It occurred to Louisa that if Hugh had attached himself to Tess because of her availability, Tess was no longer taking his interest seriously. Evenings at sunset, when they joined Senora Rodriquez in walks along the city's old ramparts, Tess's pretty heart-shaped face and lithe figure were of far more interest to the hordes of men than the ancient sights, and she enjoyed their attention mightily.

One evening while they admired the views, Louisa's heart hammered with fear when she thought she saw Conduff approach along the ramparts, but it was only a black-haired man who resembled him. For days thereafter, she kept an eye out for him, scrutinizing the crowds of miners.

Finally Hugh felt well enough to join them on the evening walks, but when he observed the attention paid to Tess, he turned quiet. He stayed at Louisa's side, causing a slight frown to crease Jonathan's broad forehead. All in all, Hugh had changed; he was no longer the gay blade she had met aboard the *Nimrod;* there was a thoughtfulness about him now, no doubt due to the shipwreck and his sickness.

For her part, Louisa enjoyed watching the waterfront activities, much as she once had in Alexandria. Panama City was built on a small promontory and faced the sea on two sides. The harbor was quaint, unchanged since the Spanish occupation. As there were no wharves, the larger vessels rode at anchor more than a mile away, and passengers were carried out on the backs of natives for hundreds of yards and placed in small boats which ferried them to the larger ships.

When they encountered argonauts who had sailed on the *Berta* with them, they learned that the men rarely fared well. Most lived in the hillside shantytown and could not afford restaurants, nor the little food available in the markets. "We're livin' on the salted foodstuffs we carried with us," they'd explain. "Some are dyin' every day. It's gettin' more 'n more desperate."

Senora Rodriguez escorted her American guests to the old forts of Morgan, the buccaneer who captured and plundered the city in 1671 when it had been the richest in South America. They visited the cathedral and the churches, too, and found great displays of gold and silver ornaments and images upon the altars, though the interiors were otherwise as dilapidated as the cracked and crumbling outsides of the buildings.

Louisa thought many of the Panamanian women handsome, especially on Sundays, when they dressed in white dresses with bright ribbons, red or yellow slippers without stockings, flowers in their hair, and gold chains around their necks.

To Louisa's amazement, the women arrived at church vigorously smoking cigars, then turned the lighted ends of the cigars into their mouths to put them out and stuck the stubs into their hair for future use! It was not unusual to see the ends of three or four half-smoked cigars sticking out from the folds of hair at the back of their heads.

"I like the way they make their hair useful as well as ornamental!" Jonathan remarked dryly.

"Perhaps I shall try it," Tess teased, "since y'all find it so interestin'!"

"And I shall make us white dresses with bright ribbons!" Louisa put in.

But interesting as the sights were, the one Louisa most longed to see was that of a ship that would carry them away to California.

Benjamin Talbot sat at his desk at the San Francisco chandlery warehouse and worked on accounts. Under "Inventory" he wrote *Two hundred wool blankets.*

He had purchased them from an unsold pile on the dock for almost nothing since no one was now in the market for blankets. He needed only to store them, then bring them out to sell in the fall. So often one merely needed common sense and a warehouse to do well in commerce, yet many of the would-be entrepreneurs failed because they brought in unsalable items like women's shoes and pocketbooks in a town populated mainly by men.

He still sat at work on the books when Daniel hurried into his office. "Governor Riley has called for an election! We are to elect delegates to draft a state constitution in September! Can you believe it?"

"God be thanked!" Benjamin said, raising his chair in excitement. "Now perhaps we will begin to make progress against the lawlessness!"

"I believe you are to be thanked, too," Daniel said. "You acted on your convictions and went to speak with Riley."

"I don't know who turned the tide," Benjamin answered, "but I surely have committed the matter to God over and over. It's a start . . . a good start, and I praise Him!"

One morning a cannon boomed across Panama City, and Louisa awakened with a start. An American ship was in! She and Tess pulled on their clothes and ran out to their balcony, where Jonathan and Hugh were already viewing the wild scene. Dawn had just begun to glimmer over the city and the sea, but every trail that led down from the hillsides was filled with argonauts who shouted with joy as they hurried to the city's ramparts. Natives cheered and danced in the streets. On every balcony in sight figures appeared to join the celebration.

Louisa looked out at the sea. A small white steamship lay at anchor. After her first surge of excitement, her heart sank. The ship would not hold many of the gold seekers.

Jonathan said, "I am going straight down to the steamship company for tickets."

Tess replied, "Wait for me!"

After breakfast Louisa installed Hugh in the courtyard and went upstairs to pack the battered green trunk they had purchased in the plaza. When she heard people arriving at the front door and great excitement downstairs, she hurried down. It was not Tess and Jonathan, but a Rodriguez cousin, Manuel, who had returned from the California diggings with a bagful of gold dust and nuggets.

The excitement had by no means diminished when Tess and Jonathan returned at midday. "We have tickets for the *Pacifica*!" Tess cried out in delight. "There was such a press of desperate men that policemen with truncheons and shotguns had to clear the way. Jonathan obtained our places through his connections with Wainwright and Talbot."

The news did not surpass the excitement with which locals and argonauts flocked in to gaze with wide-eyed awe at Manual Rodriguez's California gold.

Manuel exclaimed over and over, "Estoy rico! Estoy rico!" finally translating for the benefit of the Americans, "I am rich! I am rich!" He related, too, that a number of American gold seekers were on their way back across the Isthmus to take home fortunes in gold.

Two days later, after bidding Senora Rodriguez and her family a fond farewell, Louisa and Tess were carried across the water on the backs of natives on the way to a small boat. Being carried now struck Louisa as more humorous than discomfitting, and she called cheerily to Hugh and Jonathan, "Carried into Panama City and carried out! I am not sure whether I shall ever walk through water again!"

Despite everyone's warnings not to get wet for the sake of his health, Hugh sloshed through the shallow water himself. "And I vow never to be carried through it again," he said.

"Oh, the pride of men!" Tess called out from the back of her carrier. "You may be larger than the natives, but you would not have strained their backs. Look how much heavier some of the others are who they're carryin'."

"I like sloshing through by myself," Hugh said. He was beginning to look like his old self again, far too much like a golden Adonis for his own good, Louisa thought.

Finally they arrived at a small battered boat. Seamen handed Louisa and Tess in, then Jonathan, Hugh, and others. At last they rowed out toward the distant *Pacifica*, a magnificent white ship with the American flag waving from her bow.

"How I look forward to standing on American soil again!" Louisa said as their boat stopped beside the *Pacifica*.

Tess climbed up the swinging rope ladder first, then Louisa, who though nervous, felt more surefooted making her way up than she had climbing down the rope ladder from the *Berta* at Chagres. Tess helped her onto the deck, and they both watched the men ascend to the deck, Hugh, then Jonathan in case Hugh grew weak. They made jokes and pretended to be rope ladder experts. If nothing else, Louisa thought, the trip across Panama had turned Jonathan and Hugh into friends.

Once aboard, it was plain that the ship was overcrowded in the extreme; excited argonauts were already claiming places to sleep on the deck and hanging hammocks in the rigging. Men crowded every nook and corner.

Jonathan smiled at Louisa. "You must not look so serious. We only have to sail three thousand, two hundred or so miles."

"That far! Is it possible in only twenty days?"

"So they claim."

She glanced about at their shipmates, and found them a young and enthusiastic company.

"There are very few other women," Jonathan said. "You must be careful."

"I shall." She looked away. Since she had wept in his arms on the Chagres River, he'd retreated from her as she had from him. She was grateful, however, that he didn't pry into her past, for surely he knew that something was amiss.

"We should learn the location of exits and the rowing boats," she suggested, changing the topic. "After the *Nimrod*, I shall never again board a ship without learning the fastest routes of escape!" For that matter, she would never again sail into romantic waters; there seemed to be no fast escape routes at all from them.

Once their belongings were in the cabins, they went up

on deck in time to see the anchor weighed. The muggy air was deathly still and the *Pacifica's* sails remained furled, but instead of the ship waiting becalmed, its engine churned, the paddle wheels set up a vibration, and black smoke poured from the smokestack. Caught up in the argonauts' enthusiasm, Louisa cheered with them as the *Pacifica* began to steam away.

Her heart filled with gratitude as she looked back over the sea at the receding view of Panama City with its brightly painted houses and ancient cathedral. God had provided as fine a place as was possible for them there, and surely He would provide for her future.

Fifteen hundred miles later, they put in at their first stopping place. Acapulco was a Mexican town on a small bay entirely surrounded by hills. Night was falling, however, and they were not allowed to land because of the cholera that had been prevalent in Panama. Nonetheless the captain succeeded in landing the mails before their arrival became known to the authorities. Their next stopping place on the Mexican coast was San Blas, a village scarcely worth the visit except for the respite from the sea; the next stop was Mazatlan, where there was no opportunity to go ashore.

As they steamed out of the tropics, everyone's health improved. Most of the argonauts remained surprisingly cheerful—playing every game they could remember or devise, writing in their journals, singing their own rhymes to "O Susannah" and the like.

At night, the tables and floors of the dining saloon were used as beds and all decks were covered with men trying to sleep. Despite the poor food and overcrowded conditions, there were only desultory complaints. Even salt pork, potatoes, hardtack, and thin coffee did not seem too terrible after the conditions they had already endured.

Tess predicted, "After this kind of fare, they will come flocking to my restaurant."

"A pity your friend Pierre did not come along from Panama City to help you with it," Louisa teased.

Tess laughed merrily. "Why, he promised to come someday. He says that I have only to set up the restaurant ... as if that is going to be an easy thing in such a tent town, especially if it's as rough as everyone claims."

Louisa glanced at Hugh, but if he were jealous of Pierre, he gave no sign of it. He showed only a friendly interest in Tess, which was fortunate since Tess so enjoyed being courted on all sides by their shipmates. Only yesterday Hugh had said, "I see in Tess how I once was myself."

His interest in Louisa, however, had risen since their courtyard visits in Panama City. Worse, whenever he so much as looked at her, Jonathan appeared upset. It was a difficult impass, complicated because Hugh seemed to take out his frustrations at her rebuffs by gambling with the argonauts.

The *Pacifica* stopped in San Diego, where they saw only the landing because the town itself was some three miles up a small bay. The mere fact of steaming alongside the arid California Territory, however, dispelled the lethargy brought on by weeks of following the same routines in cramped quarters. From bow to stern, the men packed and repacked their stores, and studied maps of California.

One said, "Now, here is Ryan's Diggings, where Jack Ryan struck it rich. I am going right there myself!" and another, "I favor the lower ground where the river washes the gold right out of the hills. I don't care to dig."

Ambition soared so that when one young man said, "I shall be content if I don't get more than a hatful of gold a day," none claimed it unreasonable.

Jonathan smiled as he wrote about the scene, and Louisa sat nearby sewing. When he had finished, he allowed her to read his description of an argonaut's life at sea.

She laughed at its droller aspects and, upon finishing it, said, "You're an amusing man, Jonathan Chambers."

The warmth in his hazel eyes made her heart thump more loudly. "Sometimes I am most serious as well. I am very serious about you, Louisa—"

"No, please—" she interrupted and quickly looked out at the churning sea. Soon they would each go their own way in San Francisco, and she would no longer have to do such battle with temptation.

San Francisco soon! San Francisco!

# 10

S hafts of sunlight slanted through the thick morning fog
as the *Pacifica* swung eastward toward the California
shore. Louisa stood on deck as the ship moved through the
Golden Gate Strait into the bay, where hundreds of ships lay
abandoned at anchor, their wooden masts stripped of canvas.
They had been told that thousands of sailors had jumped
ship, but the scene still made her feel as desolate as it looked.

"Louisa, don't look so distressed," Tess said.

"It is such a discouraging sight . . . and I was thinking
that my entire future depends upon the next few days. What
if the Talbots do not welcome me? I cannot force myself on
them. And what if San Francisco is truly too rough for us?"

Tess replied blithely, "I've had so many proposals, I can
always get mar—" She faltered. "Oh, Louisa, I forget—"

Louisa glanced about and was grateful no one had
overheard. "I forget about Conduff myself, though never for
long."

She was unable to explain this morning's depression. If
she were a stronger Christian, she would turn her worries
over to the Lord. What a bad witness for Christ she was for
Tess, who had never accepted Him as her Savior. She glanced
down at the lower deck where the excited argonauts packed

for the last time, many placing their crucibles, gold tests, and sluice pans on top of their belongings as though they would immediately step out into the goldfields.

Tess observed, "Wearin' all those guns and bowie knives, you'd think they were expectin' to battle Indians and wild beasts." A moment later, she turned and added, "Look at Hugh!"

Hugh and Jonathan wound their way through the argonauts on the deck, Hugh wearing a pistol tucked in his belt. Jonathan, carrying only his journal, quipped, "If there is any protecting to do, I shall rely upon Hugh."

"Jonathan can write about me in my grave!" Hugh laughed.

Louisa, smiling with them, felt her spirits begin to rise as they usually did around Jonathan.

The *Pacifica* dropped anchor in choppy water and fired a salvo of guns to inform San Francisco of her arrival. They watched as a number of small boats were rowed toward them from the beach, then Louisa was shakily making her way down a rope ladder again—for the last time in her life, she hoped.

Finally, she sat in the rowboat and announced, "I don't care if I never sail in another ship!"

"Believe me, you are not alone in that wish," Jonathan said.

She looked out with him and the others across the choppy water at the town of San Francisco. It, too, was a disappointing sight. Thus far, its only hopeful aspect was that one of the warehouses lining the waterfront had "Wainwright-Talbot Shipping and Chandlery" lettered across its front. Nearby were trading posts, some no more than old ships' hulls, and shanties with "Saloon" painted across their weathered exteriors. Farther up the hill, there were tents everywhere—tents interspersed with shacks and sheds built of split boards, packing crates, and flattened tin cans. Only clumps of weeds separated the shacks and endless tents that climbed to the crest of the hill.

Their boatman, a red-bearded, rough-looking fellow, scrutinized Louisa's and Tess's left hands as if to see whether they wore wedding bands. "What ye ladies doin' 'ere?" he asked.

Tess declared, "Why, I am goin' to open the best San Francisco restaurant you have ever seen."

"Thet so? Plenty o' call fer it." Rowing mightily, he grinned at her. "If yer cookin's half as good as ye look, count on me. What ye namin' it?"

"Tess's . . . just Tess's."

"Oughta call it Tess's Place. That's the kind o' name the miners would like."

"Then Tess's Place it is."

He turned toward Louisa as he rowed. "An' you?"

"I hope to start a seamstress establishment."

He shook his head. "Ain't much call fer sewin' thet I heerd o'. Ain't enough women about. Cooks 'n carpenters 'n sech do right well."

"No sewing—?"

The boatman shook his head.

"Then you'll have to work with me, Louisa," Tess said. "We need only a buildin', tables, chairs, dishes, silverware and such, not to mention foodstuffs!"

"And curtains and tablecloths, which I can make," Louisa added, more hopeful.

When Hugh inquired about nearby hotels, the man guffawed. "If ye call 'em thet! Parker House be the only 'un fer decent women. It's not e'en finished, 'n already filled up tighter'n a drum. I heerd of men sleepin' in the closets, 'n takin' turns sleepin' in the beds."

"If it's as bad as that, we had better visit Wainwright and Talbot immediately," Jonathan said.

"Now them's quality folk," their boatman submitted with all seriousness. "Most of 'em come here by covered wagon afore the gold rush. Trip turned old Ben Talbot's hair gray." He nodded as he rowed. "Quality folk. Thet sort's few 'n far between since the gold come up."

Louisa was heartened to hear such sincere praise for her relations. Perhaps their situation would not be so desperate despite the appearance of San Francisco. Moreover, Hugh and Jonathan wished to find employment, and an established family might prove helpful for them.

Later, as the boatman helped them onto the beach, he said to Tess and Louisa, "The two o' ye are gonna brighten up this town. Ain't many decent women 'round. Well, see ye at Tess's Place!"

"See, we already have one customer!" Tess said to the rest of them as the boatman shoved off again.

Louisa had to smile at her friend. Then, standing on the beach, she took in her surroundings.

Around them, sea gulls fluttered up from ground littered with paper and empty bottles, and idlers stood about watching their arrival. Nearby, huge mule-drawn scoops sliced off the hillsides and dumped the dirt into the bay. Dust blew everywhere. This was her new home, she told herself. This dismal raw place. Her legs wobbled, feeling as unreliable under her as she suddenly felt about California.

"Let me help you," Jonathan offered.

Louisa grabbed his arm. "Thank you, it seems that I have forgotten how to walk."

A smile pulled at the corners of his lips. "I am not so steady on my feet myself."

They trudged up a dusty incline to an equally dusty road that fronted the warehouses they had seen from the ship. The stench of privies and rotting dead fish hung in the damp air, and uncombed, unwashed loafers stood around the saloons gaping at her. She tightened her grip on Jonathan's arm. The whitewashed Wainwright and Talbot warehouse was the only substantial and tidy waterfront building, and they headed resolutely for it. As they stepped into its office, the clerks turned immediately to them. Louisa swallowed with difficulty. "Is Mr. Benjamin Talbot here? I am a relation of his, Louisa—"

A kindly, gray-haired gentleman stepped forward with a smile of amazement. "With that beautiful red hair and those blue eyes, I thought for an instant I was seeing your dear mother." He took her hand in his. "I'm Benjamin Talbot, your uncle. We were so excited to receive your letter last week, even before you'd received our letter of invitation."

"Your letter?" Louisa asked.

"Yes. We felt led to write and ask you to come to California," Benjamin said, his brown eyes brimming with pleasure. "How much you look like your mother. Wait until the family sees you!"

They had written to her . . . Louisa fought a moment of panic, thinking how Conduff would read the letter and guess where she had gone! Yet, despite everything, Louisa's heart filled with relief. "I am most eager to meet your family and so grateful for your welcome. Allow me to introduce my friends, Tess Pierson. . . . "

"A pleasure to meet you, Miss Pierson."

"And this is Jonathan Chambers," Louisa added.

Benjamin Talbot said, "Ah, the young solicitor from Harvard. Elisha Wainwright wrote of your coming, though I had no idea you were with Louisa. Elisha speaks highly of you."

"And of you," Jonathan replied with enthusiasm as they shook hands. "I am pleased to make your acquaintance, sir."

Louisa continued, "And this is Hugh Fairfax, a friend of your son Joshua."

Benjamin Talbot invited everyone to stay at his home, then arranged to have their baggage transported from the ship. "Aunt Jessica will be overjoyed to have you with us," he promised. "And Betsy, my youngest daughter, will be pleased to have you for company."

Before long they were seated in his buggy, and he flicked the reins over the horses. "Comfortable carriages, like many other amenities, are difficult to find here," he explained as they set out. "Not only is the waterfront crude, but so is all of the California Territory. Yet it does offer advantages. I presume you gentlemen have come in search of gold."

Jonathan smiled ironically. "Only a big strike in the first day or two. I am not sure I would care for gold seeking as a lifelong pursuit."

Hugh said with a laugh, "A few hundred-pound nuggets would be fine."

"I am glad you see gold seeking in that light," Benjamin Talbot responded. "Unless you catch gold fever, as many young men have, I venture to guess each of you will last a month or so in the diggings. Fortunately, there are plenty of other opportunities for ambitious young men here. What we need is fewer argonauts and more educated men who can civilize this place."

Viewing the dusty ramshackle shops and houses as they drove past, Louisa agreed. She hoped there were more preferable sections where she and Tess might have their shops. Thus far the town appeared to be wallowing in dust, with half of the population living in tents and a third of the buildings given over to saloons and gambling houses.

Benjamin Talbot said somewhat resignedly, "In February of last year we had nine hundred people here in town. Now there are so many thousands we've lost count."

They passed through a town square, where grizzled men wandered in and out of the noisy saloons and gambling tents.

"Why do all of these men come here in the middle of the day?" Tess asked.

"Some are newcomers off the ships and others are in from the diggings, spending their gold as fast as they can on drink and gambling."

"They all need to eat while they're here," Tess remarked. "I plan to open a restaurant."

"A fine idea, young lady. I would be the first in line to patronize a good eating establishment since there are so few here."

"Is there as much gold as is rumored?" Louisa asked. "Enough for so many people?"

Her uncle nodded. "Apparently there are vast quantities of it, not only in the rivers, but up the mountainsides. Many are amazed the gold supply has lasted this long, and every month there seems to be a new strike."

Finally they left the raucous town behind them. Even Alexandria's worst section of the waterfront was not as crude as San Francisco, and Louisa couldn't imagine anything as genteel as a seamstress establishment in such a raw place.

They drove on through the countryside, over rolling hills and into dry grassy valleys. Benjamin Talbot pointed toward the crest of a hill. "There's our land, Rancho Verde . . . which is, alas, a misnomer most of the year. You will see by the color of the vegetation that we have had no rain for months.

Winter is our rainy season here."

Despite the dryness of the place, Louisa noted that the golden hillsides were dotted with clumps of live oaks that resembled old Virginia apple trees, and there were thickets of greenery along the small stream where cattle grazed.

They rode to the crest of the next hill and looked down into the valley. Below, under the shade of huge live oaks, whitewashed walls enclosed white houses with red tile roofs on the Spanish-style rancho. Just outside the walls, corrals fenced in horses near the outbuildings.

"We call the old house Casa Contenta," Uncle Benjamin told them, "and it truly was a house of contentment until the gold rush began last year. Now it's difficult to find men to care for the house and livestock. Everyone from farm hands to shopkeepers leaves for the gold fields, only returning when the rivers are too high or low."

The white buildings gleamed in the sun and great bursts of red flowers arched over the walls surrounding the entire compound. Louisa tried to recall everything that Hugh had told her about the Talbots, though the time of sailing on the *Nimrod* from Baltimore seemed years instead of a mere two months ago.

"Please tell us about your family," she said. "I only know that you were born in Boston."

"And received my education there," Uncle Benjamin added. "I married Elizabeth Brauer and went into frontier trading, so we eventually moved to Independence. Unfortunately, I was widowed while the children were still young. My sister Jessica came to Missouri and raised my children and Daniel Wainwright, whose parents were killed by Indians."

He looked at the four white houses as they rode toward the compound. "Perhaps it is easiest to tell you about the family by showing where we live. That is the main house ahead, the old casa where you will all stay with me and my sister, Jessica. Betsy, who is fourteen, is my only child still there. In the new house to the right, live Daniel Wainwright and his wife, my niece Abby, and little Daniel . . ." He told about his other married children and grandchildren, then whoaed the horses and reined them in under a sprawling live oak tree.

Before long, he was opening the carved wooden door to a red-tiled hallway and calling out, "Jessica! Betsy! Wait until you see who I have brought home!"

A gray-haired woman hurried into the entry, her brown eyes shining with curiosity. Her hair was pulled back into a bun and her slight plumpness suggested that she liked to cook. Indeed, she had just pulled off her apron and was folding it as she approached.

Benjamin Talbot announced with a grin, "I have brought your niece, Louisa, and her friends from the East." He turned to Louisa. "This is your Aunt Jessica."

Her aunt's mouth had widened with surprise. "My dear . . . you look so like your mother, just as Sarah wrote—" She took Louisa's hands in hers. "Oh, my . . . I must fight the temptation to become maudlin."

Everyone laughed, dissolving the tension.

"Here comes Betsy," Uncle Benjamin said. "Come meet your Cousin Louisa and her friends."

Betsy's clover-green eyes filled with joyous disbelief. "Cousin Louisa?"

"What a surprise I must be," Louisa said.

"A wonderful surprise. How I've been looking forward to your coming. All of us have—"

Louisa reached out to shake Betsy's hand, but her freckle-faced cousin with the long auburn braids gave her a great hug. "I am so glad you've come!"

By the time they were seated in the spacious white parlor with glasses of cold buttermilk and little chocolate cakes, Louisa was not the only one to feel welcome, for the Talbots had taken each of them—Tess, Jonathan, and Hugh—to their bosom. She felt even more a part of the family to see a portrait of Grandmother Talbot on the parlor wall. "It is similar to the one we had in Alexandria," she remarked.

"Abby made copies for all of us," Betsy said. "Perhaps she will make one for you, too. I can't wait until you meet her and Daniel, and the rest of us!"

The entire Talbot family, including all of the grandchildren, were invited for supper, and they arrived bearing warm breads, cold potato salad, and steaming hot peach pies that smelled ambrosial. "We are so happy to meet you," they said and "Welcome to California!"

With the exception of golden-haired Abby, it was simple to separate the Talbots from the others by their auburn hair. Abby and her husband, Daniel, were the ones Louisa thought she would like best as friends. She hugged their "little Daniel," who at eighteen months toddled merrily about. "How beautiful he is!"

"Forgive me, but I think so, too," Abby said, beaming. "Children are such wonders."

Louisa avoided her eyes. "Yes, they must be." If she hadn't miscarried, she would soon have had a child like this of her own.

Beside her, she noticed that Tess, who had quickly made friends with the other children, could not help stretching out her arms to little Daniel. "What a picture you make holding a child, Tess."

"I've surely had plenty of experience," Tess replied, her eyes shining so that she had to blink hard.

They adjourned to the whitewashed dining room for supper, where the crystal chandelier with wax lights reminded Louisa of one at Senora Rodriguez's house, as did the dark wooden furniture. The room was more charming, however, for Abby had stenciled an intricate coral and green border around the dining room at sideboard height just as she had in the vast hallway that led to the bedrooms.

They sat down at a long table with a bouquet of red roses in the middle of the coarsely woven linen runners. The bone china, silverware, and cut-glass crystal had come from London, but the furniture had belonged to the house's previous owners, *Californios* who had returned to Spain three years ago, before the gold rush began.

Agreeable as it all was, Louisa suspected that her relations were curious about her past as well as her future intentions. She would have to explain and make decisions soon.

"Shall we sing Old Hundredth as grace?" Uncle Benjamin suggested. "I cannot think of a better way to thank our Lord for sending us Louisa and her friends and for our many great blessings." He said to the guests, "It is our custom to hold hands as a symbol of our family's unity in the Lord." Everyone reached out for their neighbor's hand, and Louisa felt reassured as she held Betsy's hand on one side and Jonathan's on the other. They all sang out fervently:

"Praise God, from whom all blessings flow,
Praise Him, all creatures here below,
Praise Him above, ye heavenly host,
Praise Father, Son, and Holy Ghost."

They ended with a harmonious "Amen," and Louisa looked up at Jonathan. He, too, was touched. She spoke softly to him, "It reminds me of Oakley's house."

He nodded and turned to Benjamin Talbot. "Your household has that same gift of gracious hospitality that one finds at my brother's in Baltimore."

"They must know the Lord, too," Benjamin Talbot replied.

"Indeed they do. Unfortunately we have been away from godly surroundings since then. It is gratifying to be with believers again."

Daniel Wainwright, bearded and darkly handsome, sat across from them with his wife, Abby. "One cannot always choose the company one would like to keep when traveling," he said.

"Indeed," Jonathan agreed.

As they ate their ham supper, the conversation turned to the gold diggings and Benjamin Talbot remarked, "Daniel, you're driving wagons out to Oak Hill on Monday. Perhaps you can talk Jonathan and Hugh into going with you."

Louisa's heart constricted at the thought of Jonathan leaving, though she had no justifiable hold on him.

"I would enjoy showing both of you about the goldfields," Daniel said. "As usual, I desperately need drivers for the wagons since so many men are already there."

Jonathan's eyes lit up. "We would be fools not to take advantage of such an opportunity. If you can make do with a somewhat inexperienced driver, I accept your offer gratefully."

Must he be so enthusiastic about it? Louisa thought.

Daniel said to Hugh. "Your friend Joshua has opened a store at Oak Hill, and we are carrying six wagon loads of goods to help stock it. You would be doing him a kindness."

"Count me in, as well," Hugh replied. "Joshua will be as flabbergasted to see me as I am to hear he is a shopkeeper."

Louisa kept her attention on her plate as the discussion continued. It seemed that Joshua had planned to work in San

Francisco, but he had fallen in love with Abby's best friend, Rose.

Daniel remarked, "The best made plans of mice and men do often go awry, especially when love arrives on the scene!"

Louisa laughed politely with the rest of them, although in her case there was nothing humorous about it.

"Rose and her father began a church in Oak Hill out by the gold diggings," Abby said to Louisa.

"They've begun a church? I–I suppose I hadn't considered the lack of churches in such places," Louisa replied. "In Alexandria, it seems they've always been there."

"As it seemed in New York," Abby said, "but we've begun one here ourselves. We meet in the parlor with neighbors every Sunday."

"I see," Louisa said and suddenly felt uneasy. She hadn't attended a divine service since the one in Baltimore with Jonathan's family, nor had she read Scripture, but then she no longer owned a Bible . . . and with Jonathan leaving, it didn't seem of such great importance.

The next morning when she blinked awake, she was amazed not to be at sea or trekking through the jungle. Instead, she saw the whitewashed walls of the bedroom. Beside her, in a real bed, Tess still lay asleep.

Slipping out of bed, Louisa padded to the window.

In the distance, fields of golden grasses swayed gently on the hillsides, and cattle grazed beneath the trees. What a lovely pastoral scene, she thought. It occurred to her how happily she might live in such a place. She could imagine Jonathan galloping across the fields as he came home to her. He would dismount and come running, his hazel eyes aglow, his arms outstretched—

"Whatever are you thinkin'?" Tess asked sleepily.

"I–I'm still half-asleep. I didn't know you were awake."

"With such a smile on your face, you were thinkin' about Jonathan, I'd wager."

"I have no right to think about him," Louisa returned. "You are the one with your whole life ahead of you. I thought for a while that you and Hugh were in love."

Tess shrugged. "I don't know. If I'd been courted at fifteen like you, I would be married this minute and probably have children, but now it seems I can actually live my own life for a while. In any case, I think Hugh wants freedom, and I expect that's what I want now, too. Most likely, he and I were not meant to marry."

Louisa looked out the window again, trying to hide her sorrow. "Perhaps not."

At breakfast, she watched Tess and Hugh across the table. It did seem that only friendship existed between them now. What a shame it was, too, for they had made a beautiful couple when they'd cared for each other in Panama.

As she looked away from them, she found Jonathan smiling at her. She returned his smile briefly, then took a sip of coffee. Soon, she must tell him and the others about Conduff, but not now . . . not now when she was still so exhausted from the voyage.

"Hugh and I are riding into town with your uncle this morning," Jonathan said. "We want to see what opportunities are available for us here."

Louisa kept her attention on buttering her bread. "With your legal background, you will have many offers."

"I doubt that. The law is different here. They have only an alcalde who acts as judge, jury, police, and jailer."

"Then what will you do?"

He shrugged. "That remains to be seen. I must trust in God's leading."

For some reason, his words sounded overly righteous, and she replied quite simply, "I shall soon have to find work, too."

She still had a small amount of money, though Tess was worse off, having had to borrow part of her fare for the voyage from Panama to California from Hugh. Her mind returned to Jonathan's plight, and she remembered that he'd studied theology at Harvard as well as law. Perhaps God would lead him into the ministry here.

After the men left for town, Louisa and Tess strolled through the house while Aunt Jessica related its history and Betsy pointed out watercolored pictures Abby had drawn during their covered-wagon trek West: river crossings, a buffalo stampede on the prairie, the covered wagons circled at sunset in the mountains, and far more. It appeared she was a very talented artist. She had painted portraits of everyone in the family, too, and the parlor's whitewashed walls as well as the vast hallway looked like portrait galleys.

Louisa stopped before the portrait of Grandmother Talbot, which she'd noticed when she first arrived.

"It's only my poor copy of the original in Independence," Abby explained. "I've never felt I did it justice, for I'm unable to capture the glow of faith in her eyes."

Aunt Jessica asked Louisa, "Did you know that your grandmother led her future husband to the Lord before they were engaged?"

"No, I'd only been told he was a famous Boston preacher. What an interesting situation!"

"May I paint a portrait of you, too, Louisa?" Abby asked. "With that lovely red hair and those sapphire blue eyes, you would make such a good subject."

"I–I don't know. I have never had my portrait painted."

"All the more reason to let Abby do it then," Aunt Jessica said. "We are hoping to have portraits of all of the family."

"I don't have anything fine enough to wear for a portrait," Louisa objected.

"You must wear the lovely blue sprig muslin you wore when you arrived," Abby said.

Louisa laughed. "I have very little else to wear since the shipwreck!"

"People will always say, 'Louisa lost all of her clothes and other possessions in the shipwreck of a great clipper ship,' and they will think it terribly romantic to see you wearing the muslin in the painting," Abby said.

"Of course, you must, Cousin Louisa," Betsy said. "Abby even made me look pretty in my portrait!"

All of them laughed, for Betsy had no idea of how lovely she was becoming, and, in the end, Louisa gave in.

After they had discussed their relatives and the portraits at length, the sunshine drew them outdoors. They ambled through the garden, and Louisa exclaimed, "Lilacs! I never expected to see them in California!"

Aunt Jessica told how she'd brought the lilac and rose roots by covered wagon. "I was glad to have a place for them—and for us—to root into again," she said.

"How I would like to root in myself," Louisa reflected.

"Then you likely will," Aunt Jessica assured her, "for the Lord so often gives us the desires of our hearts."

Louisa shook her head, thinking about Jonathan. "I don't believe I shall have the desire of my heart."

Aunt Jessica gave her a strange look. "I shall add you to my prayers," she said firmly.

At supper, Jonathan was pleased to hear that Abby had already started the portrait of Louisa. "I'll look forward to seeing it," he said with enthusiasm.

After supper, she kept her distance from him, and she continued to avoid him during the next few days as well. On Sunday morning, however, before their divine service in the parlor, he approached her as she sat on a settee smoothing the folds of her dress.

"May I join you, Louisa?" he asked.

She swallowed uneasily. He was so handsome in his newly pressed brown frock coat and trousers. Oddly, he carried what appeared to be two black Bibles. "Yes, of course."

He smiled, his hazel eyes aglow with warmth. "I was concerned that perhaps I had somehow offended you."

"I suspect you have never intentionally offended anyone," she replied, her resistance to him crumbling.

"Then I hope that this gift will not do so either."

To her amazement, he handed her one of the Bibles.

"It will never replace your Aunt Sarah's and it is used, but it was the only one I could find in town."

"I don't know what to say, Jonathan—"

"You need say nothing. May I?" He leaned near her and opened the Bible to an inscription fronting the title page. "Evidently it was given to a gold seeker before he left Boston. One wonders how it came to be for sale in San Francisco."

She read the original inscription: February 5, 1849, May you always worship Him more than gold.

"It is such a good inscription that I saw no reason to add to it," he said. "I hope the original owner didn't sell it. In any case, I leave tomorrow and I wanted to give you a gift."

"Thank you. I shall always . . . cherish it."

He looked at her so affectionately that she turned to the Bible and thumbed through the softly rustling pages, determined to focus upon them.

Dr. Norton had often said, "The Bible is 'God's story' told

to show us how to better live our stories." If only she knew Scripture better, she might not be in such a predicament over Jonathan, she suddenly thought. Unfortunately, she had only learned the rudiments of living a Christian life since her conversion.

Looking at the Bible, the truth brought her up short. She did know the commandment against telling falsehoods, and not telling about her marriage to Conduff was a lie, spoken or not . . . it was a lie of omission.

Distracted as she was, the parlor scene unfolded before her appeared as though in a haze. Aunt Jessica played the prelude on a small pump organ, and the others—family members and the nearest neighbors—quieted. After a while, one of neighbor men said the morning prayer, then others led the worship.

Daniel Wainwright read from Scripture, and Benjamin Talbot preached about obedience to God, though none of it seemed to enter Louisa's mind. After the last prayer they sang "Fairest Lord Jesus," and beside her, Jonathan's voice held such faith she was embarrassed to sing out the last words with him:
"Jesus shines brighter
Jesus shines purer
Than all the angels heaven can boast."
She felt like a terrible hypocrite.

"Benjamin Talbot is a fine preacher, layman or not," Jonathan said to her.

She had barely heard the sermon, but she replied, "Yes, he is."

They looked at each other and Jonathan added, "I shall miss you, Louisa, but I am heartened to know you will be here with the Talbots."

"I have not yet decided—"

"But you can't live in town. It's raucous and wild, an unsafe place for a young woman."

It was sufficiently daunting to have him leave, but now he was suggesting what she must do, too. Obstinancy rose to her throat and goaded her up from the settee. "I have never said I would stay here, and I can't impose on my relatives forever. Tess is moving to town and wants me to accompany her."

"Louisa, it would be far safer—"

"Excuse me, please. I must help Aunt Jessica prepare dinner." Her voice was too curt, and she hurried toward the kitchen, Bible in hand. Kind as it was for him to have given it to her, he had no right to tell her what to do. He might be more knowledgeable than she about Scripture, but she did know she wasn't required to be obedient to him.

On Monday morning after breakfast and prayers, Jonathan, Hugh, and Daniel set out on their mule-drawn wagons to take supplies to the goldfields. The six covered wagons creaked and rumbled, stirring up dust in the faces of the cattle and horses driven behind them.

At breakfast Betsy had said, "We usually ride a short way with them, and the others are too busy with their children. Tess is going into town. Do come ride out with me, Louisa."

"All right, then, I shall."

She rode a gray mare and Betsy a chestnut toward the front of the dusty column. Tess was going into town with Uncle Benjamin this morning to sell the small raisin-nut cakes she had baked for a commercial venture. Recalling the raw town they had passed through only days ago, Louisa hoped Tess could handle the rough men. Likely she could, after caring for her rambunctious sisters and brothers. She could imagine Tess thickening her southern accent and saying, "Mind your mannuhs, suh!"

Yes, Tess would manage.

Louisa's attention returned to the scene before her: a vast blue sky, waving fields of golden grasses, and clusters of live oak trees. She had allowed her horse to drift back even with Jonathan's wagon, the second in the column. Catching his eye, she smiled slightly. She meant to urge her mount forward, then Jonathan said, "Forgive me, Louisa, if I was domineering yesterday morning. I am only concerned about your welfare."

"Thank you kindly," she replied, her tone cool. "I am concerned about your welfare in the goldfields, as well."

"Then you understand. I shall be careful, but it's an entirely different matter for young women. I hope you will not move into town with Tess."

"There is no profitable work here."

"Aunt Jessica is happy for your help in the house since most of the servants are out seeking gold."

*It is not his place to tell me what to do*, she thought heatedly and barely refrained from telling him so. She urged her horse forward to put an end to the conversation.

Finally it was time to return to the house, and she reined the mare around. Attempting to sound cheerful, she called to Jonathan, "Bring back heaps of gold!"

He grinned. "We shall fill your gold sacks with them!"

Louisa mustered a smile. She had sewn canvas sacks similar to those made by argonauts aboard the ships and presented them to Hugh and Jonathan half in jest.

She gave the men a brave parting wave. Jonathan might be successful at the diggings . . . or he might be killed. The goldfields were becoming increasingly dangerous; a murder and a lynching had taken place only last week at Oak Flats. Quite suddenly, her throat tightened with emotion and she barely mustered a strangled, "Farewell, Hugh! Farewell, Jonathan!"

She wheeled her gray mare away and blinked at the dampness in her eyes. After a moment, she lifted her chin with determination. Like Tess, she must set to work earning a living now. It would help her to forget about him as well.

San Francisco
July 15, 1849
Dear Ellie and Oakley,

It seems impossible that we left you just over two months ago, for so much has happened since then. I am now at my uncle's house, and Jonathan has left for the goldfields. He asked that I write, since he and our friend, Hugh Fairfax, had little time to even get outfitted with sluice pan, pickax, tent, clothing, and other provisions. They decided it would be foolish to be here and not try to find gold themselves. Jonathan promises to send you his first nugget.

I am attempting to find work as a seamstress, but we live in the countryside and there are no clients nearby. In the meantime, I am sewing dresses as gifts for my Aunt Jessica and Cousin Betsy, as well as one for my cousin, Abby, who is painting my portrait for the family. I have considered teaching, but most children here are too young for formal schooling. Moreover, my aunt was a teacher, and Betsy is studying to become one, so they teach the Talbot children.

My friend, Tess, is a great success. She took little raisin-nut cakes to San Francisco one morning and sold them at high prices. We have all joined her venture and bake little cakes, rolls, and raisin bread at night, and she goes into town with my uncle and sells them during the day. This will soon end as she has been offered a position in charge of a new tent restaurant. She wants me to join her, but I am unsure about it. I would especially dislike leaving Betsy, who is fourteen and enjoys our company in the house.

Louisa set the letter aside on the desk, for she felt so dismayed and dismal she was unable to think of what else to say. Perhaps later she could write more about life in California, but at the moment she wanted only to weep. Why, oh, why had she ruined her life by marrying Conduff!

# 11

Conduff strode toward Louisa like a sleek black mountain panther. "Come 'ere, honey-girl," he urged in that husky tone of his. "You jest come 'ere." He towered over her, and his green eyes held hers so intently that she was unable to tear herself away.

He slid his hand up her back and turned her slowly toward him. "With them big blue eyes and that red hair, you might jest amount to somethin' yet," he said, his tone turning as warm as honey itself. "Won't hurt none to let down yer hair."

As though entranced, she began to unbraid her thick hair, all the time watching his lips curve up in a sensuous smile. Finally her hair tumbled about her shoulders and down to her waist, a shining curtain of curls.

"Now ain't that a sight?" he asked, reaching for her. His hands grasped her shoulders softly at first, but suddenly he turned furious and was shaking her. "You cain't run off from no Blue Ridge man!" he shouted. His green eyes were bloodshot, and he reared back to slap her across the room—

Drenched with perspiration, Louisa sat up in her cot and saw she was safe in Tess's boxlike room behind the tent-restaurant. A nightmare . . . only another nightmare with images from the past. Why must she dream of him again? Was it because the miners here in San Francisco so often reminded her of Conduff?

Perhaps she shouldn't be in town, but Tess had been persuasive. "It is such a good opportunity to run a big restaurant," she'd said. "We get ten percent of the profits, and soon we'll have enough to open our own establishment. Good cookin' brings in a great deal of money in such an unsettled place."

"Unsettled place" is right! Louisa thought, and unsettled or not, San Francisco grew unbelievably. Just last week a ship had brought in Chinese carpenters and more ready-built rooms and even houses that could be put up in a day. It was only dawn, and already hammers pounded and boards thumped into place all along the street. Yesterday carpenters had hammered until dark, after which endless raucous choruses of "Oh, Susannah," "Buffalo Gals," and such had blared from saloons and gambling houses. Drunken shouts and laughter constantly punctuated the discordant clamor, penetrating the matchstick-thin wooden walls of their ready-built room.

Tess yawned widely from her nearby cot. "Listen to that hammerin'!" She wrinkled up her face in distaste, then gave a wry laugh. "I said it wouldn't be a tent town long!"

"That you did," Louisa agreed. She stood up, stiff from the iron cot. Iron discouraged the bedbugs that swarmed everywhere, Tess had explained. Louisa pulled on her shoes, for the wooden floor was splintery—"a blessing" Jonathan might call it, since few in San Francisco had wooden floors or even rooms at all. Hundreds of miners and newcomers slept on the ground in bedrolls, and even those who could afford hotels were crammed eight or ten to a small room.

Louisa hurried to their "dressing table"—a wooden

carton with a chipped white pitcher and washbowl on top. The only other furnishings in the tiny room were their trunks at the foot of the cots. She and Tess not only had a room provided by Warrick Clark, Tess's "friend" who owned the Golden Palace and its adjacent restaurant, but they had accumulated a good bit of gold dust from waiting on hungry miners last week.

Tess slipped out of her cot and pulled on her shoes. "It's exciting to be in on the beginning of a town!"

"With so many people coming in, perhaps there'll soon be call for a seamstress," Louisa replied, dressing as quickly as she could in her pale blue frock.

"I think you might get work today. Faye, one of the gamblin' hostesses, wants new dresses. I told her about your sewin', and she said she'd come by soon. She bought some Chinese silks from a ship that just came in."

"Thank you! You know so many people already, Tess."

Tess buttoned up her new pink muslin dress. "I've had the advantage of shopping for supplies and the restaurant equipment, but everyone comes around for good cookin'. You'll know plenty of folks soon yourself."

Dressed, they stepped outside and padlocked the room, then shivered as they hurried the short distance through the morning murk to the back of the big green tent.

Opening the back flap, they found the tent's air as damp as usual. Louisa lit the whale-oil lanterns, which gave off an acrid stench and clouded the very pools of light that illuminated the tent. The packed dirt floor held thirty long wooden tables and benches, and the red oilcloth tablecloths centered by the smelly lanterns provided the decor. There had been no time for sewing curtains, nor were there windows over which to hang them.

"I'll wipe off the tablecloths," Louisa offered, for they

were covered with dust and soot again.

Tess went to light the wood fires in the four black cookstoves lining one side of the tent. As the cook fires caught, more smoke filled the tent, though the burning wood at least smelled agreeable.

"Ye got coffee ready?" a bearded miner called in, peering through the front flap of the tent.

They hadn't even started it, but Tess said to Louisa, "Expect he drank too much last night. May as well open up."

Louisa hurried to the front of the tent and opened the flap, letting in the morning's murky light. A knot of miners stood there in their red and blue flannel shirts, rumpled rough trousers, and tall dusty boots.

"Ye banged the gong yet?" one of them asked, referring to the Chinese gong that announced dinner and supper.

"We don't ring it in the morning or we would awaken half the town," Louisa replied.

"Kin we come in and set 'til ye get goin'?" another asked. "Ain't had no place to set since supper. Ain't many chairs at all in this poor excuse of a town."

"Of course, come in, but the coffee's not ready. And you've beat the cook in as well."

"Aw, this fellow jest wants more time to look at ye and Tess," another miner teased and elbowed his cohort in the ribs.

The first miner grinned guiltily. "Ain't no other decent women to look at in this town. Here, lemme give ye a hand rollin' up that tent flap."

"Thank you," Louisa replied with amusement. Judging by the miners she had met, most of them meant well. It was true that there were few chairs in town, and, as for her and Tess being two of the few decent women, it was not such a compliment. Yesterday a ship had landed three hundred men and four women—and that was four decent women more than any other ship had recently brought in. From what she and Tess heard, these four were wives of gold seekers, not more women of ill repute.

As she finished lighting the whale-oil lanterns, two tables filled with hungry miners. Before long, coffee was steaming on the stoves, then the new Chinese cook, Li, was flipping flapjacks. In the ten days since the restaurant opened, Tess had taught Li how to make eggs, ham, and flapjacks—the only breakfast available—though to hear most the miners talk, it was the best food they had ever eaten.

"Here come more customers," Tess said. "Just look at them. They smell the ham and flapjacks from the street. I told Warrick we'd be plenty busy. Before long I hope we can offer a little variety to the fare."

Louisa carried tin mugs of steaming coffee to the men, then helped Tess bring out the tin plates heaped with food. Among the dozen or so new customers drifting in, she recognized the beefy Hawaiian twins, Tio and Tao, who were guards from the Golden Palace.

With broad smiles they asked Tess, "All okay here?"

"All okay," she replied.

"Warrick Clark, he tell us keep eye on res'rant, too."

"We're glad to have you around," Tess said. "Is Warrick comin' by today? I want Louisa to meet him."

The Hawaiians eyed Louisa. "Maybe . . . maybe. We tell him new girl got red hairs. He like girls with red hairs 'n girls with yellow hairs."

Louisa tried not to smile. The round faces of the huge Hawaiians were so childlike it was impossible to take offense.

"And what does Warrick think about brown hair?" Tess teased, touching a hand to her own.

"Maybe . . . maybe," Tio replied uneasily.

Tao hastily added, "He like you cookin', Miss Tess."

"Well!" Tess huffed.

"An' you fine face," Tio interjected. "You bring in lots gold dust. Fine cookin', fine face."

"It took you a while to get to that," Tess replied, not quite concealing her amusement.

The miners around them laughed, and Louisa smiled herself, knowing she and Tess not only provided food, but a kind of decent entertainment for the men. Most were not as bad as she had dreaded, or perhaps she was becoming accustomed to them. As for Warrick Clark, she was eager to meet the man who owned the Golden Palace and restaurant herself. Tess seemed most impressed with him, but since Louisa's arrival he'd been visiting the goldfields to start a gambling hall there, too.

By nine o'clock, miners filled the tent and lined up on the dusty street. The tables were filled until mid-morning, then again at eleven-thirty, when they began to serve the daily special: a thick beef stew made with onions, carrots, and potatoes. Despite the sameness of fare, the men hadn't tired of it. Indeed, most of them considered the stew a feast.

Benjamin Talbot arrived at noon with several men from the shipping office. He scrutinized Louisa as she hurried to their table, carrying a tray full of mugs of steaming coffee. "Today is the first chance I've had to come in," he explained. "How was your first week in town?"

"Busier and noisier by far than at Casa Contenta," she admitted, "but we are doing well."

"Good. Aunt Jessica and the others are eager to hear your news. Let me introduce my friends—"

Later, when they had finished their stew, Uncle Benjamin appeared half satisfied that she and Tess were fine; he seemed especially gratified to see Tio and Tao look in on them.

"We have a shipment of split peas from Hawaii if you want to try a new dish," he said to Tess as he rose to leave.

"There are no soup bowls to buy anywhere," she replied ruefully. "That's why our stew is so thick . . . to keep it on the plates."

They chuckled, and Howard, one of the men, said, "Seems to me there are tin soup bowls in a new shipment."

"I'll take two hundred to begin!" Tess said. "And the peas and twenty hams. Send them over as soon as you can, and charge it all to Warrick Clark's account."

"We received dried apples today, and there are pie pans out back, too," Howard added. He smiled at Tess, as though he liked her looks. "You could make dried apple pie."

"Two barrels of apples to start!" she ordered with delight. "Won't the miners be pleased!"

"Whole town will be pleased," Howard said. "Especially me, now that I have made your acquaintance."

Tess beamed, delighted as ever to receive a compliment.

On the way out, Benjamin Talbot said, "Glad to see things are going well. I would be happy to come here Sunday morning to take you home for the worship service."

"It's kind of you to offer," Tess said, "but there is no chance of my taking the day off."

Louisa quickly said, "Perhaps I had better not come this Sunday, either."

"Are you sure?" he asked.

She nodded. "I can't leave Tess to do all of the work."

His brown eyes were full of disappointment.

The Golden Palace Restaurant closed from three to five, and Tess went out in search of turnips that someone said had come in on a ship from Chile.

Louisa retired to their room out back, so exhausted she slept almost the moment her head touched the pillow. An hour later, she was awakened by a knock. Still half asleep, she was astonished to find one of the Hawaiians accompanying a blonde woman in a red satin wrapper and dress.

The blonde's voice was harsh. "You Louisa?"

"Yes, you must be Faye. Tess told me you might come. Won't you come in?"

The woman snatched a package from the Hawaiian's hand and ordered, "Stay here 'til I come out, or you'll hear about it from Warrick."

The Hawaiian nodded solemnly, his eyes avoiding Louisa's.

Faye entered the room and scrutinized it. "Well, I seen a lot worse in this dust-hill town."

"It—is a dusty town, isn't it?"

"That ain't the worst." She set the package on Tess's bed, then slipped off her red satin wrapper. "But San Francisco's got its good side, as they say." Turning, she proudly displayed her low-cut gown.

Louisa stood speechless.

"I brought China silks," Faye offered. "Tess says you sew pretty good."

Uncertain whether she even cared to make the kind of dresses this woman might want, Louisa finally said, "I am hoping to open a shop here in town eventually."

"Don't forget I was yer first customer."

Like it or not, she must make a start as a seamstress, Louisa told herself. What right had she to judge Faye or anyone else . . . especially when she herself had run from her husband. She unwrapped the package and found patterns in unbleached muslin, as well as pieces of red and black silk.

"I want two dresses like this one I got on, except lower in front." Faye ran a tapering finger under the cut in the dress she had on.

"Lower? I do not think it is . . . possible."

Faye lifted her shoulders sensuously. "Let me worry about what's possible and what ain't. I brought a pattern for a long chemise, too. There's enough silk for one in both colors."

Red and black chemises? Shocked at the thought, Louisa sorted through the patterns to avoid the woman's gaze.

Faye said, "Warrick's got an artist comin' to paint pictures of me, so I need them chemises right away. Give them downstairs customers something interesting to get rich for, now that I'm workin' the game rooms upstairs."

Faye pulled on her red satin wrapper and turned to leave, but not before naming the generous amount she would pay for what she called "good work."

Once the door was closed, Louisa leaned against it. She must not judge others . . . no, she must not judge no matter how appalled she might feel about the woman. What's more, she would have to begin sewing immediately.

She went to her trunk and began to extract the sewing supplies. Later, her fingers trembled as she lay the pattern pieces on the smooth silk. But when it was time to return to the restaurant, she had already cut out both chemises and was stitching the black silk.

When Uncle Benjamin came into the restaurant several days later, he brought a letter from Aunt Jessica.

"What's it about?" Louisa asked him.

"Jessica was entirely close-mouthed about the matter. In fact, she made it clear I was merely the courier and was not to ask questions."

Perplexed, Louisa opened the letter immediately.

Dear Louisa,

Benjamin will depart for town in a few minutes,

so there is only time for this short note. A man worked for us in the fields for several days after he arrived by ship. Now that he has left, I learned he inquired about you. He described you fully and said you were a Talbot, though he gave your name as Louisa Setter. Someone told him you had moved away, but nothing else.

I felt it was my duty to let you know of this. I have not spoken of it to anyone else.

God bless you, my dear. May He give you wisdom. I shall keep you in prayer.

Aunt Jessica

Conduff? Louisa wondered, chilled.

For all she knew, he was here in San Francisco. He could even be in the restaurant now! Terrified, she glanced around the tent.

"Is something wrong?" Uncle Benjamin asked.

Louisa shook her head. "It's . . . nothing."

He eyed her curiously. "Seth Thompson is preaching at the plaza this weekend. I thought you and Tess might come."

"Perhaps," she said, though she knew very well they would not attend. She thrust the note into her apron pocket. "Let me get you a cup of coffee."

She kept an eye out for Conduff all day and showed Tess the note.

"It could be anyone from Alexandria who knows you're a Talbot," Tess decided. "Everyone knew you left. And it could be anyone who stopped at the Wainwright and Talbot warehouse here and heard about you. You mustn't make so much of it."

"Perhaps—"

"You look terrible, Louisa. You'd best lie down. Take a few

hours off now. The midday crowd is about done."

"I guess I will . . . at least a while—" She pulled off her apron and could not get out of the restaurant soon enough.

That evening there was still no evidence of Conduff, and Louisa ventured back to work, her eyes wandering warily over the men in the tent. If he were in San Francisco, wouldn't he have found her by now?

Benjamin Talbot returned to the warehouse. *What had Jessica written to cause Louisa such alarm?* he wondered. Not that he hadn't blanched today himself at the letter he had received from his friend, Jonathan Wilmington, at Oak Hill.

Arriving in his office, Benjamin sat down at his desk and reread a portion of the letter.

> Unfortunately, as you know, many of the miners here are not religiously inclined. But the heights of godlessness can be so appalling.
>
> Last Sunday a ventriloquist appeared at Sandy Bar for an evening performance. It was a Punch and Judy show, and ended with a production of the devil, horns and all, who looked terrifying according to all reports. The head and shoulders of this devil appeared just above the curtain, and he said, among other things, that in this wild region where there are no infernal laws to bother, no society, no ladies, and no churches to make a great fuss about nothing, it was perfectly proper and commendable to get drunk on Sunday and to do anything for a good time!
>
> So many of the miners are mere youths, and they fall prey to the many temptations placed before them. Sometimes it does seem that religion has taken a holiday here, though that is not quite correct. Our

church continues to attract new men, but the population is so transient. . . .

He must write immediately to encourage Wilmington, who was a comparatively new Christian. While the forces of evil seemed to far outweigh those of morality and religion, God always won the final battle. All that was needed was godly people who would make a strong stand for Him.

He reached for his quill and began the letter.

Dear Jonathan,

I am sorry to hear of the "devil's" appearance at Sandy Bar and wish that he would confine himself to only one place, but, alas, he is too busy everywhere.

In San Francisco, matters differ little. If anything, conditions are even worse, for here his subtle attraction for miners is increased by the contrast between a dismal lodging and the bright interiors of the saloons with their music. Drinking has become such an accepted pattern that to refuse a drink is to insult the one offering it. With wages and profits so high and everyone drinking, even the neophyte is encouraged in debauchery.

A good many miners are sending for their wives, and I hope for an influx of decent women to change matters for the better. Their presence always elevates a society, shames vice into the byways, lessens dissipation and places wildness within limits.

Though it seems our society will never recover its moral fiber, I am encouraged about the delegates' meeting in Monterey in September to write a state constitution. They have already appointed two chaplains, one Catholic and one Protestant, to open the sessions with prayer on alternate days. I pray statehood will not come too late, for there is talk of forming yet another vigilante committee.

He reread his words, then decided he must encourage Wilmington—and himself—through the Scriptures, for they were what endured despite every kind of civilization throughout the centuries.

Putting the letter aside, he prayed for guidance. As he sat silently, the answer came for him and for Jonathan Wilmington and all who sought righteousness. He added it to his letter.

In Proverbs we are told, "Trust in the Lord with all thine heart; and lean not unto thine own understanding. In all thy ways acknowledge him, and he shall direct thy paths. Be not wise in thine own eyes: fear the Lord, and depart from evil."

This is our answer until the Lord comes. We must stand firm in our faith and trust in Him. God is faithful.

Later in the afternoon, he went outdoors to stretch his legs. At Portsmouth Square, he caught a glimpse of Mr. Krafft, a strange but good fellow who spent his time taking care of men who were sick and dying of scurvy, dysentery, pneumonia, and typhoid fever. He wasn't a doctor, only a kindly man trying to aid the helpless sick while the doctors of California were knee deep in dirt and water out at the diggings, searching for gold themselves.

From the middle of the square, Mr. Krafft shouted to all who would hear, "Your honor and gentlemen! We are very sick and hungry and helpless and wretched! If somebody does not do something for us, we shall die. All we ask is a fair chance; and we say again, upon our honor, gentlemen, if somebody does not do something for us, we shall die!"

The miners listened, but only for a moment. A parade coming down the street offered more of interest. The miners pressed forward to see a crowd of tough men in ponchos with Spanish shawls about their shoulders; they carried knives and pistols.

"It's the Hounds!" someone yelled, and the crowd began to edge away.

In front of Benjamin, a miner muttered to a newcomer, "They call themselves the Regulators, but everyone else calls them the Hounds. They pretend to do 'justice,' but they attack stores, gambling houses, and foreigners."

"They're headed for the Chilean quarter!" someone shouted.

"Why aren't they arrested?" the newcomer asked.

"Because we ain't got no police force," the miner replied. "We ain't got no courts or judges that's worth a panned-out diggin'! San Francisco practically belongs to them Hounds!"

Before long a shot sounded, then screams, which were followed by a volley of shots in the Chilean quarter. Finally the Hounds returned with a fife and drum and even a flag flying; they were loaded with belongings, and smoke filled the sky over the Chilean quarter.

"Tonight they'll be out raiding the saloons and stores," someone muttered. "They'll make off with whatever they can carry and burn the rest."

Benjamin wiped his brow and headed back toward the warehouse, remembering what Wilmington had written about the devil's appearance in the diggings. It appeared that he and his henchmen were making a great effort in the California Territory; in the end, though, men on the side of evil would have to pay their dues. The Lord God was always faithful.

# 12

T he next day at the restaurant, Louisa watched for
  Conduff, her throat dry every time a big dark-haired
man entered the tent. Her body tensed at every deep-voiced
man's words. Even a "More coffee o'er here!" or a "More o'
them flapjacks!" set her nerves on edge.

Slowly the days passed and her fear dissipated.

Little changed in the restaurant except the fare, which
now included split-pea soup and dried apple pie. The
enthusiastic miners complimented Louisa and Tess, and
some men consumed entire pies at a sitting. Word about the
apple pies spread throughout town and, even after the pie
tins were empty and every dried apple in San Francisco was
eaten, men crowded into the restaurant. With such a
constant hubbub from morning to night, and her off-hours
busy with the sewing for Faye, there was little time for
Louisa's thoughts to dwell on Conduff.

One evening at the end of the supper rush, the
restaurant's usual din quieted. "That there's Warrick Clark,"
one of the miners said. "Supposed to be the smartest sportin'
man ever turned a card in New Orleans."

Louisa, stopping in the midst of serving stew, thought:
And maybe the handsomest. He was dressed in a fine black

frock coat and trousers, and a heavy gold chain led to the watch pocket of his gray brocaded vest. His diamond ring glittered richly in the light of the nearest whale-oil lantern. He was not overly tall, but like the brilliance of his ring, his presence drew everyone's attention.

Tess was busy on the other side of the tent, and Warrick Clark stopped in front of Louisa. His deep voice was softened by a slight Southern accent. "You must be Louisa," he said.

His brown eyes were so arresting that it took an effort to respond. "Yes, I am." Despite the lazy white smile beneath his trim moustache, his eyes appraised her quickly.

"Tess was right," he remarked, "with that red hair of yours, you're a draw for the restaurant. That is, unless you want to work in the Golden Palace. More money in serving drinks than stew, I'm sure you realize."

"I don't . . . that is, no, thank you! I wouldn't be right for that kind of work at all."

He raised his dark brow and manly dimples deepened in his cheeks. "Never know until you try, do you now?"

"I know that with certainty," she replied. "Now if you will excuse me, this stew is getting cold." She moved on quickly to serve the nearby miners, but when she looked up again, he was still watching her closely.

"Just wanted to see if everything was going smoothly here," he explained when she passed by him. "Please ask Tess to send up some supper for me, will you?"

"Of course."

When he left, conversation buzzed louder than ever in the tent. Nearby, a grizzled miner remarked, "Southern gentry . . . New Orleans."

"Ladies' man, ain't he? Jes' see how smooth he works 'em," another said.

Well, he certainly would not "work" her, Louisa vowed.

222

At least her experience with Conduff had taught her something.

"What did Warrick want?" Tess asked, hurrying to her side.

Best not to mention his suggestion for her to work in the Golden Palace. "He would like some supper to be sent up for him," Louisa said.

Tess beamed. "After this crowd thins out, I'll take it up to him."

"Do you think you should, Tess?"

"I've taken supper up to him before. I just didn't tell you . . . for fear you'd look at me just like you are now. You don't have to worry. He just likes me to be there, to walk around and inspect the gaming tables with him." She smiled ingenuously. "What did you think of him?"

"I think he is far too handsome and too charming to allow for a girl's good sense."

Tess laughed. "Almost what I told him myself!"

"And what did he reply to that?"

"That I was the first girl to ever say so." Tess's eyes turned away in happy reflection. "He finds me a refreshin' change from the girls in the Golden Palace."

*Oh, Tess, watch out!* Louisa thought.

To think she had worried about Tess being hurt by Hugh Fairfax. Warrick Clark was surely far more dangerous. Despite all of Tess's recent popularity, she was still all too innocent.

One afternoon Faye stopped by the room behind the restaurant for her black and red long chemises. She held them up and inspected them with a practiced eye. "Looks like good work," she decided. "I'll be wearin' 'em tomorrow for that artist."

Louisa swallowed hard.

Faye paid with gold dust and promised to tell the other gambling hostesses of Louisa's fine workmanship, once all of her own sewing was finished.

There was still no evidence of Conduff and, by the next week, Louisa had also finished Faye's dresses.

One night before they drifted off to sleep Louisa commented to Tess, "I never dreamed of earning so much money in all of my life."

Tess laughed. "Most folks complain of high prices for rooms and food, but Warrick provides both for us. Aren't you glad after all that we came to town?"

"I guess I am," Louisa admitted. "If only there weren't so many saloons!"

"Without gamblin' and saloons, the miners would never bring their gold to town. That's what Warrick says anyhow."

"He's right, I'm sure. I suppose it's because the saloons remind me of Conduff."

"Oh, Louisa! Are you still worryin' about him?"

"Not quite so much."

"I think you're just worryin' for nothin'. I still think it was someone else from Alexandria askin' about you at the ranch." Tess sighed. "You mustn't let your past ruin your life now. Why, what would my life be like if I did nothin' but remember my past, back when I was fat?"

Not much, Louisa had to agree.

"We have to move on," Tess said.

Louisa wished she could move on to Jonathan.

Before she fell asleep, she tried to imagine him out at the diggings, but in her mind's eyes, she could only see him smiling at her, his eyes so full of love. Why, oh, why did she have to ache so over him?

When Benjamin Talbot came into the restaurant for

dinner the next day, he told about the new volunteer police force of two hundred and fifty men, armed and ready. "The alcalde was finally stirred to action," he said, "but why did it have to take so much citizen anger?" He shook his head. "Ah, I almost forgot!" He produced a letter for Louisa from his frock coat pocket. "This one's from Jonathan."

She reached for it uneasily.

"He sent it back with Daniel. They had a fine time at Oak Hill, so fine that I missed my guess about both Jonathan and Hugh. They plan to stay out at the diggings for a while."

She swallowed with difficulty. "I see."

"We miss you at the worship services on Sundays, Louisa."

She flushed. "I would come if we weren't so busy. Now if you'll excuse me—"

She hurried off before he could invite her for the next Sunday. It was all very well for them to have their Sunday worship services, but they had a fine house and everything they needed. When she had such a decent place to live, she would attend services herself. The Baptists were building a church up the hill on Washington Street and others were forming churches, too; she would go when she had time again. She slipped the letter into her apron pocket, but it wasn't until three o'clock when she returned to the room that she found time to read it.

Closing the door behind her, she tore open the envelope, her heart pounding hard as she saw the pages of bold, slanted handwriting.

Oak Hill, California
Sunday, July 22, 1849
Dear Louisa,
　　　We had a most inspiring worship service this

morning at the church here in Oak Hill, and I was
reminded of our service the Sunday before I left.
Please accept my apologies if I pressed too hard about
you remaining at Casa Contenta. Despite your
making it clear—and kindly so—that I have no rights
in the matter, I care deeply about your welfare.
Nonetheless, I was wrong, for I should have left your
welfare in the Lord's hands, which I have now done.
Forgive me for my presumptuousness.

Hugh and I have moved into Jonathan
Wilmington's cabin. He is Rose Wilmington Talbot's
father. Perhaps you will recall that Joshua Talbot,
Hugh's friend from Boston, married Rose. The three
of them have established a church here with like-
minded miners and, although we have only been
here a short time, it is a most felicitous arrangement.
Mr. Wilmington discovered gold at the beginning of
the "rush" and concentrates now on developing the
town of Oak Hill as well as the church. It is
heartwarming to see so many miners finding the
Lord. How much more valuable than finding gold.

Oak Hill is a beautiful place. There are tree-
covered mountains to the east and the golden hills
and valleys to the west. I cannot imagine living in
San Francisco, for I find this even more beautiful
than Casa Contenta. Unfortunately most of the
miners do not have a warm, snug log cabin such as
the one in which we dwell, and they have turned
Oak Flats below into a foul place.

Hugh and I have not yet struck gold, but we
have decided to try for several months, perhaps until
the end of September. We tried panning in the
riverbed below Oak Flats, but we quickly learned we

did not care to stand forever in cold water. Mr. Wilmington has introduced us to several Indians who led him to gold, and we will set out with them for the mountains tomorrow morning.

Rose, Joshua, and Mr. Wilmington all extend an invitation for you to come with Benjamin Talbot in either August or September when he brings more provisions to Oak Hill. He tells us that Abby would like to accompany him, for she and Rose are best friends.

I pray that you have forgiven me for my overzealousness and that you might be here in August, my dear Louisa. Dare I even call you that? I cannot stop myself, for at the very least, you are a dear friend.

I shall uphold you in my prayers.

Yours sincerely,

Jonathan

P.S. Letters will reach me if sent in care of Joshua Talbot, c/o Oak Hill Mercantile, Oak Hill.

She reread the letter, cherishing his words, then devoured it again. My dear Louisa, he had called her. He did care for her. Yet what good did it do either of them? What good would it do to see him at Oak Hill or anywhere else?

Heartsick, she stuffed the letter into her trunk. She'd reply later, or perhaps it would be best not to answer at all.

As the summer wore on, all sorts of newcomers arrived in San Francisco: saloon girls, gamblers from New York and New Orleans, beachcombers from the islands, criminals from the convict colony of Australia, all manner of people who had never done an honest day's work and did not intend to in the midst of a gold rush.

One morning before the midday dinner rush, Louisa stood outside the restaurant for a breath of fresh air. The streets all around were abustle. Horses whinnied and wagons creaked through the dust, drivers shouting, "Watch where you're headed!" and far worse. Auctioneers bellowed outrageous prices for everything from sluice pans to miners' clothing, and others rushed madly about their affairs. Seeing Louisa, they nodded and hurried on. She heard the loud buzz of flies around the restaurant's garbage and, disgusted, moved along herself.

The streets were lined with tents and canvas houses and few real buildings. The most imposing place on Kearny Street was Parker House, a white two-story hotel with gingerbread trim; it had finally been completed after a year of standing half built for lack of workmen. Even before it was finished it had been filled, but now gamblers, who could pay more than most, rented valuable sleeping space for their gaming tables.

In the stores she saw miners buying red or blue shirts, corduroy breeches, and black boots. Most who returned from the goldfields with their pokes full of gold dust simply put on new clothes in the stores and threw their tattered ones out into the already littered streets. By tomorrow morning, much of the new clothing would already be soiled, for many of the men would have to sleep on the ground, choking in the dust. Every day the streets and hillsides of San Francisco were more crowded; it was growing not only bigger, but richer, dirtier, more foul smelling, and dangerous.

Returning to the restaurant, she saw it with new eyes, too. Outside, the canvas was covered with dust and soot and surrounded by weeds; inside, it smelled of dampness and smoke and unwashed miners. The red oilcloths on the plank tables were already cut where miners used it instead of plates, and the actual plates were thick and heavy and chipped.

Instead of napkins, the patrons used their handkerchiefs or shirttails.

What high hopes everyone had entertained that first dinnertime on the *Nimrod*, she thought. And there had been the tall tale Jonathan told about the Californian who had lived to two hundred and fifty years. As for "the qualities of California's climate being so salubrious for one's health," many of the miners died and others looked so sickly that they might not live another week. After such high hopes, how depressing the reality of life in San Francisco was.

San Francisco
August 14, 1849
Dear Jonathan,

Thank you for your letter of July 22. Oak Hill sounds very beautiful with the mountains behind you and the golden countryside all around. Unfortunately, San Francisco is not beautiful. Everywhere there are piles of wood and raw new buildings going up to replace the tents; however, more tents are brought in daily as the town continues to sprawl over the hills.

Tess received an offer to take charge of the Golden Palace Restaurant, and I have come to help her. We are so busy that we rarely have time to go outdoors. Our room is directly behind the tented restaurant, and it is so foggy these summer mornings that we rush the few feet to the tent and then work there until late at night. I do have two hours off in the afternoon, but I am quite occupied with sewing then. Days are so alike that it seems I have been here for months.

You were right about this being a raucous town,

for it is no longer safe for a woman to be out alone. When Tess goes shopping for the restaurant, one of the Hawaiian guards from the gambling house next door must accompany her. There are also many difficulties with the food supply so uncertain. This week we had a shipment of vegetables from Hawaii that included yellow squash and yams, helping us to vary our regular fare. Sometimes we receive fish from local fishermen, and hunters occasionally provide us with fowl and venison. How I took the variety of food for granted in Alexandria!

Uncle Benjamin comes by for his midday meal at least once a week, but I have not seen the rest of the family since leaving Casa Contenta. They asked that Tess and I stay, but we could not impose forever.

Gold ships continue to arrive daily, always packed with argonauts. The old-timers complain that the men arriving now include too many scoundrels. Most of the miners at the restaurant treat us well enough, perhaps because our Hawaiian guards walk through frequently. The miners are generous when their pokes are full of gold dust. We may not be out at the diggings, but as Tess says, "We are striking it rich." We think that in a month or two we will have sufficient funds to lease a lot and buy our own tent, tables, stoves, etc. Then we shall earn far more than a small percentage of the profit.

Louisa searched her mind for something else to write. She could not mention him calling her "my dear Louisa," nor did she wish to discuss Tess's avid interest in Warrick Clark.

She reread the letter.

The truth was that her life sounded dreary. Moreover, she hadn't been entirely truthful about the miners' treatment of her and Tess, for it was changing. The endless proposals of marriage were flattering, of course, but sad, too, since many of the men proposed at first sight.

And other men—Well, the moment the Hawaiians disappeared, they began to grab her and Tess and the other women who worked in the restaurant. One man had even ripped the sleeve halfway off Louisa's dress. When she had cried out with indignation, "What right do you have to touch me?", the drunken miner had guffawed. "Any girl pretty as you settin' herself out in this town oughta expect some manhandlin'!" he'd replied, and she feared he was right.

At times she thought she might scream if the constant hammering outside did not stop or if she heard another raucous chorus of "Buffalo Gals" or "Oh, Susannah."

Worse, she thought she would lose control of her tongue when Tess went on and on about Warrick Clark. "Isn't he the handsomest man you've ever seen?" she'd ask, and "I do believe he's comin' closer to proposin'!" Scores of men proposed to Tess, but he kept her at a distance. In the midst of her popularity, he provided her with a tempting challenge.

One evening Warrick strolled into the restaurant at closing time and, stopping before Louisa and Tess, he said, "Tess, I would like to escort your friend around the Palace tonight to show her the fruits of her workmanship."

Louisa froze, for she knew immediately that he referred to the chemises she had sewn for Faye. Moreover, she thought Tess might be furious at being excluded until she saw the intimate look Warrick bestowed upon her friend.

Tess beamed at him. "Of course, Warrick. You take her. She's beginnin' to think the whole town's as ugly as this tent.

She ought to see how nice the Palace is."

He turned and smiled at Louisa. "Your apron will not be required in the Palace."

"I–I am sorry . . . I am far too busy now."

Tess said, "You ought to go see it, Louisa."

"Perhaps another time!" she replied and hurried off.

She had heard the miners talk about the pictures the painter had done of Faye in the red and black chemises. She felt guilty enough already. Moreover, she did not trust Warrick. Tess might be blind to his faults, but Louisa decided that this time she would protect herself. She'd retrieve her gold dust from the Golden Palace's safe.

Late the next morning when the breakfast crowd had thinned out, she gathered up her courage and went into the gambling palace. Keeping her eyes off the paintings on the walls, she asked for the accountant.

It was an enormous relief not to encounter Warrick, and finally she did take possession of her gold dust. Tao accompanied her to Uncle Benjamin's warehouse, where she deposited her earnings in the safe.

During the next few days she worried that Warrick might stop for her again in the restaurant, but he was apparently too busy at the gambling tables to bother with a reluctant young woman.

One evening after visiting with the Hawaiians in the restaurant, Louisa told Tess, "Tio and Tao are fond of you, and they have hinted that Warrick often trifles with innocent women."

"I refuse to believe that! And I think it's terrible and ungrateful that you've taken your gold dust from his safe!" Tess said and stalked off.

At least she had been warned, Louisa thought. For her part, if Warrick bothered her, she would seek another place of employment. But where? Sewing was impractical since there were still so few women except saloon and gambling house girls. And without sufficient funds for their own restaurant, she and Tess would be reduced to peddling food on the streets like the men who hawked tin cups of gin and buckets of pickles.

On Thursday afternoon as she sewed herself a new lavender gauze dress, a loud knock sounded at her door. Opening it, she found Faye accompanied by one of the Hawaiians.

"I'm here for my dresses," she said, stepping in. She wore a tight, low-cut orange dress as bright as the rouge on her lips and cheeks.

"Fine. I finished the dresses yesterday."

Louisa opened her trunk, took out the red and black China silk gowns, and laid each carefully across her bed.

Faye took up the red dress, then the black. "They look good, better 'n I can make 'em anyhow. Next, I want another chemise like them others from this leftover silk."

"I am sorry," Louisa replied in as level a tone as she could manage, "but I will not make such clothing again."

"Well!" Faye huffed, her chin rising. "You got no call to act better 'n me! My money's as good as anyone else's!"

"I am not better than you," Louisa replied. "I only said I will not make such clothing again."

"I know what yer thinkin'," the blonde responded, taking a cloth pouch of gold dust from her pocket and throwing it on the bed. "You ain't so perfect yerself. Warrick figures yer hidin' somethin'—"

Louisa stiffened. "Why would he say that?"

"He has a sixth sense about women. How do you think he gets young girls workin' for him?"

Louisa clenched her hands. "What about innocent

girls like Tess?"

Faye gave a bitter laugh. "The innocent ones he reels in slow but sure. A little flirting here and there, then the next thing she knows, she's gettin' in deeper 'n deeper. He knows how to work a woman like a fisherman works a fish." She drew a slow breath. "I ought to know, I was one of 'em."

"Oh . . . I'm sorry."

"Don't gimme yer pity!" Faye snapped. "Anyhow, he'll drop Tess as fast as he dropped Roxanna, the girl before me. Don't matter anyhow. I'm leavin' this dust-hill town and goin' back to New Orleans as soon as I get a big enough stake for my own place. 'Faye's' I'm gonna call it, just 'Faye's.' Warrick'll be sorry."

"Is—isn't there some other kind of work you could do?"

Faye blinked with indignation. "Cookin' and sewin' and such ain't for me. Had enough of that once. Meantime I got to let that artist paint more pictures of me."

"You could have your choice of miners to marry here," Louisa said.

"You're right about that," Faye agreed with a brittle laugh, "but I don't want no houseful of squallin' brats. Besides, the men I go for . . . they don't take to marryin'."

"You could make a new life, Faye."

Faye glowered. "Now, don't start in on me with religion."

"But I didn't intend to. Where did you get that idea?"

Faye handed over the money for the clothes. "Don't know why I told you about me goin' to New Orleans. I hope you don't tell no one."

"I promise I won't."

Faye gathered up the dresses. "Thanks. And don't feel sorry for me either, 'cause if there's one thing I know, it's how to attract men."

"I guess you do," Louisa said. Unfortunate as that was for

her client . . . and probably for them, as well.

Late that evening while Louisa and Tess served supper in the restaurant, the grizzled boatman who had rowed them to shore from the *Pacifica* came in. "Heerd about ye two workin' in the Golden Palace Restaurant, 'n I figured ye were grubstakin' yer restaurant." He grinned broadly as he sat down at a table near the serving counter.

"How did you know it was us?" Tess inquired.

"I heerd it was the prettiest two young ladies in town!"

They all laughed, and Tess said, "For that fine compliment, I'll take your order."

Seconds later, to Louisa's and Tess's astonishment, Warrick Clark entered the tent.

"I'll wait on him," Tess said quickly. She hurried through the tables and benches to him, her face aglow.

When Louisa served the boatman his plate of stew, Tess returned to the serving counter. "He wants a piece of peach pie. Good thing I set a piece aside."

The boatman eyed her askance. "Ye ain't tied up with thet gambler, are ye?"

Tess's eyes narrowed. "What if I am?"

"If so, ye'll be sorry. Ye won't be the first girl he's taken in. When he sees fit, he'll drop ye like a hot potato."

Louisa caught Tess's arm before she could flounce off. "Please listen, Tess! I spoke to Faye this afternoon, and she says the same thing."

Tess wrenched away, furious. "I am not Faye!" she cried out. "I can take care of myself!"

# 13

A strong wind raked the city the first week of September, stirring up a terrible dust and setting everyone's nerves on edge. It whistled through the cracks of Louisa's and Tess's room, making the bedside candle flicker wildly as Louisa undressed for bed. How could they endure a winter here? Louisa wondered. As it was now, the room's temperature varied little from the weather outside. Worse yet, she felt homesick for her Alexandria brick house; in fact, everything about Virginia seemed preferable, except Conduff's presence.

Exhausted, she blew out the candle and crawled into bed, falling asleep to the raucous music from the gambling halls and saloons. It seemed only minutes later that she was roused by the ringing of the restaurant gongs.

"Fire!" someone shouted. "Fire! Everyone wake up!"

She sprang from her bed in the eerie pink light and inhaled the acrid smoke. "Tess, fire!"

Tess groaned in her sleep.

"Tess! Tess!" Louisa threw open the door to their room and was amazed to see the night sky illuminated with a frightening redness. Flames crackled and flared at the Golden Palace, and fiery cinders filled the sky.

She stood rooted to the floor in disbelief, then cried, "Tess! The Golden Palace is on fire! The Golden Palace and far more! Quick, put on your robe!"

"I'm comin'!"

Leaving the door open for light, Louisa pulled on her blue cotton robe and her shoes. "Our trunks! Pull them out!"

At their doorstep, a miner shouted, "I'll help ye!" He and another man shouldered the trunks and carried them out onto the street a safe distance from the fire. Others pushed and pulled their ready-built wooden room away from the restaurant, downwind of the flames.

"The wind's dropping," a man observed with relief, "but this whole ramshackle town could burn anyhow."

Men sprinted toward the fire with buckets of water, then began to form a bucket brigade; others spaded up a firebreak on the ground by Tess's and Louisa's room. Warrick Clark and Faye came running out of the smoke in their nightclothes, coughing and covered with soot, followed by the bartender and three of the saloon girls.

Tess rasped, "Warrick told me he wasn't seein' Faye!"

"Stay here by our trunks, Tess," Louisa urged, tugging her friend back before she created a scene she would surely regret.

Yellow and orange flames flared from the Golden Palace and spread rapidly to a neighboring saloon on the other side, then raced across the dried weeds to the restaurant tent, where they began to devour the canvas.

When Louisa and Tess started forward to help, the men shouted, "Out of the way!"

Throats dry with despair, they watched the flames race across the tent, ignite the whale-oil lanterns and burn the oilcloth-covered tables and wooden benches. Louisa thought she would never forget the flames' tortured dancing in the very place she had worked, nor the horrified fascination on people's faces as they gathered to watch.

The bucket brigade and the spaders toiled on, and at long last the flames flickered out beyond the tent at the firebreak where Tess's and Louisa's room stood.

A crowd of miners milled about, and Louisa was amazed to see Warrick Clark and Faye thread their way through them to approach her and Tess. His eyes moved to their ready-built room. "Glad to see you saved it. It's not much, but Faye and I will have a place to sleep."

Tess cried out in dismay, "You think you're going to sleep in Louisa's and my room?"

Warrick's brows drew together. "My room, Tess. I paid for it. I am the one who owns the lots."

"That's outrageous!" Tess replied. "What about all the money we made for you with the restaurant?"

"There's not as much profit in food as there is in gambling," he returned. "I'd planned to double the Golden Palace and, since we have to rebuild, we'll do it now. That means, Tess, no room on the land for a restaurant."

Tess asked angrily, "And what are we supposed to do?"

He lifted a dark brow. "You can stay the rest of the night in the room with Faye and me."

Tess reared back to slap his face, but he caught her wrist in midair. "As for later, you and Louisa can always work for me in the Golden Palace."

"Never!" Tess replied. "I will never work for you again!"

"Then go back to whatever you did before you came here. I imagine it wasn't as virtuous as the two of you pretend."

"How dare you!" Tess lashed out.

A smile tugged at his lips, and he kept his grip on her wrists. "I dare because I am the proprietor, the owner of the place, such as it is."

Tess finally extricated her hands from his grasp. "I never want to see you again!"

He laughed. "Fine. You're spirited enough, but I have always been more partial to blondes and redheads."

Tess's eyes widened with disbelief, then she whirled away. Louisa pulled her arm. "Come, Tess—"

Faye stood at Warrick's side in her soot-smeared red silk wrapper, smiling smugly. "You kin always sew for me," she said to Louisa, "but you know the sort of clothes I'll be wantin'."

"It is kind of you, Faye, but no, thank you."

Tess cried out at Warrick, "You have my gold dust—"

"Be quiet, you fool! Don't you have any sense? You'll have every thief in town combing the ashes. I've sent Tio and Tao to guard what's left of the Palace."

Louisa looked at the smoking ruins of the gambling palace and saw one of the hulking Hawaiians standing guard out front, pistols in each hand. Nearby, the miners watched as the fire slowly burned out, smoldering and sputtering here and there among the charred debris. Doubtless there was more than one shiftless man among them who would like to get his hands on the gold in the safe. Earlier, during the fire, she'd heard someone suggest that a disgruntled gambler had probably put a match to the place. "The Golden Palace is known to be crooked," he'd muttered. "Looks like a case of revenge."

"Come, Tess," Louisa said, pulling her friend away from Warrick and Faye. "We can sit down on our trunks to watch the Hawaiians search."

Tess allowed herself to be led back to the trunks. At length she said, "What a fool I was."

"Perhaps more of an innocent."

Tess nodded hopelessly and sank onto her trunk, shoulders slumped with dejection. "I daresay I know less about men than I thought."

"You are not the first one of us to learn that," Louisa returned.

While the ashes and charred wood of the Golden Palace cooled, the Hawaiians continued to search for the safe, but could find it nowhere. "Maybe somebody steal, then make fire," Tao suggested. "Maybe . . . maybe."

"Come, Tess, we'll go down to Wainwright and Talbot's," Louisa said to her tearful friend. "Uncle Benjamin said we are always welcome at Casa Contenta."

"At least I kept some gold in my trunk lately," Tess said as they began to drag their trunks behind them through the dust. "If nothin' else, I have enough to repay Hugh, and that's more than what I arrived with."

As they made their way down toward the bay, early morning sunlight danced on the silvery water. It might have been a splendid sight without the abandoned ships that stood as askew as drunken derelicts. How beautiful San Francisco must have been before the goldseekers had turned it into such a wretched place, Louisa thought. Unfortunately she felt as wretched as the town looked.

When roosters awakened them on Sunday morning at Casa Contenta, both Louisa and Tess had slept for ten hours. Tomorrow they would leave for Oak Hill, and Louisa, dressing in her best frock, felt her stomach churn uneasily at the thought of seeing Jonathan.

Dressed, she and Tess joined the Talbots and their neighbors in the white adobe parlor to worship and to hear Benjamin Talbot preach.

"Come sit with me," Abby said to Louisa, patting the

space beside her on a settee. "Daniel is going to assist with the service."

Louisa joined her, and Tess sat down beside them with little Daniel in her arms.

Abby said, "I am as excited as a girl about going to Oak Hill tomorrow. I haven't seen Rose since spring."

"I am becoming excited, too," Louisa replied. She was uncertain, though, whether she felt more delighted or distressed. It was so utterly senseless to subject herself to being near Jonathan. She looked down at the Bible in her lap, ashamed that she had hardly opened it since he gave it to her.

"Oak Hill must be one of the most beautiful places on earth," Abby vowed, her blue eyes sparkling.

Tess bounced little Daniel on her lap, eliciting gleeful chortles from him. "I'll be glad to see Hugh," she admitted, "though I am not so eager to tell him of my foolishness."

"Must you tell him?" Abby asked. "You're not betrothed to him, are you?"

Tess flushed. "No, but I would rather he heard what a fool I was from me than from anyone else." She sounded so concerned that Louisa wondered whether her friend felt a new appreciation for him.

Aunt Jessica began to play the prelude at the small pump organ that had come around the Horn, her hands moving over the keys with assurance.

Everyone quieted, and Louisa opened her Bible and thumbed through the pages. Here was the Bible Jonathan had given to her. His face rose before her from memory, causing her heart to ache.

As the service proceeded, Daniel read from Scripture in his low, resonant voice. "Now the Lord had said to Abram, 'Get thee out of thy country, and from thy kindred, and from thy father's house, unto a land that I will show thee.' "

How like her life, Louisa thought. She had left her country and her father's house, too.

" . . . I will bless thee," Daniel read on, "and make thy name great; and thou shalt be a blessing: And I will bless them that bless thee. . . . "

Benjamin Talbot stood up beside the organ to begin the sermon. "One of history's greatest moments occurred on that ancient day when God sought out a trusted servant, Abram, and showed him a path designed to change the course of events in heaven and on earth.

"When that covenant was born, the stage was set for a plan that would bring reconciliation—through Jesus Christ—between God and the 'scattered' who were estranged from Him on earth."

His eyes met Louisa's across the room, and it appeared he was speaking to her.

"God's plan for triumph began with this covenant. First the promise, 'I will bless thee' . . . then an obligation, 'And thou shalt be a blessing' . . . then a prophetic note, 'By thee all the families of the earth shall bless themselves.'"

Louisa recalled Dr. Norton's words in Alexandria: "I sense great potential for the Lord to use you."

How she had failed God. She was a blessing to no one . . . to no one at all. What a failure she had been in God's plan for mankind.

Benjamin Talbot continued, "I often think of God using us like prisms. As he blesses us with His light, His love is diffused through us to extend to those around us until His light extends over the entire earth. Scripture tells us, 'Let your light so shine before men, that they may see your good works, and glorify your Father which is in heaven.' "

The words of the sermon unfolded in her mind and her

heart. How determined she had been to follow the Lord upon dedicating her life to Him—yet since leaving Alexandria, she had wandered ever farther away. Her downfall had begun with not telling about her marriage, with her lie of omission. Soon after, she had stopped reading Scripture, then gradually she had forgotten to pray except when she was desperate. She had even avoided attending worship services, and finally she had begun to slide over the edge by sewing the shameless garments for Faye.

"Heavenly Father, forgive me," she prayed. "I was so determined to be independent of others that I became independent of Thee as well. Forgive me . . . forgive me. As for Jonathan, I have been yearning for him. Worse, I slowly allowed him to take Thy place when I know Thou should be first in my heart . . . and that Thou art all-sufficient for me."

The passage of recent months unreeled in her mind in counterpoint to the sermon. Hundreds, perhaps thousands, had died on their way to California, but God had saved her from the shipwreck and preserved her through their ordeal in Panama. Surely He had done so for a purpose. If so, she would learn as His path opened before her; He would impart His directions to her daily. For now, it was sufficient to know that she was blessed . . . blessed to be a blessing.

Benjamin Talbot said in conclusion, "If there are any here who wish to dedicate or rededicate their lives to the Lord, let them do so now."

Louisa prayed, "Oh, Heavenly Father, I do rededicate my life to Thee and ask that Thou wouldst use me to Thy glory . . . help me to be a blessing to others—renew that first great joy in me. . . . "

When she opened her eyes, light shimmered in the white adobe parlor as though it were filled with the radiance of the eternal place. Everyone in the room appeared transformed in her sight, looking wondrously beautiful no matter how old or wrinkled, how ill-favored of face or form, how richly or poorly dressed. The radiance was so dazzling that it seemed to be a foretaste of heaven. "I thank Thee, Lord! Oh, how I thank Thee for allowing me to see these people through Thy loving eyes . . . for filling me with Thy love for them." Her heart felt as if it might burst with gratitude and love, and she sang out the final hymn with the others with a fervency she had never before known:

"More love to Thee, O Christ,
More love to Thee!
Hear Thou the prayer I make
On bended knee;
This is my earnest plea,
More love, O Christ, to Thee,
More love to Thee . . .
More love to Thee."

After the benediction and postlude, she made her way to Benjamin Talbot and softly informed him, "I have rededicated my life to the Lord this morning."

He beamed. "I thought perhaps you had. You seemed to fill with joy and love. May you always be a great blessing wherever you go."

"Thank you," she said politely, though her heart thundered exuberantly.

Monday morning was glorious as she rode through the golden countryside. She held the reins lightly as the four mules pulling the supply wagon moved steadily onward. Never in her life had she dreamed she might drive a wagon, but with so many men at the diggings, there had only been four neighbors to hire. She felt aglow with joy, though it had nothing to do with going to Oak Hill.

"Whatever has gotten into you?" Tess asked as she rode up alongside the wagon on a bay mare.

"The joy of the Lord," Louisa replied. At her friend's bewildered expression she added, "It's not the kind of happiness you can work up yourself. At least, I have certainly never been able to."

Tess smiled, her heart-shaped face looking sweet under the white sunbonnet. "I feel happier now, too. And I don't care if I never see San Francisco again."

"Nor I." Louisa turned to gaze out over the mules at the magnificent golden countryside ahead. "To think that I hoped to find happiness . . . or fulfillment there or anywhere else without Him—"

"Without Jonathan?"

Louisa shook her head slowly from side to side. "Without allowing God to be of foremost importance in my life!"

A slight frown marred Tess's smooth brow. "Aren't you worried that we'll be disappointed in Oak Hill as well?"

"I know in my spirit that He is going before me to work matters out, that He holds my future in His hands. I have never before felt so sure, so entirely certain."

Tess appeared ill at ease. "After our midday stop, I'll trade off ridin' for drivin' the wagon."

"If you like . . . or if Abby wants to exchange places with you." It truly didn't matter, she realized, for she was more content than she had ever been in her life. She had taken time to read Scripture before leaving and recalled what Paul had written to his beloved Philippians in the first century: "for I have learned, in whatsoever state I am, therewith to be content." Happily, once she had turned to Him, the Lord had filled her with sweet contentment, too.

When the sun beamed down from directly overhead, they stopped for their noon meal. Aunt Jessica had sent beef stew, biscuits, and apricot pie with them from the hacienda, and they built a campfire to make coffee and heat the stew. Louisa helped the other women set out food and utensils, then they sat down on the ground with their "eating pans" which they held by their wooden handles.

"I wonder if Hugh will be happy to see me?" Tess asked.

"Certainly he will!" Louisa assured her. The weather was warm, even sitting in the shade, and she was glad that Aunt Jessica had talked her into wearing a sunbonnet.

"And Jonathan?"

"It is no longer quite so important to me," Louisa replied. It was true. She no longer ached at the thought of him. In her mind, he took his proper position as a friend. "The Lord has changed my thinking," she told Tess, who eyed her askance. It occurred to her that she must pray more often for Tess.

An hour later they commenced their afternoon ride, Louisa continuing in the wagon so that Abby might enjoy riding the bay mare and be free of her motherly duties while little Daniel napped.

The turning wagon wheels brought to Louisa's mind the wheels turning through this golden countryside in the past. Aunt Jessica had spoken of the Spanish padres bringing their knowledge of Christianity to California and the carretas they had introduced to the land. Now wagon wheels like these rolled to the goldfields. With so many emigrants arriving, surely there would be carriages and who knew what other conveyances rolling through this countryside for years to come. How many would carry someone who shared her joy? She hoped it would be many, a great joyous multitude who loved the Lord.

Everyone was agreeably tired when they stopped for the evening. After supper they sat around the campfire and exchanged tales of their travels to the West—coming "over," "under," and "across" as everyone called the modes of travel to California. "Over" referred to overland by covered wagon; "under" was sailing under South America around the Horn; and "across" meant the trek across Panama or even Nicaragua or Mexico. The horses, loosely corralled in the middle of their wagons, occasionally snorted as Abby and Daniel told of their trek by covered wagon from Independence.

One of the drivers who had doubled the Horn by brig told of the endless sea voyage. Louisa and Tess shared some of their harrowing adventures in traveling across Panama, though poling up the vine-choked Chagres River in a native bungo now sounded more like an adventure than an ordeal.

The stars came out, and Benjamin Talbot led the evening's prayers, then the singing. Louisa wished for an instant that it was Jonathan leading out so joyously with "Amazing Grace," but she immediately turned the wish over to the Lord.

The men decided on guard duty hours, then it was bedtime and everyone readied themselves to sleep under the starry sky. Louisa crept into her bedroll, her heart brimming so with gratefulness that she could not help praying, "I thank Thee, thank Thee, for this beautiful day. Oh, Lord, how I thank Thee for blessing me so."

Day after day, the weather remained warm and glorious as they drove the six supply wagons through the golden hills. Only the food became tiresome as their supplies dwindled to onions, carrots, potatoes, and a bit of salt pork. There were, however, wild greens to add as the trail led higher into the hills. If all went well, the journey would take less than a week. Louisa continued to give thanks and to read on in the Book of Philippians.

The scenery changed, growing ever more magnificent as the mules and horses churned up the dusty trail into the mountains. They rode alongside a stream, and above them stood foothills forested with oak, cedar, and pine, and occasional glimpses of distant cloud-crowned mountain peaks.

Riding past her wagon on horseback Benjamin Talbot explained, "This stream leads up to Oak Flats and then higher to Oak Hill."

"Then we are almost there!"

"By midday," he replied, smiling at her excitement.

Louisa reminded herself that Oak Flats, crowded with argonauts, might be a disappointment. Perhaps even Oak Hill would not be as beautiful as Jonathan had written. Yet as they wound through a ravine toward Oak Flats and the miners' tents came into view, the forested hillsides imparted a majesty to the scene.

Before long, they rode on a rutted trail alongside the stream and tents, then into the camp. The miners gawked at them, especially at her, Tess, and Abby.

"What ye carryin' fer sale with ye?" they shouted.

Benjamin Talbot had been riding near the women's wagons. "Sluice pans, shovels, pickaxes, clothes, boots, and foodstuffs. You have to buy it up at Oak Hill now. I am selling directly to the Mercantile."

"Why's that?"

"They pay their bills promptly, and they are always here to serve you," he replied.

"Expect we'll come up there then," one of them with a fierce sunburn answered. "The fly-by-night tent stores here ain't so good. When they've got all our gold dust, they don't care if we never buy from 'em again."

Louisa scrutinized the miners as she rode past. Nearly all

were bearded, their red and blue flannel shirts faded and torn, black boots and wide-brimmed hats scruffy, trousers a muddy brown. Some wielded pickaxes in the hills, but most stood knee deep in the stream, swirling water in metal pans. They all looked as worn as their ragged clothing.

Benjamin shouted to one of them, "Still finding gold?"

"Ain't as good as last fall. Be better come spring when the river's full."

Another added, "Wasn't nothin' but puddles this summer, but it's started rainin' in the mountains agin."

It was a wonder they didn't die or at least get rheumatism, Louisa thought as she observed their living conditions; she was glad that Hugh and Jonathan had given up panning.

The actual tent town of Oak Flat was located in a gap between the hills. It reminded her of the seamier sections of San Francisco, though set among the mountains. Benjamin Talbot had told them there would be lots of saloons, several gambling tents, and a few stores—and on the whole, no place for young women. As usual, he had been right.

Beyond Oak Flats, the stream made a wide bend and the land rose steeply. Blackberry vines tangled the underbrush that lined the rocky trail up to Oak Hill. It was so steep that at first Louisa worried whether the mules would be able to pull the heavy wagons, but they plodded on steadily until they arrived at the top.

The sun stood directly overhead as they rode up into the clearing where a cluster of log cabins stood shaded under feathery pines, fringed cedars, and acorn-bearing oak trees. Behind them were log outbuildings and a corral that held burros and horses, and beyond was a pasture with a dozen or so grazing cattle. Higher up, miners pickaxed at the rocky hillsides.

"I'll let them know we're here," Benjamin Talbot said, and he rode ahead, leaving puffs of dust behind him.

Before long, someone yelled, and people ran from the largest cabin. Apparently it was a church, for a wooden cross stood over the doorway. To Louisa's delight, Jonathan came out with the others, and waved enthusiastically upon seeing her.

"You came!" he called out, his face wreathed in a great smile. "And you are wearing a sunbonnet!"

She laughed, for she had nearly forgotten about it. She reined in the mules at the nearby hitching post. "Tess is three wagons behind me."

"So I see," he replied, waving and calling back a welcome to her. "Won't Hugh be pleased!"

As the mules stopped, he took the reins from her. "Here, let me help you down. I never thought I would see you driving a mule wagon. You must be worn out."

"Oh, I have become ever so strong now." He was taking her hand, helping her down, and her body was still aquiver from the hours of bouncing on the wagon seat. His hazel eyes probed hers with such interest that she found herself adding, "I am strong in the Lord now, too, Jonathan."

Wonder-struck, he set her down on the ground. He hesitated, then caught her in an exuberant embrace. "Oh, Louisa, I have prayed endlessly for that! I cannot think of anything that would make me happier, unless—"

"You look fine, too, Jonathan," she interrupted, pulling away, "just fine." He did indeed look wonderful, somehow taller and his shoulders broader. "Like a miner, but without a beard, thank goodness."

His smile had faded slightly, but not entirely as he said, "I am a miner. And I remembered to send my first nugget of gold off to Ellie and Oakley . . . unfortunately a small one."

Perhaps he thought she was being circumspect because people were about, and, of course, she was . . . but for more than that reason. She loved him now only as a Christian brother. Nevertheless, she was glad that she had worn her dark blue sprig muslin dress, for he looked at her with such pleasure.

"You are wearing the dress Abby painted you in," he observed, the cleft in his dark chin deepening.

"I am surprised you remember." In fact, it was surprising that he would know.

He replied in an odd tone, "It's the sapphire shade of your eyes. It is unlikely I'd forget."

"Well—" she said, "there are Hugh and the others."

Hugh was helping Tess down from her wagon, looking strong and healthy, even from a distance, and Abby was embracing a young woman, who must be her friend, Rose. Nearby Benjamin Talbot shook hands with a man whose hair was the same chestnut shade as hers, probably Louisa's cousin Joshua, then with an older man, likely Rose's father.

Hearing the soft rush of the river and the wind in the pine trees, she stood for a moment to admire the scenery. "You were right about Oak Hill, Jonathan. But even after you told me, I didn't expect such beauty."

"It is not nearly so beautiful as you—"

"No, please. I–I must clarify my position. I should have some time ago." She saw the others congregate at a hitching post near the church, awaiting them. Now was no time to explain about Conduff. "Later, I must speak with you. This afternoon perhaps, if we could walk."

"Yes, of course. Did you receive my last letter?"

"I only received one."

"I sent another several days ago." He looked disappointed, then a bit relieved, and the tension in the air between them lessened. "Come, let me introduce you to Rose and Joshua Talbot, and to Jonathan Wilmington."

Tess and Hugh were just behind them, Hugh, bearded and smiling his Adonis smile. "What a pleasure to see you again, Louisa," he said. "How do you like Oak Hill?"

She looked out at the cluster of log houses and the church under the trees, at the flowers blooming around the buildings. On the other side of the river, the steep slope of oak, cedar, and pine shimmered in the midday sunshine. "It is the most beautiful place I have ever seen, but then I am unaccustomed to mountains."

"Has Jonathan pointed out his cabin?"

"His cabin?"

Jonathan nodded uneasily. "There, the new one on the end." He hastened to add, "It is not nearly completed. The others helped me begin it only three weeks ago."

The new log cabin, its wood still pale, stood at the edge of the feathery pine trees.

He said, "It is not nearly so fine as your house in Alexandria . . . or Oakley's in Baltimore."

He was looking at her so earnestly that she turned to the cabin again. Matters still stood as they had between them months ago, she reminded herself, but how she'd like to live here with him as his wife. In any case, there was no sense in wishing for things that could not be. "It is very nice," she replied without so much as a quaver in her voice.

Moments later, she was being introduced to the others. Rose Wilmington Talbot, a raven-haired young woman with circles of high color in her cheeks, opened her arms in welcome. "How happy I am to meet you, Louisa. I have heard so much about you."

Jonathan introduced her to her chestnut-haired cousin, Joshua Talbot, who owned the Mercantile, and to Rose's father, Jonathan Wilmington. "And here come Maddy and Moses," he said about the free-black couple who worked for them.

"Before we get too comfortable," Benjamin Talbot said, "let's drive the wagons to the Mercantile and be done with them so we can enjoy dinner. Rose says there's venison."

"Then let's be under way!" Hugh exclaimed laughingly.

Jonathan said to Louisa, "Let me drive your wagon in. Town is only a short distance away, and you will want to get off here with Abby and Rose."

Louisa hesitated. "They would probably like to visit alone for a while, and I am eager to see the town myself. I would, however, be more than happy to relinquish the reins."

Jonathan smiled hopefully at her, finally saying, "I am eager to show you my new cabin, too."

She knew very well that she should not encourage him, but there was nothing to say except, "After dinner perhaps?"

"Yes, after dinner."

Rose's father decided he and Moses would bring their own wagon into town so everyone could ride home in it while the supplies were unloaded at the Mercantile.

Jonathan sat down beside her on the supply wagon seat, and she thought how fine it felt to be with him. They set off, bouncing with the other wagons through the woods for the Mercantile. Before long, she was laughing delightedly at the "town" of Oak Hill. "It is only a few log stores, the Mercantile, and a restaurant with red gingham curtains!"

"And a blacksmith and laundry down the way. It's not Alexandria or Baltimore," Jonathan said, "but I am becoming far more partial to log buildings than I was to so much brick."

"I believe I am, too," Louisa decided. "And what a blessed contrast this is to San Francisco."

"That's why I would like to live here, to set down roots. Wagon train emigrants with families are coming in now, and many of them want to live in a decent town, too. The lawless element usually stay around Oak Flats, but they come up for supplies because of our lower prices."

The dozen or so bearded miners in town added vitality to the place. They strolled in and out of the Mercantile and the restaurant, looking at the supply wagons, then turning surprised glances at her and Tess. Unfortunately, several were lurching down the dusty road drunkenly.

Jonathan whoaed the horses and jumped down from the wagon seat. "Here, let me help you."

She was halfway down from the wagon when she noticed that nearby a tall, black-bearded miner had staggered to a halt, his green eyes roving over her before they filled with recognition.

"Well, now—" the miner began, his voice far too familiar. "Always reckoned on findin' you out here 'round Talbots, and it looks like I finally did."

Conduff! It was truly him!

Louisa's feet hit the ground with a thud.

"Cain't get away from yer husband, cain you, honey-woman?" he asked with satisfaction. "Well, now . . . you won't be runnin' away agin."

# 14

Once it had frightened Louisa to see Conduff ravaged by drink, but now she felt strangely calm. Even the gun and knife stuck in his belt did not alarm her. *I do thank Thee even in this, Lord,* she prayed silently. *Show me what to do.*

"Louisa—" Jonathan began.

She knew he would take command if she gave the merest hint of a request. "Thank you for your concern," she responded quietly, "but this is between me and . . . my husband."

A smug smile spread across Conduff's face, his yellowed teeth showing through his unkempt black beard. His voice deepened to a suggestive rumble. "Be mighty handy havin' you 'round agin . . . honey-woman."

*He still considers himself that sleek black panther of a Blue Ridge charmer,* Louisa thought through her numbness.

"Got you by surprise, I reckon," Conduff went on smoothly. "Bet you wonder how I knew you'd be here."

"Yes, I do."

"I got aholt o' thet letter you sent Tess and then o' one yer fine Talbot kin sent askin' you to come. After thet, it was easy enough to follow a red-haired woman."

She tensed.

"I only come to claim what's rightly mine."

Tess and Benjamin Talbot began to step forward, but Louisa stilled them with a movement of her hand.

"You kin move out to the diggin's with me now," he added.

When she made no reply he took hold of her arm. "Likely make yer share o' gold dust washin' for miners, even if you are a Talbot. Them washin' women find more dust in a day's washin' than most miners grub up in a day."

His sour breath assaulted her senses, but she did not allow herself to back away, nor to be angered at his suggestion. Her voice was controlled. "I am saddened to see you are still drinking as heavily as ever, Conduff."

"Ain't yer affair! You know I don't take no naggin'. Now you come along—"

Tess spoke up furiously. "You killed Louisa's father, and you killed her child with your awful beatin's. You are a brute and a monster, Conduff Setter! You've no right to my friend."

Conduff blinked at Tess's onslaught. "A husband's got the right to beat a wife if he wants. Didn't know about a brat—"

Louisa's eyes closed with hurt for an instant, though her calm remained. "Conduff, I will go back with you, but on one condition. You must give your life entirely over to Christ, for only He can save our marriage and deliver you from drink."

"Never!" he spat. "I heard enough o' that in the Blue Ridge, 'n then from you!" His fingers dug deeply into the soft flesh of her arm. "No church!"

"You can pray anywhere to receive Him into your heart—"

His fingers dug in painfully again. "I ain't gettin' religion nowhere!"

Mr. Wilmington's wagon rumbled to a stop at the hitching post. "Let loose of that woman, Setter, or we'll run you out of town again!" he yelled. He leapt down to the dusty road. "There's plenty of us here to do it, too!"

Startled, Conduff released Louisa's arm.

"I shall wait for your decision until Sunday, Conduff," she said, stepping away. "If you give your life over to the Lord, I shall go with you wherever you wish."

"You ain't seein' me in no church!" he retorted.

"I leave that to you. The Lord wants each of us to decide for ourselves—either yes or no."

His green eyes roved over Jonathan, Hugh, Joshua, Moses, Benjamin Talbot, Mr. Wilmington, and the other wagon drivers, then he retreated a step. Turning to Jonathan, he said, "I seen how yer lookin' at her. You ain't puttin' nothin' past me!"

"Louisa is a decent young woman," Jonathan replied stiffly, "and you had better speak to her as such in my presence."

Conduff's eyes glittered. "I'll kill you first!"

Appalled, Louisa expected him to reach for his gun, but he was either unaware of it or wished to avoid facing all of them. She gulped. "I hope to see you on Sunday then, Conduff."

His lips worked angrily, but he made no reply.

Benjamin Talbot said to Conduff, "Let me buy you a cup of coffee in the restaurant . . . dinner if you like."

"I don't take no free coffee or dinner from no one!" After delivering a last infuriated look at Louisa and the others, Conduff staggered away.

Relieved to see him head down the road toward Oak Flats, Louisa silently prayed, *I thank Thee, Lord, for giving me such calm. Help me to endure whatever lies ahead.*

"Let's go home," Mr. Wilmington suggested into the quiet. .

Louisa dared not meet the others' eyes as they started for his wagon. Finally sitting down in it, she mustered a humiliated, "I am sorry. I should have told all of you, but I . . . simply could not."

Tess sat down on the seat beside her, slipping an arm around her shoulders. "You didn't owe it to anyone to tell."

On the other side of her, Jonathan said not a word.

Sudden tears blurred Louisa's vision. "I must tell you all now. I prayed for Conduff for years. I prayed mightily. Finally my pastor in Alexandria suggested leaving as a way of defense, though I cannot use Dr. Norton as an excuse. It was my decision to leave Conduff, and perhaps a hasty one—"

Tess interrupted, "But your father had just died . . . and you'd lost the child!"

Louisa nodded, not wishing to say more.

"Gid-dup!" Mr. Wilmington urged the horses before speaking out with feeling, "I can understand why you would leave. I'd have done so myself, had I been in your shoes."

Benjamin Talbot nodded from the next wagon.

"Thank you." She appreciated their support, but she wished Jonathan would say something.

Hugh said, "Setter's wild and unprincipled. We had to run him out of town just last week."

"If only someone had shown me how unprincipled he was when I was fifteen," Louisa said, though it seemed a lame excuse.

Mr. Wilmington added, "I admire what you said to him. Only the Lord can change us. I had to learn that the hard way myself. We must all pray for Conduff."

"Worst of all," Tess said, "her own father pushed her into marrying him." She hugged Louisa more tightly. "How could you be so calm with him? I daresay I'd have boxed his ears good."

Louisa replied softly, "Fighting Conduff with fists is useless. The only possibility is with God's love."

The wagon bounced along the grassy trail, and an uneasy silence filled the mountain air. Louisa bowed her head and began to pray for him . . . and for Jonathan to forgive her for not telling him about Conduff long ago.

When they arrived at the log settlement, Jonathan helped her down from the wagon, his voice tight. "Is that what you wished to tell me on our walk this afternoon?"

"Yes." She looked down in guilt. Forgive me, Jonathan! her heart cried, but she ached too terribly to get the words out. She must be content to be married to a changed Conduff, for God would turn him into a new creature if he only gave his life to Him. "Please pray for Conduff's conversion."

Jonathan nodded. "I am . . . and I shall. If I can . . . help in any other way, you must let me know."

"Oh, Jonathan, you're so good. Please forgive me."

"I have, Louisa. I forgave you for whatever the problem was between us a long time ago."

Rose had not only prepared venison, but carrots, corn bread stuffing with onions and mushrooms, and potatoes with gravy. "It is just like our Thanksgiving dinner last fall," she said, trying to cheer them. "We're two months early, but it's suitable, for we are so thankful to have all of you here. Poor Maddy did most of the work."

The rotund black woman, wearing a white turban around her head, beamed as she bustled back toward the kitchen. "It be a blessin' to have such fine folks to cook fo'."

The dinner proceeded as though nothing had happened

by the Mercantile, though Jonathan, seated at the far end of the table, remained overly quiet, as did Louisa. Abby and Rose exchanged news across the table, and Tess and Hugh renewed their friendship.

For dessert they ate rice pudding, and Hugh told how he and Jonathan had discovered gold in the mountains with the Indians. "Enough for a good start and enough to invest in Oak Hill," he said.

When Tess asked Jonathan about his plans, he appeared uncertain and confessed, "I still await the Lord's leading."

As do I, Louisa reflected. It seemed that her future hung as never before in the balance.

The afternoon stretched into an eternity for her, though the others were kind. Rose drew her apart from the others and said, "Joshua explained to Abby and me what happened today. You'll see, Louisa, God will work matters out. It wasn't so long ago that I was praying for Joshua's conversion. All of my despair then was as nothing compared to my joy now."

"Thank you, Rose. I do thank you for telling me, but you were not married to Joshua then, and I am . . . to Conduff."

Rose nodded. "The men think you should stay here in my cabin when you and Tess aren't sleeping at Father's. They are worried that Conduff might try to kidnap you."

"I have thought of that. He might try if he knows where I am, but he becomes confused when he has had too much drink. Oh, Rose, I am sorry to have brought this trouble to you."

Rose took Louisa's hands in her own. "Even though we don't yet know each other well, I believe you would stand with me if I were in your place, Louisa."

"Yes, I expect that's true. I would try to help you."

Rose squeezed her hands comfortingly. "Would you like to help us make cushions for Jonathan's cabin?"

"I'll try."

It would be preferable to make cushions for almost anyone else's home, but she must stay occupied.

That afternoon as she sewed, she reflected on her past. How she had hoped that leaving Alexandria would make life better. Then she had pinned her hopes on the move from San Francisco to Oak Hill. It appeared one couldn't run from problems, for like Conduff, they followed.

Later, Abby approached her. "I know how difficult this must be for you, my dear cousin. I want to tell you that Daniel prayed unendingly for my salvation, and I shall never be able to thank him enough. I have thought and thought about your trouble, and I know it was God's leading when you spoke to Conduff. We must pray fervently for him, no matter what we prefer ourselves."

"You are a confirmation for what I told him," Louisa said.

"Come, let us hold hands and pray," Abby said.

Later, Maddy said, "Moses 'n me is prayin' hard fo' you, Miss Louisa. We're truly bearin' down."

Tears of gratefulness welled in Louisa's eyes.

The men were working on Jonathan's log cabin, hoping to finish it before the autumn rains began. Louisa hadn't visited the cabin with Tess and the others, but she saw from the parlor window that it overlooked the river and the mountain slope. Jonathan had mentioned a newly acquired grizzly bear rug and a few pieces of furniture. Louisa tried not to think of living in such a house herself, living with Jona— She forced her thoughts away and prayed, God's will be done.

While she stitched the blue squares of fabric together for Jonathan's dining room chair cushions, she listened vaguely as Abby and Rose discussed their lives in the West. How happily married they were: Abby with her "little Daniel" and

Rose so delighted to be expecting a child herself. If only—

Louisa firmed her resolve; she couldn't allow herself to envy them. She already had a husband.

That night when she and Tess retired to the guest room of Mr. Wilmington's cabin, Tess admitted, "I do care for Hugh again. I daresay I have learned some valuable lessons about myself and men on the voyage, and in San Francisco. Hugh says he's learned some himself. It seems he couldn't stop his gamblin' until Jonathan and Joshua helped him."

"Did you tell Hugh about Warrick Clark?"

"Yes. Ashamed as I was, I told him. To my amazement, he was furious with Warrick, absolutely furious! Oh, Louisa, I know I shouldn't bother you now, when you have enough trouble with Conduff, but I think Hugh is goin' to declare himself. He says he has missed me beyond belief."

"And what did you tell him?"

"That I'd missed him, too. I finally got all that 'livin' my own life' done with, not to mention playin' the southern belle with men. I finally realized it was my mother's way, but it needn't be mine, too."

Louisa smiled at her friend before blowing out the candle. "I'm happy for you. When I first saw you and Hugh together in Chagres, I thought you looked as though God had meant you for each other."

"Did you truly?"

"I did. And I still do."

Tess made no further mention of Conduff or Jonathan, and before long she was breathing deeply with sleep while Louisa tossed and turned and prayed throughout the night.

Saturday seemed endless, a timelessness. The seconds and the minutes and the hours overstrained and then overstretched themselves. When Louisa wasn't helping to prepare meals, she stitched on carefully, thinking how lovely matching blue curtains would be on Jonathan's dining room windows. It was just the shade of her sprig muslin dress that he liked so well. No, she must not think of that either! "Dear Lord, I pray for salvation for Conduff . . . I pray for his eternal soul. Please soften his heart, Lord . . . please soften his heart."

Benjamin Talbot glanced out toward the cabin doorway. Miners had come for Jonathan Wilmington, and they spoke with quiet concern to him. After a moment, Wilmington waved him over, then introduced them.

"We have a problem," Wilmington said, "but I believe God has sent you as the answer."

"Me?" Benjamin asked with a surge of wariness.

The men nodded, and Wilmington said, "The seminarian who usually preaches for us is sick, and we need someone to give the sermon tomorrow. We know you are experienced—"

"But only in my home with my family and neighbors," Benjamin objected. "I have never preached publicly. I am not an ordained minister."

The men looked at each other, and one said, "Your father was a famous Boston minister, wasn't he?"

Benjamin nodded. "But that doesn't make me one. I don't have a great talent for it—"

"We have no one else," Wilmington said. "No one."

Benjamin hoped one of them would say, "Here am I, God, send me!" but they all continued to look at him.

Quite suddenly he knew God's will. And despite all of his real and imagined objections, he knew he must be obedient. "I shall do it," he finally said, "but only on one condition."

"Yes?"

"That each of you pray fervently for me and the congregation from this moment until I have finished tomorrow."

"Done," Wilmington said.

"You have our word for it," the others promised.

It was a far easier thing to go to Monterey to coerce the governor into political action, he thought unhappily, to be salt and light in the community—and then to wait an eternity for the wheels of government to turn. But this . . . this speaking to the hearts of miners, some of them like Conduff who had gone far astray—He had never preached to those who had given themselves entirely over to the other side.

In the midst of his objections, it struck him that believers were called not only to be salt and light, but to tell the world of Christ and His power to transform lives.

One of the miners said, "We be glad to pray for ye, but ye have a better promise yet. The Lord, He promised never to leave or forsake ye. Scripture says He's prayin' fer all o' us this very minute at the right hand of His Father."

"Thank you for reminding me, my brother," Benjamin said.

And when they left, he added a silent, "Thy will be done, Lord. Thy will be done."


On Sunday morning, the forested slope across the river shone a bright green in the sunlight. The bearded miners began to arrive by ones and twos up the trail from Oak Flats alongside the river. They smiled and spoke with enthusiasm, as though life were worth living no matter how rough their accommodations down in the Flats. It occurred to Louisa that there must have been godly miners in San Francisco, too, but she had been too far away from God herself to recognize them.

Hopeful, she stood waiting under a feathery green pine tree in front of the log church. Lord, help me to pray in the right way, she thought. I am truly concerned about Conduff's soul.

After a moment, she struggled to imagine Conduff striding up the trail to make his decision for God. What a different man he might be. Perhaps he was now passing by the tangles of blackberry vines in the underbrush . . . or perhaps even riding a burro as did several of the worshipers who now arrived. Someone Conduff could be like them, pleasantly greeting those who stood in front of the church, his face aglow with the anticipation of worshiping God together. It was difficult to believe, but with God all things were possible.

"Come, Louisa," Abby said, gently taking her arm. "It is time to go in."

"Already?"

"Yes. Worship will begin in a minute."

Glancing back at the trail down to Oak Flats, she reluctantly allowed herself to be led toward the church door. "He might still arrive," she whispered to Abby and Rose.

Rose nodded. "God so often moves at the last moment, when all seems lost. It would not be the first miracle to take place in this church."

Despite her reluctance, they escorted Louisa through the rows of rustic pews toward the front of the log church. She was only vaguely aware of the chinked log interior and the gray slate floor that Rose had helped lay. Sitting down, she quickly bowed her head in prayer.

Benjamin Talbot led the service, looking joyful and full of faith. His words sounded familiar and heartwarming, though she could not quite focus on them. She did, however, note Moses stepping forward to sing from a front pew, where he had been seated with Maddy. One never saw colored people sitting in the front of an Alexandria church. That they might here, that people's hearts had been so softened, was a miracle in itself. She glanced toward the back of the sanctuary. More miners had arrived, but not Conduff.

Standing in front of the rough wooden cross, Moses sang a spiritual in a rich baritone, and Louisa glanced back again, wishing that Conduff could hear the words. Her eyes caught Jonathan's, and she quickly turned forward toward the simple altar.

Benjamin Talbot spoke about faith, about the great cloud of witnesses, and she admonished herself: she must have sufficient faith not to glance back for Conduff again. God was omniscient, omnipresent, and omnipotent; she must not limit Him. The invitation to make a decision for Christ would come after the sermon and final hymn.

At last they sang the final hymn, "Rock of Ages," and she sang out with the congregation, praying through every word.

Then Benjamin Talbot said in his deep, strong voice, "If there is anyone amongst us who wishes to accept Christ as your Savior or to rededicate your life to Him, you may now come forward."

Louisa buried herself in prayer while the congregation sang, "Blest Be the Tie That Binds." Heavy boots clumped up the slate aisles, and she couldn't help opening her eyes. Two sandy-haired men had come forward. No Conduff.

The last verse of the hymn washed over her:
"From sorrow, toil, and pain,
And sin, we shall be free;
And perfect love and friendship reign
Through all eternity."

That was how it would be with the Lord in glory, she thought. From sorrow, toil, and pain, and sin, they would be free.

More people stepped to the altar, and she was astonished

to see Tess and Hugh come forward, too. *I thank Thee, Lord . . . oh, how I thank Thee!* Louisa prayed, joy momentarily overcoming her sadness at Conduff's absence.

After the prayer and benediction, it occurred to her that she had indeed limited God; despite what she knew, she had limited Him to act during the service! Hopeful for Conduff again, she went forward to embrace Tess. "I had no idea, no idea at all. Oh, Tess, I am so happy for you, my dear friend! This decision will change your life so wonderfully."

Tess smiled with mystification. "I had no idea either, but suddenly I felt as though God was saying, 'Go forward, go forward now, Tess. Don't wait 'til too late like—." She faltered, flushing. "Then Hugh rose from the pew, too!"

Beside her, Hugh beamed, and Louisa shook his hand heartily. "I am unsure how it happened myself," he said, "though I have seen your faith and Jonathan's. I knew it was different than just going to church at Christmas and Easter, as my family did while I grew up. And I saw, too, that, curious as it seems, to know Christ is to know true freedom. Last night Tess and I spoke of it, and I knew I wanted to believe that fully, too."

Tess turned to Louisa. "I saw how your life changed when you first accepted the Lord in Alexandria . . . and how your spirits fell when you grew away from Him . . . then, lately, your peace since you rededicated yourself to Him."

"You saw it that clearly?"

"Yes, that clearly."

"Oh, Tess—" She embraced her friend again. "It's true that without Him, I am nothing." The thought flashed to mind that—thanks to God—she had truly been blessed to be a blessing for Tess. And for Hugh, too.

Benjamin Talbot shook hands with Tess and Hugh. "To think that I didn't want to preach, that I was just barely obedient. I shall never forget the sight of you two and the others coming forward. I thank God for goading me onward."

Many in the congregation came to congratulate their new sister and brothers in the Lord, and Louisa stepped back, giving way to them.

As she walked up the aisle, she saw Jonathan speaking seriously with two of the late-arriving miners.

"Louisa, please come outside with us," he said, his expression solemn. "These men have something to tell you."

The men appeared discomfitted, and an ominous feeling swept through her. "About Conduff?"

"Yes, ma'am," the gray-haired miner replied, "about Conduff Setter."

They followed her out of the log church while she prayed, "Lord, let it not be what I think."

Stopping in the shade of a pine tree, the miners shifted their feet uneasily. The gray-haired one said, "Well, there was fightin' in the saloons agin last night. Setter was drunk as ever, 'n one miner accused him o' stealin' his gold dust. Next thin', they shoot, 'n Setter's dead. Afraid he brought it on himself. They buried him this mornin'.'"

Louisa stared at the miner. Brought it on himself, he had said. Brought it on himself.

"I reckon that's all to tell."

Conduff dead. Dead and buried. His soul forever separated from God, according to Scripture. If only she had been a better wife to him, if only he hadn't followed her here—*Is it my fault, Lord?* her heart cried out. *I truly tried!* Light beamed through the pine boughs, swirling and pinwheeling before her eyes.

"Come, Louisa, you look pale," Jonathan was saying, his hand at her elbow. "I had better take you to Rose's cabin."

"No . . . please. I want to be alone. I'll walk along the river."

"If you're certain—"

She nodded.

The miners looked at her, abashed, "Didn't know you was kin to him, ma'am. Our sympathies."

She nodded, her heart full of agony. She must get away from all of them. Turning, she started toward the river.

A grassy footpath led behind the church and the six log cabins, and she walked it with dry eyes. After all of her prayers for Conduff, what a horrible person she must be not to even weep for him. In her mind's eye, she could imagine Conduff stealing the other miner's gold dust . . . even the gunfight in the saloon with him drunk. . . and then his lying on the floor dead. No, she must not think of that.

She visualized him alive again, his yellowed teeth flashing through the unkempt black beard and that salacious tone as he said, "Be mighty handy havin' you 'round agin . . . honey-woman." How different he'd looked from the handsome charmer she had met over three years ago. "Ain't used to settin' with a man, are you?" he had asked then, his green eyes gleaming with pleasure, and "Honey-girl, I kin teach you anythin' you ever want to know."

How proud of him she had been at their wedding, then how awful their wedding night. In retrospect, all he had ever taught her was to distrust him. He had treated her like the slaves he'd paraded to the auction block and beat in their prison cells.

She walked the path for a long time, until she saw the Mercantile. "Well, now . . . got you by surprise, I reckon . . . . Expect you kin move out to the diggin's with me now."

She turned abruptly to retrace her way up the footpath through the trees. Perhaps if she had returned to the diggings with him he wouldn't be dead now.

"Louisa?"

Looking up, she saw Jonathan on the path before her.

"Forgive me," he apologized, "but you looked so pale and shaken, I felt I must follow you. There are often bears hereabouts. And desperadoes, as Aunt Jessica calls them."

She replied, "Only now, one less desperado."

He nodded unhappily. "Yes, one less."

"If I had gone with him yesterday, he would still be alive—"

"And perhaps you would be dead, adding a murder to his Judgment Day account. If you are blaming yourself for trials he brought on himself, Louisa, you must not."

"But I was his wife! Scripture says wives are to be submissive—"

"And husbands are to honor them and love them as Christ loves the church. Did he do that? Or did he, as Tess claims, beat you half unto death?"

Louisa pressed her trembling lips together, still full of remorse at Conduff's death and his unregenerate soul.

"None of us would have allowed you to be carried off by him . . . nor allowed you to go of your own volition," Jonathan said.

She closed her eyes, then opening them saw how heartsick Jonathan was, too, how fine and compassionate he was. "Oh, Jonathan—" she cried, "if only he hadn't killed Da and my child!"

He reached out to her with sympathy, and she flung herself into his arms, tears bursting to her eyes. Sobs broke from her mouth and her throat. "I fled home before I'd even had time for grieving . . . and then . . . and then—"

"And then you were under way to California," he supplied. "You looked so stricken when you came into the shipping office that day. I thought 'Who has wounded this young woman so terribly? Who?'" He rocked her back and forth in his arms. "I remember praying for you that first day in the office . . . and then later knowing that God wanted me to take you to Baltimore . . . to care for you."

Tears streamed down her cheeks, running down onto his white shirt and black frock coat. She was unable to tear herself away from his comfort. He was security, strength, and protection, and she'd had so little of them in her life.

"Louisa," he said soothingly. "Louisa—"

Finally her heartache eased, and she fumbled for the handkerchief in her skirt pocket. "Forgive me. I've acted like a wanton, throwing myself into your arms." She blew her nose and wiped the tears from her face. "I expect I don't look like a wanton now!"

He spoke gently. "You have never looked like one to me. Come, let's start back to the settlement."

"How can I ever face the others?"

"The Lord will help you . . . as He helped me when I had grief in my heart. As I recall, He used you to help me the first time I returned to church in Baltimore."

She cast a glance at him, then looked down at the river far below.

After they had walked on the path for a long while, she began to realize that the river still rushed far below and the birds still chirped among the trees. It reminded her that God was still in heaven, and in her heart.

Benjamin Talbot recruited miners to drive the wagons back with him and Abby. When he left he told Louisa, "Not all people make decisions for the Lord. He does not coerce us. You cannot take the blame for Conduff."

She nodded, but it didn't stop her from doing just that.

The days passed slowly, one, then another.

Louisa moved about the cabin helping Rose as though in a dream. Her only solace was reading from the Bible Jonathan had given her, and walking out toward the river. She realized he was avoiding her now—and no wonder. She had thrown herself into his arms on the very day her husband had died, just as at fifteen she had thrown herself into Conduff's arms. What a genius she had for doing the wrong thing—and now with a man who'd once thought he might become a pastor, and still might.

Midweek, a miner returning from San Francisco delivered a letter to her, and she opened it mindlessly. From Jonathan! This was the letter she had not received in San Francisco.

Dear Louisa,

I have waited such a long time to tell you how much I care for you, and I feel it is now time to speak out. I love you, Louisa, as I have never loved another woman, in every way it is possible to love. I am building a cabin here in hopes that you will come and love me and love Oak Hill.

Perhaps this is rash, but I can no longer stop myself. Please come and marry me, dear Louisa, and I shall honor and protect and cherish you all of my life. I feel that God will soon set aside whatever it is that has stood between us.

You have only to say the word, and I shall come—

She tore the letter to shreds. He had written it before knowing she was married. True, he had been kind to her the afternoon she'd learned of Conduff's death, but Jonathan was a fine man. He had probably even been praying for her all of this time—but now he knew how she'd deceived him. If he never wished to see her again, she would not blame him. What right had she to think of him! As for the love of men, it always brought her heartache in the end.

The river gave her respite from her guilt. When she heard its rushing water, she was reminded of the Lord saying, "Whosoever drinketh of the water that I shall give him shall never thirst; but the water that I shall give him shall be in him a well of water springing up into everlasting life."

The September air was warm and dry, not humid as it had been in Alexandria. It pleased her that the evening air cooled, for she began to sleep deeply at night, and even when she did awaken, she heard the soothing sounds of the river.

Oak Hill was beautiful and peaceful but, abhorrent as the thought was, she began to think about returning to San Francisco to work.

Finally it was again Sunday afternoon.

Jonathan had kept his distance from her, even in church, but when they stood up from Rose's dinner table he asked, "Would you like to see how my cabin is progressing?"

Hope rose in her heart.

She must overcome her grief and remorse, she told herself, for she was now of no use to anyone. "Yes, I—I . . . would like to see it." The others were watching them, and she turned with embarrassment.

Silently, she and Jonathan made their way up the path to the log cabin. She recalled the first time she had seen it, and he had said almost apologetically, "It is not nearly so fine as your house in Alexandria . . . or Oakley's in Baltimore."

Now she said, "How beautiful the cabin is with the trees and mountains all around it . . . with the river rushing down below. It is one of the loveliest places I have ever seen."

He brightened. "Yes, I always think so, too." After a moment he added, "Daniel brought window glass, and we installed it this week . . . before, as Maddy says, varmits settle inside for the winter."

She had to smile. "Varmits indeed."

He looked at her rather tentatively as she stepped over the threshold and into the entry. "It is like Rose's and Joshua's cabin."

He seemed as unnerved as she felt, and she said to fill the silence, "The logs are more fresh and fragrant than in their cabin."

"Yes."

Stepping into the unfinished parlor, she admired the newly mortared stone fireplace. Likely it was the mortar that gave off such a pungent odor now, but the tension between them had grown so great that she dared not speak of it or anything else.

Her gaze moved on, then stopped as fear paralyzed her. A bear! It stood beyond the parlor in the shadows of the bedroom, its glassy eyes glittering at them. She spun away, and ran directly into Jonathan's arms. "Run!" she whispered, so terrified the word scarcely came out. "A bear!"

He gripped her strongly as she struggled forward. He would not move, then he himself began to tremble.

"Jonathan, run!"

It took a moment to realize that he did not intend to move, then another to realize he was shaking with laughter.

"Look at the bear again!" he laughed.

Confused, she turned with him. The bear had not moved . . . nor would it. "Your grizzly bear skin! Oh, Jonathan—" She attempted to back away from him, but it was obvious he did not intend to move now, either. He held her firmly.

"The skin is only hanging to dry until the floor is finished," he explained somewhat huskily. "I shouldn't have laughed, for I wouldn't want to frighten you for anything . . . not after what you have endured, Louisa."

His voice had softened, and she looked up into his eyes. "A bear rug would be warm on the floor in front of the fireplace," she said hesitantly.

"That's what I thought." He gulped audibly. "Come, I want to show you the painting in the dining room."

She followed him into the white plastered dining room, surprised at this touch of elegance, for the other walls were of chinked logs. Then she saw the painting that hung on the wall . . . the portrait Abby had painted of her in her blue sprig muslin dress.

"I talked Abby into making a copy for me and made her promise not to tell you or anyone," he said.

Louisa gazed at him, speechless.

"I should not have hung it already, but it inspires me to work harder on the cabin."

"Oh, Jonathan . . . she made me far too beautiful."

"Not nearly as beautiful as you are."

"The blue in my eyes and of the dress—It is just like the color in the chair cushions I've been stitching."

"I wanted the rooms to suit you."

She stood looking at him until he finally said, "Come, let me show you the rest of the cabin. I fear that I overspoke. I know it's not seemly to speak my mind to you yet." It obviously cost him an effort to continue. "Louisa, I fear that after what you have endured, you may prefer not to . . . marry again."

"Not to marry—"

He nodded. "Yes, marry. I should like to marry you, Louisa, though I shall not ask you now."

She gazed in wonder at this man who was so kind and considerate, this man who had made her life worth living again. "How can you trust me or love me when I deceived you all of this time?" she asked.

"I do, nonetheless. I love you and trust you."

"And I thought you must find me far too forward . . . for throwing myself into your arms."

"Never," he replied. "I have always been the one reaching for you, and I worried that, in the end, it would have the opposite effect. I pray that I haven't frightened you away. . . . When do you think it might be seemly for me to speak of this properly, Louisa?" he asked. "Customs are not so strictly adhered to on the frontier as they are in the East."

Mourning for Conduff, he meant. She tried to think when her marriage to Conduff had ended. Certainly long before she had fled him last spring . . . long years ago. And when had Jonathan begun to court her? From what he'd confessed on their walk last Sunday, it had been at their first meeting in the shipping office in Alexandria.

Before she could respond, he said, "I'll wait. I shall wait if it takes forever, though it already seems an eternity."

How God had blessed her with this dear, loving man, she thought. Possibly He had even arranged for her to see the grizzly bear skin as a menace so she'd fling herself at him again.

At the hopeful look on Jonathan's face she said, "I can't live with Rose's family too long, Jonathan. I think that . . . your speaking might be seemly very soon."

His eyes brightened. "Dare I ask next month?"

He reached for her hands, but she stepped heedlessly into his surprised embrace. "Next month would be fine," she whispered against his chest, "though right now would not be too soon to speak, either."

"Oh, Louisa," he whispered, "I love you so."

She could no more stop her words than the sun could cease its shining or the moon its glow. "And I love you."

Brimming with love and joy, a prayer rose from her heart. *Thank Thee, Lord, thank Thee for blessing me so through Jonathan. Thank Thee for Thy forgiveness and mercy, for this second chance. And help us to be a blessing to others now, too.*

As his arms enfolded her, she thought that if Aunt Sarah or Dr. Norton or Benjamin Talbot were here at this moment, they would each and every one of them say a most joyous and fervent "Amen!"

# ABOUT THE AUTHOR

Elaine Schulte is a wife, mother of two sons, and writer whose short stories, articles, and novels have been widely published. Although she writes both contemporary and historical novels, she says, "I identify strongly with our pioneers, whether they were moving here from other countries or from New York or Missouri to new lands and new hopes. I can't imagine a more courageous, more adventurous people.

"In 1846, Walter Colton, the navy chaplain in California, said, 'The American people love valor, but they love religion also. They will confer their highest honors only on him who combines them both.'

"Many of the pioneers who came to California were valorous men and women of God. They spoke eloquently of their faith—and of their trials—in their diaries and autobiographies. I hope that my writing about them will help to counteract today's stories about the pioneers that dwell mainly on the sordid and ignore those people who were worthy of honor."

*The Journey West* is Schulte's first book in The California Pioneer Series about the Talbot family and their covered wagon journey to California in 1846.

The second novel is *Golden Dreams*, which describes Rose Wilmington's travels to California by clipper ship, while Benjamin Talbot carries out his call in the new city of San Francisco.

*Eternal Passage* is the third novel in the series, and it, too, is fiction based on facts. In the fall of 1849, for example, evangelist William Taylor and his wife sang "The Royal Proclamation" with one thousand miners on San Francisco's notorious Portsmouth Square, then told them of God's grace.

Betsy Talbot is the heroine of the fourth novel, *With Wings as Eagles*, which takes place in the gold rush town of Oak Hill in 1854.